The Improbability of Sainthood

Tim Reardon

The Improbability of Sainthood

ISBN: 9798989451340

Library of Congress Control Number: 2024939532

Cover Design by All Things that Matter Press

Cover Image: Deirdre Molloy

Published in 2024 by All Things that Matter Press

This one's for all the SF 80's dorks, jocks, preppies, punks, headbangers, thrashers, cholos, and stoners. It's for the drama kids and the spirit crew, the wannabe surfers and fake valley girls. It's for the brainiacs and the burnouts and even the Marinites and the Peninsulites. And of course, we can't forget the Sunset District Irish (SDI) with their Derby jackets and Ben Davis pants, their Chuck Taylors (sunset slippers) and Pendletons, their Mickey's Big Mouths and Bud Talls—you guys were in a class all your own, the architypes for a collection of legendary characters who re-emerge surreptitiously with every passing generation as if spawned in fog and Guinness. You're all a great inspiration for this tale.

Acknowledgments

I'd like to thank Kate Reardon and Lizzy Reardon for their careful and thoughtful reading. As always, I need to express my utmost appreciation to my loyal, local editors, Laura Ferry Kelly and Dan Harlan. You guys are extremely important partners in my process. You never hesitate to help this sometimes-lazy scribe. And as graduates of the class of '86 (St. Rose and SI respectively), you were particularly helpful on this project as you were able to provide important analysis like, "We didn't say that in '85," and "That song didn't come out until '88." Also, a quick thank you to Mike Mayer, Riordan class of '70 for encouraging my writing and providing the bones of the Blue Comet story that appears in these pages.

Special thank you to the incredible SF artist, Dede Molloy, for her beautiful cover art.

And finally, a special shout out to Deb and Phil from All Things That Matter Press. You make it easy to be a writer.

Splashdown: The Pirate's Plank Disaster 25 Years Later

A Six-Part Documentary Series

Produced by NorCal Newsreel. Presented by Small Town Consortia in association with The Joint Center for Civic Review and The Sonoma County Film Institute

2010

Episode One: Residuary
TRT 29 min

[Transcript]

Music: Paul Simon's Slip Slidin' Away
Stillshot: The carcass of a waterpark. Weeds overgrown around the gates. Faded blue slides (slightly out of focus) in the background.

Narrator: How did the tragedy affect you personally?

Monty Phelan (Former Lehane Mayor): I was running things. The town was thriving, and this ended it. I lost the next election. The people didn't know who to blame, and I guess I was on the short list. So, I'll say that it affected me in a disproportionately negative way. In other words, I got screwed.

Narrator: Do you feel any responsibility for what happened?

Monty: I loved this town. The downtown development project was all me, and the plans were already drawn for the new resort and spa in the south end. I was very popular among my constituents. Sometimes things happen. You know? But people need to point the finger at someone.

Narrator: Do you think the current leadership can spark the kind of growth they're seeing up in Healdsburg or Geyserville?

Monty (laughing): Lehane is cursed, ma'am. So, no.

PROLOGUE

Summer 1985

Jerry Hawkins and his friends had just finished smoking some choice weed from a makeshift pipe that Carolyn Roddy had crafted by using a Bic pen and her house key to hollow out a Granny Smith apple. About fifty other members of their rising senior class were sprawled out on blankets and towels across the picnic area at the edge of Pirate's Plank. The water park was in Lehane, CA, just forty miles north of their San Francisco homes.

It was a bit overcast, but hot and filled with a strange kind of crackling energy that Jerry had always associated with earthquakes.

The whole crew had staked out the far corner of the park's expanse so that they could drink jungle juice and smoke weed without being bothered by Pirate's Plank staff. The end-of-summer trip for the group of soon-to-be seniors had become over the years an unofficial tradition for the boys from St. Xavier and the girls from St. Mary's. The park was just far enough away from the city fog for them all to pretend for another day that they didn't have anything to care about except the sun and beer and who was going to make out with whom. The management at the Plank didn't seem to mind the barrage of unchaperoned teenagers setting up camp for the day, so the conditions were ideal.

Jerry had a nice combo-buzz going. The weed and the booze and the vibe were all cooperating to make everything shimmer in their little bubble, separated from the rest of the world. He could hear his buddy Edgar talking and laughing with Dave, but the words weren't registering. Bob Segar was singing something raspy out of someone's boom box, but Jerry couldn't make out the song.

Instead, he was letting himself stare at Carolyn Roddy.

She was wearing a fluorescent green bikini top and a matching pair of terry cloth shorts with white trim. Her shoulders were freckled and glossed with baby oil and perspiration, and her smile was dazzling. She was leaning back on her elbows and staring right back at Jerry. "You're stoned," she said, her eyes shaded against the glare by her green-tinted sunglasses.

"Feeling good," said Jerry and thought maybe he was a little bit in love with Carolyn Roddy at that moment. There were a few other St. Mary's girls whom he'd dated and liked. And of course, everyone at St. X was hot for Chrissy Lang, who was sitting with three other girls on a Navajo blanket about thirty feet away. But Jerry was more than content hanging out with the girl who could take fifteen minutes to make a perfect pipe out of an apple and then take just one hit.

"I'm not a stoner," she'd said while she was packing the first bowl. "I'm an artist. I can make a pretty good one with a Coke can too. I can even do one with a bunch of Starbursts squished together."

"Impressive," Jerry said and looked over at Edgar and Dave who were nodding in appreciation as Carolyn balanced the apple between her knees, and with both hands, tightened her ponytail. Jerry wondered if Dave and Edgar were also a little bit in love with Carolyn Roddy.

"Whose buds were those?" she asked after they'd passed the apple around for a few minutes and then watched Dave place it on top of the Igloo as if it were some kind of good luck charm.

"Edgar's," said Jerry. "I don't ask where he gets it. Like you, I'm not much of a stoner either."

Carolyn laughed, "Said the stoned guy who keeps staring at me."

"Sorry," he said quickly. Suddenly very self-aware. "Maybe I *am* high. Sorry. Seriously."

She sat up Indian style and laughed again. "I don't mind," she said.

"Carolyn," said Edgar Cortes, leaning forward now. "Did you say you could make a pipe out of a Starburst?"

She shook her head. "Not *one* Starburst, Ed," she said. "A whole pack stuck together."

Edgar and Dave found this hilarious. Dave said, "How about Now & Laters?"

Carolyn looked at Jerry. "Are you guys serious?" she said. "Now & Laters are too hard. You need to be able to smoosh 'em together and then poke a hole through."

Dave and Edgar looked strangely thoughtful and said nothing for a moment until Edgar replied, "How about Bubblicious?" and then burst into unrestrained laughter.

Jerry was letting his mind wander, quietly laughing at the random thoughts that were coming into his head.

"You enjoying this conversation?" Carolyn said to Jerry.

"Oh ... no," he said. "I was thinking about something else."

"What?" she said.

Before Jerry could activate his filter, he was already talking. "You know how Popeye always had a pipe in his mouth?" he said. "What if it was filled with weed?"

Dave and Edgar were laughing again, but Carolyn just smiled and shook her head. "He was a fitness guy," she said. "I don't think weed was part of his regimen."

"What about Frosty the Snowman?" said Dave. "Or would that expedite the melting process."

"Expedite the melting process," said Edgar and then snorted out another laugh.

Carolyn took off her sunglasses and said, "How about the rich guy on *Gilligan's Island*?"

Her smile revealed hints of dimples and made her almond-shaped eyes crinkle at the corners. Jerry's mind was doing the same kinds of somersaults it did every time he smoked even a little weed. He was wondering why he hadn't noticed Carolyn last year. He knew her and liked her. But something had happened to her over the summer. She'd gone through a transformation—the whole butterfly thing. A lot of the girls looked different, but not all in good ways. Right now, sitting on the grass next to Carolyn, Jerry was almost dumbfounded by the change.

"Thurston Howell III," said Jerry, happy to be riffing off Carolyn's contribution to this ridiculous game. "There was probably weed all over that island."

Edgar said, "I guess the dad on *101 Dalmatians* also liked his ganja."

"And how about Sherlock Holmes?" said Dave. "How did he ever solve a case?" Then he opened his mouth to say something else, but stopped, and his eyes shifted above Carolyn's and Jerry's heads.

Jerry turned around to see what was behind him. It was Chrissy Lang and a few of her buddies. "Hi, Carolyn," Chrissy said and smiled but then turned her attention to Jerry. "Hey, Hawk. Time for the clog. You in?"

Chrissy was wearing a red one-piece. She was a volleyball player. She had long legs and long blonde hair that had been wet but was now drying in golden waves. She looked like the girl from the Hawaiian Tropic commercial. This was the first time she'd ever called him *Hawk* even though they'd gone to grade school together, and people had been using that nickname since he was in the fourth grade.

Jerry Hawkins stood up and followed Chrissy and the others, who were heading for the biggest slide. He took only a couple steps before he caught himself, turned back, and put his hand out to Carolyn.

She looked over at Chrissy and then back at Jerry. "That's okay," she said.

"You're not doing the clog?"

"I actually never learned to swim."

"Really?"

"Yeah," she said. "Really."

"But the water's only three feet deep."

"I'll watch you guys," she said. "Off you go, *Hawk*."

Jerry knew he'd blown it. He was embarrassed now. "It's supposed to be a tradition," he said, and Dave stood up to join him.

Carolyn looked over at Edgar, who was lying back now with his hands behind his head. "Edgar and I will watch our stuff," she said.

Jerry nodded. "Okay," he said. "We'll be back in a few."

"You better," she said and broke the tension when she flashed that smile again.

Jerry and Dave jogged to catch up to the group that had grown to about twenty kids, split pretty evenly between St. Mary's girls and St. X boys.

Dave was walking shoulder to shoulder with Jerry. "She's looking at you," he said out of the side of his mouth.

Jerry turned around to look back at Carolyn, but she was talking to Edgar.

"Not her," said Dave.

Jerry turned back around to see Chrissy Lang waiting for him near the ramp. "There's a girl lifeguard up there," she said, looking strangely serious. "We need a cute boy to distract her."

The group had paused to watch this exchange. Jerry felt like it was a trap. If he said he'd do it, then it would look like *he* thought he was cute. Or, that he thought *Chrissy* thought he was cute. But he also didn't feel like he could ignore the request because she was looking right at him. Or was she? He'd just had several hits of pretty good weed, and now he felt like maybe he was misinterpreting what was happening.

Dave saved the day. "Hawk'll do it," he said.

Chrissy smiled and kept her eyes on Jerry. "Just think of something to say to her. Then try to keep talking when we rush the slide."

Jerry nodded.

Dave said, "Then jump on after the last person."

"I'll go last," said Chrissy. "Come in behind me."

Jerry's brain was firing sporadically. He was simultaneously trying to think of what he was going to say to the lifeguard while also processing what Chrissy had just said. *Come in behind me.* He actually took a deep breath to try to get his mind right. He'd heard about the clog from previous classes. The folklore maintained that the record was eighteen people on the slide at the same time. He was in no shape to count, and he didn't really care. In fact, he certainly would have skipped the whole endeavor if Chrissy hadn't beckoned him to join.

Everyone was hustling up the ramp, but they stopped at the stairs to let Jerry move past them. Their faces were bursting with anticipation. Many of them were dripping from their previous trip down the slide. Some were laughing and nodding at him. *Let's go, Hawk.*

He was laughing now too, thinking of this as a challenge. For everyone else it was a physical dare, but his role required him to utilize both his physical and mental skills. He was going to have to use his wits to occupy the lifeguard.

When he turned the corner, there was a short line in front of him. The lifeguard was standing on the left side of the chute, saying, at uniform intervals, "Go ahead," and then watching the slider make the first turn and waiting a few more beats before saying, "Go ahead" to the next person.

She looked about their age. Maybe older. She was a bit overweight and had a nice face, sunburned on her nose and cheeks. She was wearing a Pirate's Plank t-shirt with her bikini bottoms as well as the park's requisite pirate's hat, complete with skull and crossbones. She looked bored, like she'd been doing this her whole life. Her name tag said Trixie. Jerry wondered if he was reading that correctly.

When Jerry was fourth from the front, he stepped out of line and said brilliantly, "Hi, Trixie. What time do you guys close tonight?"

Trixie didn't look away from the top of the chute. "Go ahead," she said to the next slider. Then she glanced at Jerry and pushed her sunglasses down her nose to get a better look before she pointed at the sign behind her that listed park rules and hours of operation. "Go ahead," she said again.

Jerry looked over his shoulder and saw Danny Harlan at the front of the line. Harlan looked at Trixie and then at Jerry. When Trixie said, "Go ahead," Harlan put his hands on the sides of the slide to slow his descent .

Trixie watched him for a second and then turned to Jerry. "Are you guys doing that stupid clog?"

Jerry shrugged and watched Trixie's eyes widen. By the time she turned back around, five more people were jumping on the slide. Trixie stepped around Jerry and shouted, "Stop."

But it was too late. St. Mary's and St. X kids were jumping on the slide two and three at a time. Trixie's head snapped back at Jerry, and now he felt bad. She looked like she was going to cry. She stepped up to the mouth of the slide and extended her arm like a railroad crossing gate. But kids flew right past her. She looked back at Jerry one more time just as Chrissy arrived.

Jerry took a step to scoot around Trixie and join the others, but then he heard a loud cracking sound, and he skidded to a stop in standing water. The cracking ripped through the air, and everything froze for a moment. He imagined the sound was akin to lightning splitting an old sequoia or some ancient schooner running aground. It was followed a moment later by what sounded like an enormous Velcro strip being torn apart.

Jerry's eyes went directly to the sound, where he saw the slide coming apart and his friends plunging thirty feet toward the hard dirt in the shadows beneath the slides. There was no sound anymore. He knew everyone was screaming. *He* was screaming. But his ears and his brain weren't communicating. Then he saw, closer to him, the top part of the slide bending away from the platform.

Chrissy was looking at him and trying to hold onto the slippery edge of the slide that had separated from the other segments. Jerry took a step toward her with his arm extended, but she was ten feet away from him by now. She held on as long as she could, but when she gave one last effort to pull herself up, her hands slipped, and she got herself turned upside down with her feet pointed at Jerry and her eyes still locked on his as she plummeted away from him, head-first into the shadows.

And then this happened.

Jerry Hawkins took a long step up on a support beam, grabbed the railing with one hand, and catapulted himself over the safety barrier.

He could later describe the feeling of the heat on the slick metal railing and the rush of warm air in his ears as he fell. He remembered the smell of suntan lotion mixed with something chemical. He could speak at length of the feeling of his bare feet hitting the soft mound of sand on which he'd landed. He would later find out that the sand had just been dumped there that morning as a reserve supply for the artificial beach near the lazy river.

But he hadn't noticed it before he jumped.

He could talk about the people beneath the slide looking like casualties of some foreign war. Some had actually landed on top of each other and were groaning, sprawled out on the dirt, moving in strange, broken ways.

He could even remember in detail Chrissy's damaged skull, which had hit the concrete slab beneath one of the support posts. He'd run over to attend to her, but she was already gone, eyes dusted over and absent of light. He looked away from her face and down the length of her body, which was stretched out and still. Water was splashing all around her, and Jerry stood over her in some misguided attempt to keep her dry.

He felt the cold water on the back of his neck.

The dirt was already turning to mud. He was surrounded by mud. And now he was beginning to hear again—mostly the splattering of water and the screaming of his friends.

In the midst of the mayhem, strange combinations were splashing around in his head, making it hard for him to stay on his feet. Not images or even ideas. These were mishmashes, raw and urgent emotions mixed with something beyond thought. Lust and violence.

Fear and death. Insignificance and power. Revulsion and hope. Too many impressions to consider at once.

He was spinning, dizzy with nausea and panic as he slid through the mud away from Chrissy. He found Dave, sitting on the ground, head between his knees. Dave actually looked okay until Jerry watched him use his left hand to hold up his right hand so that Jerry could see the bone coming through the skin above his wrist.

"Jesus," said Jerry and nearly gagged.

"I think I'm in shock," said Dave. "For some reason this doesn't hurt yet."

"Chrissy's dead," said Jerry.

"You should go help the others," said Dave.

"I know," said Jerry.

At some point, Dave was going to ask Jerry about his clog experience and why Jerry was unharmed. Edgar and Carolyn would as well. And his parents. As would the police and maybe some news organizations. He assumed that only Trixie and maybe Chrissy had watched him jump, but he wanted to be ready if anyone else had seen.

As he was examining his fallen classmates, all besides Chrissy apparently still alive, he was already developing a strategy—something that would placate the curious, something that would make sense even though he couldn't even explain to himself why he'd done it. He should have been thinking about all his classmates, but he was instead wondering if this was what people meant by the term *temporary insanity* and then he further wondered if it was only temporary.

Splashdown: The Pirate's Plank Disaster 25 Years Later

A Six-Part Documentary Series

Produced by NorCal Newsreel. Presented by Small Town Consortia in association with The Joint Center for Civic Review and The Sonoma County Film Institute

2010

Episode Two: Periphery
TRT 29 min

[Transcript]

Allison "Trixie" Walsh: It was just a summer job.

Narrator: But didn't they train you on how to prevent something like that?

Trixie: Yeah. They told us not to let them do it. But what are we going to do? They don't give us guns. We weren't going to throw our bodies in front of the slide. We'd tell kids don't do that and hope there weren't twenty of them. That was the training. If a couple kids did it, and we could catch them, we'd kick them out of the park for breaking the rules. That was the training.

Narrator: How old were you when it happened?

Trixie: Nineteen

Narrator: Do you think they should have had someone older up there? Someone with more authority?

Trixie: Yeah, right. What kind of person with any authority is going to take a job for four dollars an hour? There was a park manager, and then there was just us. A bunch of kids just out of high school. We thought it would be fun to have a job outside instead of delivering pizzas or bagging groceries. And now I'm here still talking about this shit twenty-five years later.

Narrator: Do you still live in Lehane?

Trixie: Where else am I going to live?

1

Edgar Cortes decided to make an appearance at Speedway Meadows where he knew he'd see a bunch of St. X guys getting loaded before the game. Varsity football games in the city were always played on Friday afternoons, but because St. X and St. Mary's had half days on Fridays, the kids would rush to Golden Gate Park for a few beers and then try to get back to St. X before the end of the first quarter.

Edgar hadn't seen anyone in over a month. He was no longer enrolled at St. X.

The keg was over in the trees behind the public bathrooms. From across the meadow, he was almost certain he could see Jerry Hawkins pumping the keg and handing out Baskin Robbins cups. They had friends who worked at the 31 Flavors on West Portal, and those guys had been supplying the keg cups since sophomore year.

Jerry stepped out of the shade and squinted just as Edgar approached the outer perimeter of the gathering. Jerry used his hand as a visor and said, "Holy shit," and then smiled a big smile before taking a long sip from his waxy paper cup. "I thought you joined the circus or became a roadie for Bob Marley or something."

"Marley died four years ago," said Edgar. "But that would've been fun."

"Well, what the hell is going on?" he said and motioned with his head for Edgar to follow him back to the keg. "First your mom told me you were visiting relatives, and then she just stopped answering the phone." He poured a cup with too much foam, passed it over to Edgar, and then topped off his own. "And when I went to your house, she told me you'd be coming home soon, but that was weeks ago. They stopped calling your name at school after the first week."

Edgar felt himself frown and let his head drop. "I fucked up," he said.

"Okay," said Jerry, leading him back to the sunshine, away from the rest of the group. "And ..."

A few people nodded at Edgar and gave him the thumbs up, but he could see in their eyes that they were all wondering about him. "Just stupid shit," he said, stalling. He wasn't ashamed, but he never wanted to disappoint Jerry, who mostly tried to do the right thing. "What the hell are *you* doing here?" Edgar said and shrugged at Jerry.

"Me?" said Jerry.

"Yeah," said Edgar. "Why aren't you playing?"

"Oh," he said. "Yeah, I quit after doubles."

Jerry started at free safety as a junior. He wasn't going to play college or anything, but he was a damn good high school player. A hard hitter and really smart. "I thought you loved football," said Edgar.

"It was all right," said Jerry. "I wouldn't say *love*."

"How come you quit?"

"You know Dave's arm is still fucked up?" said Jerry.

"Worse than they thought?"

"He's not going to make it back even if we get to the playoffs."

"So, you thought you shouldn't play either?"

Jerry didn't say anything for a long while. He took a sip of his beer. And then another sip. "So, where the hell have you been, man?" He grabbed Edgar's shoulder and shook it. "You just disappeared."

"I was in juvie for almost a month," he said and turned away from Jerry. He looked back up at his old classmates and worried that they wouldn't be friends with him anymore—that their parents wouldn't let them. "Hawk, I screwed up my life."

They were sitting side by side on the grass. Jerry nudged Edgar's shoulder and said, "Dude, we're just kids." Then he looked out across the meadow and said, "Did you know that Ronald Reagan went to juvie when he was our age?"

"Really?" said Edgar.

"Probably not," said Jerry. "But he could have and still become president. When you turn eighteen, it'll be like it never happened."

Edgar laughed and swallowed the last of his beer. "I can't picture Reagan in juvie."

"I can picture his wife going in there and telling kids to *just say no*."

"Good advice," said Edgar. It would have been so easy to avoid the shit he got into, but he didn't even question it when he was doing it. "A week after the accident, I started hanging out with my cousin and got into some stupid stuff."

"What did you do to end up in jail?"

"The official charges?"

"Just tell me what you did," said Jerry as two St. Mary's girls crossed the meadow in the direction of the keg.

When they got close, one of the girls said, "Hey, Hawk, do we pay *you* for the cups?"

"Harlan's up there collecting money," he said.

When they walked by, Edgar noticed that the girls were whispering to each other.

Jerry must have noticed because he said, "People were worried about you, brother."

"Yeah," he said and looked up toward the keg. Harlan was pouring beers for the girls, but he was looking at Edgar.

"Good to see you, buddy," he shouted and raised one of the beers in salute.

Edgar raised his own cup toward Harlan. "Good to be seen," he said and then looked back at Jerry. "My cousin is a bad dude."

"I know it," said Jerry. "What did he make you do?"

"Julio didn't *make* me do anything," said Edgar. "I got into his world willingly for some reason."

"Why?"

"I can't explain it," he said. "But after the waterslide, I was kind of fucked up for a while. Weird dreams. Fights with my mom. Smoked way too much weed. And started hanging out with Julio."

"Did you feel like some kind of outlaw?"

"Absolutely."

"Like what kind of stuff did you do?"

Edgar closed his eyes for a moment and let a quick slideshow of the Julio days run through his head. Pulling runners from The Tennessee Grill. Purse snatching in the Mission. Weed sales in the Bayview. Smash and grabs from tourists at the wharf. Fights. B&E. Vandalism. Trespassing. Something different every day.

"We were just breaking the law all the time," he said. "In the beginning, I felt like I didn't care if I got caught. By the end, I actually wanted to get caught. Like I deserved it."

Jerry had this look on his face like he understood even though Edgar felt like this was all nonsense, unnatural thoughts.

"I haven't been doing stuff like that, but I think I get it," said Jerry. "Like you were trying to punish yourself even though you didn't do anything wrong."

"I did a lot of things wrong," said Edgar.

"No," said Jerry. "I mean when you decided to start doing things with Julio. That was you kind of punishing yourself."

"Maybe," said Edgar. "I felt guilty all the time."

"How did you end up getting caught?"

"You know that Big 5 sporting goods store in Serramonte?"

"Yeah."

"Julio and Keith went in to steal a bike."

"Julio wanted a bike?"

"Yeah," said Edgar. "He wanted to trick it out and turn it into some kind of lowrider bike, like the Harley Davidson guys do with their choppers, with the handlebars way up high."

"And then do what with it?"

"I guess ride it around the neighborhood. Maybe sell it? I don't know."

"And what happened?"

"I was driving the get-away car."

"Julio's big old Delta 88?" said Jerry.

"That's the one," said Edgar. "Which was good because the trunk is so big, we were gonna just throw the bike in the trunk and boogie out of there."

"But ...?"

"But they came running out into the parking lot with a security guard chasing 'em," said Edgar, feeling the tightness in his stomach like he did that day. "And instead of just riding the bike, Julio was pushing it, so this fat rent-a-cop was keeping up with him."

"Why didn't he ride it?"

"He said later that the tires weren't pumped up yet."

"Damn."

"Yeah, so Keith takes off in a different direction, and Julio comes right for the car. But instead of putting the bike in the trunk like we'd planned, he just starts jamming it into the back seat, and then he gets into the back with the bike, but the bike's hanging halfway out the door and the security dude is about two feet away, and Julio says, 'go, go, go,' so I put the pedal to the metal."

Jerry's face looked sad then. Like he knew what happened. Like he knew that Edgar never turned to look before he hit the gas.

"But there was a van right in front of us, and I slammed into it."

"Dude," said Jerry, shaking his head now and tilting his cup to take a drink even though the cup looked empty.

"It was a YMCA van with a bunch of little kids in it," said Edgar. "And after I hit it, I put it into reverse and hit another car. I was driving like a mental patient. So, Julio jumped out and ran in the same direction where Keith went, up toward Montgomery Ward."

"What about his car?" said Jerry. "And his bike?"

"It was over by that point, so he just took off. He couldn't get busted again on account of he was already on probation."

"So, you took the rap?"

"I wouldn't say it that way."

"Why not?"

"Because I actually did the crime," said Edgar. "I didn't steal the bike, but I was the get-away driver, and I crashed twice in a parking lot."

"Did any of the kids get hurt?"

"No. I don't think I was going fast enough."

"I guess it could've been worse," said Jerry. "Five weeks isn't that bad considering."

"Yeah," said Edgar. "But I might have to go back for more time after sentencing next month."

"*More* time?" said Jerry.

"The lawyer thinks they'll credit me with time served and put me on probation because it was my first offense. I'm just supposed to stay out of trouble until my hearing."

"Remember when you threw that water balloon at Sister Margaret?"

"Fifth grade," he said. "She walked right in front of Sam Mogannam."

"Yeah," said Jerry, laughing a little bit now. "You were framed."

2

The keg was still half-full, so Edgar helped Jerry lift it into the back seat of Harlan's old Dodge. Harlan actually put a seatbelt around the half-barrel to secure it so that it would still have some carbonation after the game. Jerry sat up front next to Harlan, and Edgar sat in the back next to the keg.

Edgar and Jerry got fresh Baskin Robbins cups from a bag on the floor and filled up for the short drive from the park to school.

When Harlan pulled away from the curb, Edgar said, "Thanks for the ride." Then he took a sip of his beer. "I took the bus down here because they revoked my license."

"No problem," said Harlan. "You should hear the stories people've been saying about you."

Edgar glanced over at Jerry, but Jerry was looking out the window. "What are they saying about me?" he said.

Harlan glanced into the rearview mirror and said, "Don't get pissed, dude. But I heard you killed some little kids in a drunk driving accident in the Serramonte parking lot." He turned his eyes back to the road. "I know it's probably not true, but I heard someone in the cafeteria spewing that bullshit."

Edgar took a long pull on his beer. "Did they say I did it on purpose?"

"Huh?" said Harlan. Then, "I don't know. I didn't really hear the full conversation. Wait. Did you really kill some kids, Ed?"

"Nah," he said. "But I did crash into a YMCA van."

"And that got you sent to juvie?" he said.

"Yeah," said Edgar. "There's more to it than that, but I fucked up. I deserved it." Before Harlan could reply that people shouldn't go to juvie for car accidents, Edgar said, "Did you get hurt in the fall?"

They'd just stopped at the long stoplight on Sunset Boulevard, so Harlan turned around, all serious now. "I landed on my feet," he said, slowly, like he was trying to explain this to a very old person or a very young person. "I was able to hang on for a few seconds, so I was one of the last people to land." His eyes looked suddenly glassy. "I fell with the water. I was *in* the water. And when my feet hit, the ground was already muddy, so my feet slipped out from under me. And then I slid some ways down the slope on my ass." He shook his head at Edgar. "I didn't really feel anything except burning in my feet and knees. But a few days later, my back started hurting." He shrugged. "Now it hurts all the time. When I drink beer, it doesn't hurt as much. But sleeping is a bitch right now, man. I get about two hours a night. Every way—"

A horn blew behind them, and Harlan stepped on the gas before he turned away from Edgar. They shot out into the intersection, and then Harlan looked in the rearview mirror again. "I have no idea why my legs didn't break, but I think that would have been better than this back thing."

Edgar drank some more beer and thought about the sound of that slide snapping and then the screaming. He'd had his eyes closed when it happened, and he felt like his sense of hearing was enhanced. He was fifty yards away from the slide, but it sounded like something coming out of an amplifier. He remembered sitting up and opening his eyes but not being able to focus on what was happening.

Then Carolyn was up and running.

Edgar never got up though. He figured out what had happened, but he didn't do anything. He was tempted to grab that apple and take another hit as people were running past him to get over to the slide. But he didn't. He just sat there and tried to save everyone with his mind. He didn't think what he was doing was praying. He thought it might be more than praying. He'd been pretty stoned and was trying to use his mind to make things okay. He wasn't an ambulance guy or a doctor, so this was the best he could do, and in the end, he still thought he might have saved some of his friends. Chrissy was the only one who died.

"I had a similar fall," said Jerry. "But I got lucky with that sand being there."

"You did," said Harlan and reached over to pat Jerry on the knee. Then he cranked the wheel into a hard left turn and said, "I'm gonna park on the other side of the boulevard, you guys. I don't want any parents seeing the keg in the back."

Edgar and Jerry nodded, and Harlan pulled up near the sidewalk strip of trees on 36th Avenue near Rivera. All three boys got out of the car. Jerry and Edgar were finishing their beers when Mr. McNaughton, their religion teacher, pulled up behind Harlan's Dodge.

Mr. McNaughton walked with his toes pointed at forty-five-degree angles away from his body. When kids thought they could get away with it, they'd make duck noises in the hallways when he walked by wheeling his briefcase behind him on his little briefcase cart. "Hi, boys," he said and smiled. "31 Flavors?"

"Yeah," said Jerry. "Stopped by on the way to the game."

"Oh?" said Mr. McNaughton. "When did they start selling beer? I smell beer."

No one said a word.

The boys were all leaning on the car. McNaughton walked around them and peered into the back seat. "This isn't good, my friends," he said.

McNaughton was pretty cool. Edgar had him sophomore year. He was the kind of teacher who pretended like he didn't see or hear everything going on in the classroom or the hallways. It was like an inside joke that he shared with his students. *Don't do anything too stupid, and I won't see it.*

The question now was whether or not he *wouldn't see* this. This was definitely stupid. While McNaughton was still standing near the car, looking through the window and shaking his head, Edgar decided to take this into his own hands. What did he have to lose? "This is my car, Mr.McNaughton," he said and walked over to where the man was standing, hands cupped around his eyes, face right up against the glass.

"And that keg too?" he said.

"That too," said Edgar.

McNaughton put his hand flat on the roof of the car and tapped down twice before saying, "And you don't go to St. Xavier anymore, do you Ed?" He met Edgar's eyes and half-smiled, not showing any teeth, but squinting a little bit and nodding now.

"I sure don't," said Edgar.

"Why is that?" said McNaughton.

"As you can see," said Edgar. "I'm a bad influence on St. X kids."

"Is that so?" said McNaughton, looking over at Jerry now, who'd poured out the rest of his beer and crushed the cup down to the size of a ping-pong ball, which he was holding in his fist as if he planned to throw it at someone.

"These two are good guys," said Edgar. "I shouldn't have met up with 'em today."

McNaughton had his hands on his hips now. The cuffs of his corduroy jacket came down over his hands, all the way to his knuckles, like the jacket was a hand-me-down from an older teacher who'd given up trying to help kids who were this stupid. He shifted his weight from one side to the other and then scratched at one bushy eyebrow. "Mr. Harlan, I seem to remember seeing you driving around in this beauty at some point," he said and pointed at the car, which was making ticking noises as it cooled off from the short drive from Speedway Meadows. "Did you sell the car to Mr. Cortes?"

Harlan looked right at McNaughton and said, "This car?"

McNaughton turned his attention to Jerry. "Shouldn't you be out on the field, Hawk?"

"Probably," he said.

"Why do you say that?"

"Because then I wouldn't be here."

McNaughton looked over at Edgar and said, "Take care of yourself, Ed." Then he shuffled off in the direction of the field. "Maybe you other two better check in with Father Stricker when you get to the game," he said but didn't turn around.

When McNaughton got to the crosswalk, Jerry said, "Thanks for trying to take the heat, Edgar."

Edgar shrugged. "I don't have anything to lose at this point," he said.

Harlan grabbed him by the arm. "Didn't you say you need to stay clean before your hearing, or they're gonna make you go back to jail?"

Edgar glanced at Jerry, who was still squeezing the remains of his keg cup. "What're the odds?" he said.

"Of me going back to juvie for this?"

"No," said Jerry. "Of McNaughton parking behind us?"

"What're the odds of anything?" said Harlan.

3

Carolyn Roddy had been going to St. X games since she was a little kid. Her dad had played for St. X and remained a fan, so she'd tagged along with him for years. Now that she was a senior at the sister school, St. Mary's, her dad didn't go to the games as much anymore, and today, she didn't really want him around anyway. Carolyn had a single purpose: she wanted to talk to Jerry Hawkins.

Things had been weird for the past month. All the guys were doing their thing, and the girls were doing their thing, but the two groups hadn't met up much since the accident. Some parents were setting ridiculous curfews. Others weren't letting their girls drive anymore. Carolyn's dad, a San Francisco fireman, had been less strict than other parents, but he was asking more questions now—more interested in her social life than at any time in her life up to this point.

As far as Carolyn was concerned, everyone had lost their minds. What were the odds that another freak accident could happen to the same people who were just in one? The way she figured it, all the kids who were at the waterslides that day were now shielded against future freak disasters. At least through senior year. No one in her group was going to get struck by lightning or have a safe fall on her head. It simply couldn't happen. Again, the odds were against it as far as she was concerned.

She couldn't understand the full-on panic coming from the Catholic school universe. She understood the sadness. She felt that too and understood that she, too, had gone full mental for a few weeks like everyone. But this extended panic didn't make sense to her. And she also couldn't figure out why Jerry Hawkins had disappeared. She'd visited Dave at the hospital and checked in on some of the other kids who'd gotten hurt in the accident, but Edgar and Jerry seemed to be hiding out for some reason.

She didn't mind going to the game by herself. As a senior, she'd lost the anxiety she used to have of appearing to be without friends. She knew she had friends and didn't care if people saw her arriving alone. It was liberating to her. And when her friends' parents wouldn't let them go out last weekend, she had no problem seeing *St. Elmo's Fire* by herself at the Empire on West Portal. The movie totally sucked, but she liked the solitude she found in the dark with a big tub of popcorn, a large Coke, and a couple of hours to herself.

But today she wanted to see Jerry before her whole senior year slipped away. She'd met him at a party near the end of junior year and thought there was a spark. Then, when she had the nerve to plop down on his towel at Pirate's Plank and carve the apple pipe, she *knew* there was a spark. He was a little shy, but when he was stoned, he was relaxed and funny. And she knew he was into her.

When she heard that he'd quit football, she thought she might be able to talk to him in the stands if he showed up. And about halfway through the second quarter, there he was. Carolyn saw Jerry, Edgar, and Dan Harlan coming down the stairs by the upper field .

She wished that she'd changed out of her school uniform. There'd been time after school, but she didn't want to miss the Art & Publicity meeting, so now here she was in her plaid skirt and bobby socks. The last time Jerry saw her, she was looking good in her new swimsuit. There wasn't really any accessorizing that could spice up the St. Mary's uniform.

She rolled the waistband in her skirt two more times. Then she unbuttoned the second button on her blouse and tucked the blouse into her skirt. She took out her ponytail and used her fingers to comb her hair out of her face. She looked at her reflection in the snack bar window and was satisfied that she didn't look like a monster. She tucked a strand of hair behind her ear and nodded at her reflection. She was ready to go see Jerry when the soccer player selling hotdogs from behind the counter slid open the window and said, "Lookin' good, Carolyn. What can I get you?"

"Oh," she said. "Sorry, Tony. I was using your window as a mirror."

"Any time," said Tony Chiesa and smiled. He was a nice guy. Most of the kids called him *Cheese.* "You going to the party tonight?"

"Maybe," she said. "Boathouse?"

"No," said Tony. "I think someone's having a house party. He doesn't go to St. X."

Carolyn gave Tony the thumbs up and looked over her shoulder to make sure she didn't lose Jerry, who was walking toward the stands.

"Stop by before the end of the game. I'll have the address by then," he said. "You want a free hot dog?"

"No thanks, Tony," she said and jogged around the snack bar line to see Jerry and his buddies sitting away from the cheering section in the corner of the stands near where her dad used to sit.

She sat on the bench directly behind Jerry, leaned forward, and whispered in his ear, "Why are you avoiding me?"

"What?" he said and turned at the waist to look back at her. He was already blushing.

"I called you twice and left messages with your mom," she said.

Harlan was watching the game, but Edgar turned and said, "Hey, Carolyn."

"Hey, Ed," she said and smiled. "I think I called *you* too. No callback."

"Sorry," he said. "I've been—"

"I heard," she said before he could finish. "Some junior girls told me when I first got here."

"I guess everyone knows?" he said.

"Not everyone," she said. "And the girls weren't being judgy. They knew we were friends and just asked if I'd heard." She worried about Edgar a little. He was totally mellow, but she thought St. X was good for him, and now he had to be at one of the public schools and maybe wouldn't get the discipline he probably needed. "You had an excuse for not calling me back," she said. "But this guy ..." She pointed a thumb at Jerry.

Jerry wasn't looking her in the eye. "I know," he said. "I guess that was stupid."

Carolyn didn't want to scare him off, so she said, "I'm just jerking your chain, Jerry." Then she put both hands on his shoulders like she was going to give him a massage. She didn't know what she was doing, so she kept talking. "I've been ignored by guys much stupider than you."

Jerry turned all the way around on the bench and looked at her now. It forced her to take her hands off his shoulders. She was wondering if she was blowing it, but then he smiled and said, "I think I've turned into a weirdo since the accident." He shook his head but kept his eyes on hers. "I can't even tell you why I didn't call you back, and I don't blame you if you think I'm a jerk."

"Don't worry," she said. "Everyone's gotten a little weird."

Dan Harlan jumped out of his seat, and the cheering section started going nuts. Jerry didn't even turn around.

"Sorry," she said. "I'm making you miss the game."

"I don't give a shit about this," he said and nodded back toward the field, where he stole a quick look at the scoreboard.

"Then why'd you come?" she said and immediately regretted it. She was talking without a filter and saying moronic things that might offend him. She reminded herself that she needed to calm down.

Edgar leaned all the way back so that he was leaning against Carolyn's bench. He said, "You should have come to the keg before."

"I know," she said. "I had a meeting after school. What are you guys doing after?"

"We just got busted by our religion teacher with the keg in the back of Harlan's car," said Jerry. "Edgar took the heat for me and Harlan, but the teacher told us to check in with Father Stricker at the game."

"He's the dean, right?"

"Yeah," said Jerry. "I think the game plan is to avoid him and hope everyone forgets by Monday. Maybe there'll be a fight or something, and Stricker will have something else to worry about."

Carolyn nodded. These guys getting busted was a bummer. She didn't want it to ruin the mood for her first conversation with Jerry in a month. "Tony from the soccer team said there's some party tonight. Did you guys hear anything?"

"Cheese?" said Jerry.

"Yeah."

Jerry and Edgar both shook their heads. "We just got here," said Jerry. "And no one at the park mentioned it."

"Cheese knows some strange dudes from the independent schools," said Edgar. "I wonder if one of those rich kids is having something at his house."

Harlan turned around and said, "Hi, Carolyn." Then he looked at the boys. "Remember, we have a keg in the back seat of the car," he said. "That might be our ticket into a house party. Those guys from Urban and University never let us in. Sometimes they call the cops as soon as they see us."

Carolyn took all this in. She didn't care about the party. She just wanted to change out of her uniform and hang out with these guys tonight. "Well, Tony said to check in with him before I left," she said. "So, I can find out about the party and then we can decide if we want to go or not." She knew she sounded presumptuous, but she could walk that fine line without being pushy. "If you guys don't mind me tagging along tonight."

Jerry was quick. "You're in," he said. "If you don't mind sitting next to the keg."

4

Jerry couldn't remember why he hadn't returned Carolyn's calls. He always had it in his mind that he wanted to, but he kept procrastinating until it felt as if he'd waited too long. It all seemed foolish now as he sat with her in the stands. She was behind him, so he was turned nearly all the way around in his seat, but it didn't matter because he didn't care about the game. He cared only about this girl.

She was in her St. Mary's uniform, but she was the kind of girl who looked pretty without even trying. She had a way of smiling while she was talking, and her smiles—even the ones that didn't show teeth—made her look beautiful.

"Do you want to take a walk?" she asked. "We can keep an eye out for Father Stricker."

Jerry was already standing up when he said to Edgar and Harlan, "I'll be back." Harlan didn't look away from the game, but Edgar gave him an approving nod.

Jerry and Carolyn walked down the stairs to field level and then walked around the track toward the visitors' side and out the west gate past the sand dunes and down toward West Sunset baseball field. During the walk, on two occasions, his hand brushed against hers as they made their way down Quintara Street. He almost made an attempt to hold her hand but chickened out and decided he would maybe try on the way back.

They sat in the splintered stands behind the visitors' dugout and looked out through the chain link fence toward the Golden Gate Bridge and the Marin Headlands. Bottlecaps littered the cement beneath their feet.Two seagulls were yapping and fighting for something in the garbage can at the bottom of the stairs. It usually smelled like stale beer in these stands, but not today. There was only the faint smell of cut grass and something sweet, like candy. It might have been Carolyn's shampoo, and it smelled something like a watermelon Jolly Rancher.

"Did you not return my calls because I reminded you of the day Chrissy died?"

"I'm gonna sound like an idiot," he said. "But I have no explanation for why I didn't call. Maybe I was a little nervous and put it off too long and then thought I'd see you somewhere, but then I didn't see you for a few weeks after you called, and then I quit football, and I don't know why I did that either ..." He let the words trail off and met her eyes briefly before looking back out toward second base.

"Well," she said. "It sounds like it could be a lot of things that were all hitting you at the same time."

He could feel her looking at him, but he didn't turn toward her. The truth was that he should have been trying to figure out why he was feeling the way he was. He should have at least discussed with someone his desire to end his football career before he told the coach. It's not like he really regretted it. He didn't miss playing. But he did want to understand *why* he didn't miss it. Maybe Carolyn was right. "Yeah," he said. "I guess it was a lot of things."

"And the waterslide was one of those things," she said, still looking at the side of his face as he kept his gaze away from those eyes that he knew might break through to something in his mind that he preferred to keep locked up for now.

"Could be," he said.

She put her hand on his knee, and he felt a tingle emanate from that spot, up through his torso, until it settled in his ears, which he could feel getting warm. The same thing had happened when she touched his shoulders up at the football field.

"Why don't you want to talk to me about it?" she said in a voice that sounded more like a soft song.

"I do," he said and looked at her, risking the power of those eyes. "I just don't know what to tell you."

"Do you mind if I ask you some questions about that day?"

"I don't mind."

She took her hand off his leg but moved very close to him so that their hips were touching. "Don't answer if you don't want to," she began. "I'm not trying to mess with you. I'm trying to figure out what happened to everyone."

"I'll answer," he said but didn't like hearing his own voice. It sounded robotic.

"I read something in the paper," she said. "*The Santa Rosa Press Democrat. The Chronicle* had just the one article, but I wanted to know more, so I asked my cousin to send me anything that came up in her hometown paper. There were a bunch of articles in the *Press Democrat* because Pirate's Plank is only a few miles north."

Jerry hadn't even read the article in *The Chronicle*. He didn't need to. He was there. He'd talked to a few reporters that day because all the other kids who'd fallen were with the paramedics and firefighters. He couldn't even remember the questions. "What did they say?" he said to Carolyn.

"Who?"

"*The Press Democrat.*"

"Oh," she said. "They had most of the same stuff as *The Chronicle*, but they also had an interview with a girl who was working that day."

Jerry thought about Trixie. He could picture her face. The panic in her eyes when she figured out what they were doing. Her moment of bravery when she tried to block the mouth of the slide before it gobbled up his friends and then spit them out in chunks across the muddy ground. "What did she say?" he asked.

"From what the lifeguard said, combined with what I've heard from some of the kids who were there that day, I think she might've been talking about you."

"About me?" he said and felt his intestines squeeze into a knot that settled just under his sternum.

"The lifeguard said that one boy leaped over the railing to help his friends." She put her hand on his knee again.

5

Edgar watched the game for a few more minutes but wasn't really interested. He wandered around the outdoor basketball courts for a while and then stopped to talk to a few people near the snack bar under the press box. No one mentioned his stint in juvie, but it was all he could think about because today was the day.

While he was locked up, he met some interesting characters, none more intriguing than Sawyer Puck. Sawyer had offered him a cool deal while the two of them were roommates. And if Edgar was going to follow through with the arrangement, he stood to collect a lot of money. There were three problems: he didn't want to do it alone; he wasn't sure if he could trust Sawyer Puck, and he was running out of time.

Sawyer should not have fit in at Juvenile Hall. But he strangely did. By the time Edgar had arrived, Sawyer seemed to know everyone. When Edgar first got there, he'd seen Sawyer telling stories to the corrections officers but also moving from group to group in the cafeteria, shaking hands with kids and sitting down to tell jokes. He acted like a social director at a frat house.

But his persona didn't seem to make sense in this particular environment in which being able to kick someone's ass was the most valuable kind of capital. Sawyer was one of the few white kids in there, and there wasn't a single thing about him that looked tough. He had soft, almost girlish features. His hair was always impeccably combed, a sharp part on the left side and some kind of product that held it all together that way. All the kids wore the same clothes—department issued jumpsuits. But they kept the shoes they came in wearing. Most inmates had worn-out Chuck Taylors or low top Nikes with black swooshes, but Sawyer wore penny loafers.

Edgar had heard of penny loafers, but he didn't know why they had that name, and he didn't know anyone who wore them. So, he was surprised when he saw that there were actual pennies in slots on top of Sawyer's shoes and that the shoes appeared to have been recently shined.

Edgar was further surprised when, after about a week, he and Sawyer had become friends. It was an unlikely partnership considering Edgar grew up in the Mission District and Sawyer's house was in Pacific Heights. But the two had the same sense of humor and were both smart enough to quietly make fun of the other kids in the facility. Most of these kids were morons.

When Edgar had gotten word from one of the counselors that he was going to be released—at least temporarily—in two days, he'd told Sawyer the news, and Sawyer raised his eyebrows. "You leaving me in here with these barbarians?" he said.

"I think you'll be alright," Edgar said and jumped off his bunk.

"I know I'll be alright," he said. "But this place is fucking boring, man."

"Understood," said Edgar. "How much longer do you have?"

"Shit," said Sawyer. "Long enough to know I'm gonna lose my mind in here."

Then he walked over to Edgar and extended his hand. Edgar shook it and nodded.

Sawyer said, "You might have to come back and break me out."

Edgar laughed. "We can start digging the tunnel tonight," he said. "Maybe we can get you out at the same time as me."

"Y'know what?" he said. "You actually might be able to help me in a different way since you'll be on the outside."

"Okay," said Edgar. "Let me know what I can do."

***

Edgar was sitting on the bench in the empty tennis courts when he saw Jerry and Carolyn walking over to him.

They were holding hands.

Jerry opened the gate and let Carolyn pass through in front of him. When they got close to the bench, Jerry let go of Carolyn's hand and jumped over the net like Jimmy Conners. Carolyn smiled at Edgar and shook her head.

"That's higher than it looks," said Jerry. "I almost didn't make it."

"You guys have a good walk?" said Edgar.

"We went down to West Sunset," said Carolyn. Then she made eye contact with Jerry and said, "We talked a little bit about the waterslides."

Edgar nodded and tried to imagine how that conversation might have gone. Edgar still hadn't talked to anybody about that day. When his mom had asked him about it, he told her the truth, that he'd missed it all. He wasn't near the slide when it collapsed, and he didn't have anything to say about it. But he figured Jerry and Carolyn probably had a pretty serious talk, and maybe he had to stop putting off talking to them about Sawyer Puck.

"There's a thing I'm supposed to do tonight," he said. "And I could use some help."

Carolyn sat next to Edgar on the bench, and Jerry stood, leaning against the net with his feet crossed at the ankle.

The horn went off down at the field, and Edgar figured it was the end of the third quarter. From his angle, he couldn't see the scoreboard, but he didn't think it was good for St. X. He had to tell himself that he didn't need to care anymore. He could already see kids leaving, headed off to get ready for whatever would be happening later.

"What kind of help, Ed?" said Jerry.

"I met this guy in juvie," he said. "Sawyer Puck."

"What the hell kind of name is that?" said Jerry.

"Sawyer Puck?" said Edgar. "I don't know. But it fits him."

"How can we help, Ed?" said Carolyn, and Edgar wondered if it would be best to keep her out of it.

"Well," he said, "I really only need one other person, I think ..." Then he looked over at her. She wasn't smiling, but she had understanding eyes.

"I don't mind going along for the ride," she said. "If you don't think I'll get in the way."

"It's not that," he said. "It's more like you might not want to get involved in this."

"But you think *I* want to get involved?" said Jerry, who uncrossed his ankles and walked over to the bench where he sat next to Edgar.

"You might not either," said Edgar. "I'll tell you what Sawyer wants me to do, and then you can let me know if you want to help out or not. And either way, you guys are the best. It's not a big deal if you don't want to do it."

"All right," said Carolyn, and she was smiling now. "Let's hear it."

"Okay," said Edgar. "Sawyer's mom and his stepdad sold their house. It was his real dad's house, but the mom got it in the divorce and couldn't afford it anymore. It's vacant right now, so Sawyer wants me to break in and get something he's got hidden in the basement before the new owners occupy."

"Jeez," said Jerry. "That sounds pretty serious." He ran his hand through his hair and glanced at Carolyn. "And didn't you just tell me you're supposed to stay clean so you don't have to go back to jail?"

Edgar ran his tongue over his lips. They were dry and so was his throat. He was actually fine doing this by himself. He just wanted someone around in case something went haywire. But there was no reason to think there'd be a problem. This was an easy job. The house was empty. No alarms. No dogs.

"I don't really have to break in," he said "because Sawyer told me what to do and gave me a map and everything. So, it's not really burglary, I don't think."

"I don't know, Edgar," said Jerry. "It feels like it's at least trespassing or breaking and entering. I don't know the official term for going into someone's house and taking something that doesn't belong to you, but it sure sounds like burglary or robbery or theft or whatever, right?"

Edgar didn't like the way Jerry was wording it. He sounded like the lawyer who put him in juvie. "I can just say that I'm retrieving a friend's property."

"What does he want you to take?"

"He was my friend in there," said Edgar. "He kind of took care of me. And I'm not breaking in. I'm just gonna walk in the side door that has a broken lock."

"Okay," said Jerry. "What does he want you to take?"

"It's his baseball card collection."

Jerry's voice went suddenly high-pitched. "What?"

Carolyn laughed. "He just wants his baseball cards?" she said. "And the house is empty?"

"Apparently, they're really valuable cards," said Edgar. "I'm just supposed to go in and grab the bag and hold it for him until he gets released."

"And then what?" said Jerry.

"Then he's supposed to pay me."

When Carolyn maneuvered herself on the bench so that she was facing Edgar, her skirt slid further up her legs. Edgar forced himself to adjust his eyes when he heard her say, "Why didn't he just tell his mom to get the cards before she moved out?"

"I asked the same thing," he said. "I think it has something to do with his stepbrother, and the stepbrother saying the cards are his. That's why he hid them in the first place."

Jerry sat down next to Carolyn but leaned out so that he could look past her at Edgar. "How do you know this guy Sawyer isn't bullshitting you?"

"I don't really care at this point," said Edgar. "If the cards are there, and he's going to pay me for them when he gets out, that seems like a good deal to me." He paused for a second and thought it through again. Jerry and Carolyn were two of the best people he knew, so their opinions were important to him. The whole thing was simple though, so he said, "And as far as I know, I'm not committing any crime. As I said, I'm retrieving a friend's property."

There was a long silence in the tennis courts. The din of the distant crowd and the sound of the 29 bus braking hard on Sunset Boulevard filled the void. Jerry was up walking again. Edgar was resigned to just do the job by himself.

Then Carolyn said, "We'll help you out, Ed."

6

Sawyer Puck didn't tell any of the other kids in juvie why he was there. If they knew he'd been found guilty of attempted murder, he felt people would be reluctant to trust him. Most of the guys were aware that their fellow inmates lied about their crimes anyway, so no one pushed him too hard on the details of his own incarceration, though Sawyer knew there were rumors.

He believed it was a flaw in the justice system that those convicted of *attempted* murder received shorter sentences than those who'd actually accomplished their goal, but he was personally pleased with this particular statute as it would mean that he wouldn't grow old in jail.

It was his opinion that people who tried and failed at homicide were more likely to take a second crack at finishing the job when they got out. It didn't follow logic that people were rewarded for being lousy at something they were trying to do. And this applied to all crimes. Attempted robbery? Attempted arson? Attempted money laundering? Same idea. *Attempted* just means they failed. It didn't make sense to Sawyer that those people—himself included—were rewarded with lighter sentences for their ineptitude even though they had the same intentions as people who were more accomplished at committing their respective crimes.

Though his sentence wasn't really all that lenient—he still had to wait until he turned eighteen before he'd be reevaluated—but if he'd succeeded in his act of violence, who knows how long he'd be stuck there or whether he'd be transferred to San Quentin or Pelican Bay when he turned eighteen.

When other inmates asked him what he'd done to end up at San Francisco's Juvenile Hall, he simply told them it had to do with a family dispute. And that was true. If his mom hadn't cheated on his dad and then married the asshole with whom she'd cheated, none of this would have happened. Things would probably have been better for him.

This isn't to say that he was an angel. He did have a habit of getting into trouble even before his mom did what she did.

But he'd never done anything like the crime for which he'd most recently been imprisoned. That was a moment of weakness for him, and he wasn't proud of it. This particular misconduct was far beyond his standard troublemaking—childish pranks, disrespect for authority, underaged drinking, bookmaking, sex, drugs, and rock 'n roll. He wasn't averse to any of those crimes. Most of them were victimless. And rock 'n roll was rock 'n roll.

He'd been arrested for attempted murder on a tip provided to the police by his own mother. Before that, the last time he'd been picked up by the police was for graffiti. He'd spray painted W.P.O.D. on a neighbor's garage door. WHITE PUNKS ON DOPE. The Tubes song. The San Francisco band had written it ten years before as an absurd anthem of wretched success.

And that's how he thought of his parents. Money had made them awful people, absurd and wretched. And now he was an awful person too.

He was released after two days for the graffiti, but he wasn't so lucky after the murder attempt. Which is a poor description for what he'd done. Yes, he could have killed someone. But, no, that's not what he was attempting to do. He didn't think about taking someone's life when he reacted the way he did. In fact, he didn't even think about it when he did it. It was a reflex. So how is that attempting anything?

In Juvenile Hall, he tried not to think about his trial and his attorney's botched defense, but the guards constantly peppered him with questions. Apparently, most of the other kids were in there for lesser crimes. None of them knew what he'd done. But the guards all knew. Even the ones who didn't say anything to him had a way of looking at him. He could tell they knew and were judging him, watching him like he was some kind of savage. But how could a savage keep his shoes shined in this shit hole?

Isaac was his favorite guard. He was probably only about twenty-five or twenty-six. He was some kind of mix of white, Mexican, and Black. He worked the night shift and never judged Sawyer. Isaac liked to talk to him in the rec room right before lights out, and he didn't seem to think Sawyer's crime made him a bad person. But he was curious about the details. "If you weren't trying to kill him, what were you trying to do?" he asked, a thin smile on his round face.

"Teach him a lesson, I guess."

"Ya' think he's smarter because of your lesson?" he said, the smile even wider now, his eyes just slits above his flat nose. He put his hand on his belly and laughed like you'd see a character do in a Saturday morning cartoon.

"I don't think so," said Sawyer. "Certainly not from that day. But I think he might be figuring some things out about me now that he's had some time to reflect."

"But you in jail," said Isaac. "And he on the outside." Isaac put the emphasis on the first syllable of *outside.* Sawyer liked the sound of it and made a mental note to start saying the word like that. He thought it might give him street cred with the other inmates, though he'd already won most of them over just by being smarter than they were.

"True story," said Sawyer. "But not forever."

Isaac played with his handcuffs when they talked. He practiced sliding them out of the case and fanning them out like an expert blackjack dealer. He'd gotten better since Sawyer had arrived months before. Tonight, he slid them out and immediately cuffed the back slat of Sawyer's chair. "Not bad, huh?" he said and raised his eyebrows at Sawyer like a little kid who'd just learned to walk the dog with his yo-yo.

"Yeah," said Sawyer. "You're getting good, but the chair doesn't fight back."

"True story," said Isaac, removing the cuffs from the chair and placing them back in the case on his duty belt.

"You want to practice on a live model?" said Sawyer.

"You?"

"Why not?" said Sawyer.

Isaac laughed and looked around the empty rec room and then peered out the open door. "You just a little bit of a thing," he said. "It probably wouldn't be much of a fight."

Sawyer had a way of smiling without moving a muscle in his mouth. He felt it more in his eyes and nose, like the bubbles from a big sip of 7up entering into his sinuses. The smile was hidden back behind his teeth and his tongue, but it was there when he said, "I'm not going to resist, man. I'm just asking if you'd like to practice cuffing my wrists rather than the back of a chair?"

"Oh," said Isaac. "I got you." Then he walked over to the open door and looked both ways down the hallway. He checked his watch and said, "Okay, let's see what I can do."

Sawyer was actually rooting for Isaac. He considered him a friend and an all-around good guy. "What should I do?" he said.

"Sit in the chair," said Isaac. "Then I'm going to have you get up and turn around, and I'll cuff you."

Sawyer stayed in his chair. Isaac walked in front of him and said, "Get up, punk."

Sawyer did as he was told but walked away from Isaac just for fun. Isaac must have been doing his thing where he grabs the cuffs out of the case and fans them out because he didn't notice Sawyer walking toward the door. Sawyer was three steps away when Isaac said, "Hey, stop!"

Sawyer was closer to the door than he was to Isaac, so he kept going and said, "You have a few things to work on, Isaac."

"Hold up," he said. "Come back. I know what I did wrong."

Sawyer stepped back into the room and shrugged at Isaac. "Chairs are easier," he said.

"Yeah," said Isaac. "I was supposed to hold your wrist before I went for the cuffs. Rookie mistake."

"How much longer will you consider yourself a rookie?"

"I've been here for six months," he said. "So, I got six left, I guess, and then I'm not a rookie anymore."

Sawyer nodded. "How many kids have been in and out of here since you started?" he asked.

"You missin' Edgar?" he said.

Sawyer took a moment. He'd asked Edgar for a favor on the outside, but Edgar had wavered and told Sawyer that he'd *try*. It was a high-stakes favor, but Edgar didn't know that. As far as Edgar knew, the job was simple. And it was. The door would be open. The bag would be easy to find. Then all he would have to do is create a hiding place at his own house. That's it. But the stakes were, indeed, high. So, Sawyer didn't want Edgar to *try*. Sawyer wanted Edgar to do him this solid, and they'd both get a nice reward for their efforts.

"Yeah," said Sawyer. "Edgar was cool, and I'll miss him. But I'm glad he got out."

7

Andrew Caine looked out the window of the bus as he bounced down Stanyan Street past the panhandle. He spied a pack of fake hippies in tie-dyed T-shirts. They were sitting in a circle on the grass and passing around a joint. Andrew was nineteen, and these wannabes didn't look much older than he was, so he wondered why they were paying homage to the Summer of Love nearly twenty years after it happened. They would have been little kids or even babies back then. But here they were sitting around trying to summon Janice Joplin and resurrect the free love movement only to later go back to their parents' houses in Ashbury Heights to have tuna casserole and watch *Family Ties*.

He got off on Haight Street and immediately picked up the alluring trace of the deep fryer at the McDonald's on the corner across from Kezar Stadium. He had at least twenty bucks in his pocket, so he walked in and ordered a Big Mac and an orange drink. He finished in about two minutes and was back on Haight, stepping around a few thirty-year-old skateboarders and their pit bulls.

He looked across the street at Rockin' Robins and the I-Beam. It was late afternoon now on a Friday, so people who got off early or didn't work at all were already hanging around the bars, getting ready to start their weekends. Outside Rockin' Robins, there was a group dressed like characters from Grease, only there were two Sandys. They must have been sisters. Their faces were nearly identical. But one Sandy had a blonde ponytail and was wearing the yellow dress and white shoes from the scene at the sock hop. The other girl had a mess of curly hair and was wearing the tight, black outfit and red high heels from the final carnival scene.

Andrew found himself stopping to stare. It was a strange and almost surreal feeling to be seeing Sandy's id and superego talking to each other on the street, while a too-short Danny Zuko popped the collar on his leather T-Birds jacket and lit a cigarette.

When the Sandy sisters stepped into the bar with little Zuko and a chubby Kenickie in tow, Andrew couldn't help thinking about his own sibling. His stepbrother, Sawyer. The last time he'd seen him was an ugly scene that he would love to forget, but that would be impossible because Sawyer had thrown, at close range, a kitchen knife at Andrew that left him with a deformed ear.

He knew *deformed* was overplaying it a bit, but the truth was that a section of his ear had been gashed open and stitched back together by an ER doctor who'd smelled like cigars and smoked meats.

Andrew's scar was visible if he combed his hair behind his ear. When he washed his face, and his fingers would touch the damaged cartilage, it made him feel sick to his stomach, and a strange combination of rage and curiosity toward his younger sibling.

He was pretty sure Sawyer hadn't planned to murder him that day. But because Sawyer hurled, from such a short distance, the large, extremely sharp knife in the direction of Andrew's face—and just barely missed—it was hard for Andrew to think of Sawyer as anything other than a violent criminal.

As Andrew moved east on Haight, he heard the muffled sound of The Romantics' *That's What I Like About You* thumping from behind the door of Rock & Bowl. He'd been there a few times and liked it. It was the old Park Bowl. He was not good at the sport, but at Rock & Bowl, the bowling was just a periphery activity. It was more about the lights and the music and not caring whether or not you rolled a gutter ball.

Andrew wasn't usually very impulsive, but he was wandering aimlessly today, and there was always the chance he could score some weed from someone inside. He stepped through the doors and drifted to the bench that looked out on the lanes and the video screens. The giant room was lit by blue lights then pink lights then back to blue lights again.

The Romantics' song ended, and the video for *Money for Nothing* by the Dire Straits took over the big speakers and the monitors mounted on the wall behind the pins. The song started with Sting crooning that he wanted his MTV, and then the weird animation started up. Geometric-looking working-class dudes in overalls just trying to get through the week, judging the band for getting their money for nothing and their chicks for free.

Andrew couldn't stop thinking about the money that Sawyer had stolen from him. It wasn't really money, and, technically, Sawyer didn't steal it. But Andrew felt that he'd been cheated out of something valuable.

Before Andrew's uncle moved to Mexico, he'd given Andrew some cards. They were of baseball players, and his uncle had organized them in binders. There were whole teams from certain years and even cards for every player from the 1955 season. His uncle had also included packs that still weren't open and had sticks of gum inside. There were pages of rookie cards held down by laminate sheets.

One of the cards was extremely valuable.

But Sawyer Puck had left that part out when he'd suggested a trade: an ounce of good weed and his sworn silence in exchange for the cards. Sawyer had found some very private materials in Andrew's closet, and he told Andrew that he wouldn't tell a soul if Andrew just gave him the stupid baseball cards. This was a simultaneous act of barter and blackmail.

Andrew didn't want his dad to find out his secret. At least not like that. So, he handed over the cards to his stepbrother, accepted the substantial bag of weed, and hoped that Sawyer would forever keep his mouth shut.

He later learned that people were paying a lot of money for this kind of collection and that one card in particular—a Roberto Clemente rookie card—could be worth tens of thousands of dollars. Sawyer had kept that information to himself, and when Andrew found out the truth and asked Sawyer to return the collection, Sawyer lost his mind. "We made a deal," he'd said and pointed a finger at Andrew. This conflict escalated and ultimately ended when Andrew nearly lost his ear, or his life, depending on how you interpret it.

And now that Sawyer was going to spend some time locked up, Andrew wanted to find that bag of cards. He knew they were hidden somewhere in the house. Andrew had been looking for the cards for months, ever since his stepmother—Sawyer's mom—had turned her biological son in to the police for the knife business. Andrew guessed that she'd become scared of Sawyer. *Children of the Corn* had come out the year before, and some people had a general fear of kids.

Andrew had turned the house upside-down and couldn't find any trace of the cards. And now, because Andrew's dad and Sawyer's mom were both idiots, the house no longer belonged to the family. The two of them had already spent most of his stepmom's divorce money, and Andrew's dad had quit his job and been out of work for nearly a year. They desperately needed money, but the big decision wasn't to get jobs. It was to sell the house and downsize.

The new owners hadn't moved in yet, but three different times Andrew had pretty much given up trying to find the cards. He'd already pried up floorboards and shined a flashlight into crawl spaces and the backs of cabinets. He nearly fell through the ceiling when he was searching the attic and his foot slipped off a joist and put a hole in the old plaster. Ultimately, he half-decided that Sawyer had either already sold the cards or had them hidden at someone else's house. But another part of him knew that it would have been nearly impossible for Sawyer to unload those cards. He couldn't have known there was going to be the blow up in the kitchen and that his mom would call the police.

So, the cards still had to be somewhere in that house.

Sting and Mark Knopfler finished up their song, and now the Rock & Bowl DJ was bringing the house down with Tears for Fears. Andrew liked their look, but he listened to just the first verse and then headed for the door. When he got to the threshold, he heard the explosion of what must have been a strike and then a chorus of cheers.

When he got outside, the sun was just starting to set, and Haight Street had an orange glow. After being immersed in the blue and pink flashing lights in the bowling alley, he had to squint at the Friday afternoon activity that was beginning to swirl around the neighborhood.

He passed a second-hand clothing store and a headshop and then saw a *Psychic Readings* sandwich board tucked between a Chronicle stand and a parking meter. The sign was in front of a half of a storefront. At some point in time, the old building must have been split in half, and the result was two very narrow stores—a skate shop and the medium.

The psychic place had faded purple curtains, pulled together behind the window. The door was also closed, but there was a sign stenciled directly below the address—*RING BELL FOR FORTUNE TELLER.*

Andrew passed by the door and looked into the skate shop. It was mostly skateboards, but one shelf had rows of roller skates for rent. And behind the counter, they had something new. It was built more like a hockey skate with a single row of wheels. Andrew hadn't seen any on the street yet, and he doubted that they'd ever catch on. Too weird looking.

When a worker wearing shorts down past his knees and an old pair of slip-on sneakers made eye contact, Andrew took a step to move in the direction of Ashbury, away from the salesman and the store. But something stopped him. He didn't take any time to analyze the instinct. If he did, he would have kept walking east. Instead, he turned on a dime, walked back past the skateboard guy, and rang the psychic's doorbell.

8

As soon as Carolyn had agreed to help with Edgar's odd job, Jerry felt a nervous energy pumping through his veins. A lot was happening, and he was trying to process it all. He was anxious about this adventure, but he was excited that Carolyn was now involved.

"I think we should wait until dark," said Edgar. "Even though this should be easy, we might as well do it under the cover of night."

"The cover of night," said Carolyn and raised her eyebrows. "Sounds very dramatic. I feel like Nancy Drew."

Edgar smiled. "I have no idea why I said it that way. I don't have much experience with capers, so I think I'm just using language from Scooby Doo."

"I like it," she said and then turned her attention to the gate, which had just clanged open.

Jerry followed her gaze and saw Father Stricker entering the tennis courts and heading their way. "Shit," Jerry whispered. "Here we go."

"Gentlemen," he called when he was halfway across the court. When he got a bit closer, he added, "And lady." He seemed a bit out of breath from the walk, but he bowed to Carolyn.

"Hi, Father," she said and stood up from her place on the bench.

"Father, this is Carolyn Roddy," said Jerry, and he was surprised how composed he sounded even though he was almost certain he was about to get lambasted because of the incident with Mr. McNaughton before the game.

"Hello, Carolyn," said Father Stricker. "Is your dad Jim Roddy?"

"Yes," she said.

"A good man," said Father Stricker. "I believe I taught him theology back in the day."

"Wow," she said and squinted at Stricker. "It's hard for me to even imagine him in a religion class."

"How's my friend Sister Marilyn doing?" said Stricker.

"She's doin' good, Father," said Carolyn. "She got her voice back last week."

"Sure, I heard," he said. "The doctors were worried she'd never talk again. It's a blessing you girls have her."

Carolyn nodded.

Father Stricker looked at Edgar and smiled. "We miss you, Ed."

"Thanks, Father," he said.

"You're at Lincoln now?"

Edgar nodded.

"Don't let your worst moment define you, son." Stricker was wearing his black slacks and black shirt, but he'd loosened his top button and let the white collar hang half-free from its customary position just below his Adam's apple. "Becoming a saint these days is quite improbable," he said and glanced over at Jerry.

"I know it, Father," said Edgar. "But I'm taking full responsibility for my past sins, and I told my mom I'm getting back to hanging out with better people. I got a little lost for a bit."

"Do you think you're losing your way had anything to do with the tragedy at the waterslides?" Stricker said and scratched at the sideburn under the arm of his glasses.

Edgar pursed his lips and looked up at the sky, which was turning pink way out behind the Farallon Islands. He said nothing for a long moment.

"I think the tragedy's affecting the parents more than us," said Carolyn. "A lot of 'em are afraid our senior class is cursed, and that something else is gonna happen. Do you believe in curses, Father?"

The priest looked up at the sky in the same direction Edgar was looking. Then he turned his attention back to Jerry and his friends. "I think a lot of the time when we're considering curses, we should really be holding mirrors up to our own souls, and maybe into each other's souls when we can."

Jerry considered this and wondered whether Father Stricker was somehow trying to get them all to feel some sense of responsibility for what happened to Chrissy. But why would he want that? How would that make them any better? How would that help them heal? If healing was, indeed, something they needed at this point.

And then Jerry's mind went back again, like it always did, to Chrissy's face. Then Harlan's face. Then Trixie's face. Then Chrissy's again. Then Dave's. And water. When he did this, he always felt like the water had entered him and was rushing and splashing and splattering inside his body. Gravity forcing it down from his brain and letting it wash through his spine and over his bones like waves crashing against the pilings of an eroding pier.

"How about this one from frosh theology, Jerry?" Stricker said and then nodded at Jerry hopefully. "Christ hath redeemed us from the curse of the law, being made a curse for us."

Jerry paused. The verse was barely familiar except for the fact that he remembered not understanding it when he'd first heard it. Like Carolyn, he didn't like the word curse. It especially didn't make sense to him in this context.

"Corinthians?" Jerry said finally.

"Incorrect," said Father Stricker. "It's from Galatians."

Jerry glanced at Carolyn, who seemed to be enjoying this.

"Edgar," said Father Stricker. "What does it mean?"

To Jerry's surprise, Edgar said, "I remember it, Father."

"Yes?"

"It's basically the cornerstone of everything we believe," he said. "Jesus was told to come down here and die for us. That was his curse."

"Do you like that idea of God?" asked Father Stricker. "Someone who'd curse his own son?"

Edgar took even longer this time. But it wasn't an uncomfortable silence. The four of them seemed relaxed in the moment. Jerry saw movement on the other side of the chain link fence. It was Harlan, walking fast. He pointed in the direction of his car and then jogged up the stairs to 37th Avenue. He was covering the side of his face with one hand in case Stricker looked over at him. Edgar was breathing quietly and looking at the sunset again.

"I don't think I do," he said.

"You don't like that idea of God?"

"I don't," said Edgar. "And that's not the way I think of him anyway. A father wouldn't curse his son like that. I think he just sent him to do a really tough job."

"A job that required sacrificing his life."

"Yeah," said Edgar. "But then he got to rise from the dead, so it wasn't a curse after all."

Father Stricker nodded. "Like I said, Edgar, we miss you."

Then he told Carolyn it was nice to meet her and to give his regards to her father and Sister Marilyn. "And Jerry," he said when he was near the gate. "I guess you and I should talk on Monday. Come see me in my office before third period and bring Dan Harlan."

***

Harlan was leaning against his car when Jerry, Carolyn, and Edgar arrived. Jerry peeked in the back seat and saw that Harlan had put a towel over the keg. The result was that it looked like there was a keg with a towel on it in the back seat of Harlan's car.

"Nice camouflage," said Jerry and pointed at the towel.

"I don't know," said Harlan, "it's better than nothing."

"I guess," said Jerry.

"What did Stricker say?"

"It's hard to be a saint," said Jerry.

"Huh?"

"He wants to see us in his office on Monday."

Harlan closed his eyes for a second. "My parents are gonna kill me."

"Yeah," said Jerry. "Me too."

"He's not gonna kick us out, is he?"

"I don't think so," said Jerry. "He misses Edgar too much to lose us too."

Edgar laughed. "That was weird, right?" he said.

"Not so weird," said Carolyn and put her hand on Edgar's shoulder. "I think he'd be bored if the whole school was filled with choir boys."

It was quiet for a moment, and then Harlan said, "Well, since I'm going to be grounded until graduation, I'd like to have some fun tonight." He shrugged and looked at Jerry for approval.

"Good," said Jerry. "Do you want to drive the getaway car for a home burglary in Pacific Heights?"

"I was thinking more of going to a party," he said. "But you have the neighborhood right."

"Seriously?" said Edgar. "I've never been in one of those big ass houses."

"What's an *ass house*?" said Carolyn.

"Huh?"

"St. Mary's High humor," she said. "Forget it."

Harlan furrowed his brow at Carolyn. "I think I get it," he said. "But I feel like the moment has passed."

"It has," she said quickly.

"Cheese is the one who told me about the party," said Harlan. "He said to tell *Carolyn*." Then he gestured to her with his chin. "He said you wanted to go."

Jerry felt a tightness in his stomach. He liked Cheese, but the guy liked to chase girls. Jerry tried to pretend like this wasn't affecting him, but then Carolyn took a step closer to Jerry, put her arm around his waist, and rested her head near his chest.

"Tony invited me," she said. "And told me that he'd give me the address later."

"Apparently," said Harlan, "it's at some drama kid's house on Lyon Street. I guess he goes to one of those independent schools. Rich kid."

Jerry had actually been to an event at one of those schools during his freshman year. A friend of a friend had set him up with a girl, and he'd gone with her to a dance at the school, which was a beautiful, converted mansion on Broadway. The girl was nice, but he'd felt out of place all night. He couldn't remember if he'd ever talked to her after that. "What's the kid's name?" he asked.

"No idea," said Harlan. "But I have the address."

"I think we should go," said Edgar. "But, Harlan, we're serious about the getaway car thing."

"No problem," he said. "Then maybe later we can rob a bank."

Splashdown: The Pirate's Plank Disaster 25 Years Later

A Six-Part Documentary Series

Produced by NorCal Newsreel. Presented by Small Town Consortia in association with The Joint Center for Civic Review and The Sonoma County Film Institute

2010

Episode Three: Wary
TRT 29 min

[Transcript]

Narrator: Did the boys seem different when the school year started?

Bill McNaughton (Former St. Xavier Teacher): I don't know. I felt like they were, but I think I was also looking for it? You know? Self-fulfilling prophecy and all that. I thought they needed me. I probably wanted them to need me. To make me feel like my job was important.

Narrator: So, you didn't think your job was important?

McNaughton: Actually, I knew it was important. Maybe I just wanted the boys to know it as well. I was there to support them. We all were.

Narrator: What were the signs that they'd been through something traumatic?

McNaughton: There were really two different groups. All the kids who went to the waterslides that day. And then all the kids who weren't there but saw their classmates come back to school with neck-braces and broken bones and whatnot.

Narrator: And what kinds of behaviors did you witness?

McNaughton: The group that went to the park could actually be separated into two categories—the ones who were on the slide and the ones who weren't. What surprised me was that the kids who didn't participate in the clog were just as messed up—maybe more affected—than kids who ended up in the hospital.

Narrator: How did their feelings manifest?

McNaughton: We had kids who'd just stand up and walk out of class in the middle of a lecture. Students were turning in tests with nothing written on them. Kids who'd never seen their counselors before were going once a day. And they were challenging their teachers, like they thought we were lying to them or something. Like they had reason to believe that we were somehow misleading them about the world. They didn't trust anyone.

Narrator: What about the kids who were on the slide?

9

The air inside the fortune teller's shop was thick and smelled like eucalyptus. After Andrew was buzzed in, he had to walk through another doorway that was obscured by a curtain of hanging beads, like Greg Brady had used—during his rebellious stint—for his rad apartment over the attic.

Andrew didn't have time to consider what the fortune teller might look like. He'd only decided to come in for a reading a few seconds before he pushed his way through the bead curtain. But he certainly didn't expect what he saw.

She was sitting in a tall-backed chair in front of a round coffee table. Her wavy blonde hair was held back from her face with a soft headband tied in a bow on top of her head. She wore a leather jacket over a black, lacey bustier. And she had black tights under her skirt.

Andrew's eyes went first to the bustier. He was intrigued by the fashion statement. He eyed the collection of necklaces that dangled nearly to her navel. Crosses and celestial bodies and jagged shapes and beads of various sizes. To Andrew, it was all beautiful, even though at first glance, the jewelry looked like tangled fishing gear.

She also had giant crosses for earrings, heavy eye makeup, and a beauty mark under her right nostril. The room was dim, and Andrew was still blinking the scene into focus when he actually gasped and opened his mouth, ready to shout,"Oh my God—"

But before he could say anything, she stopped him. "I'm not her," she said.

Andrew took another step into the room, and his eyes were beginning to adjust to the light. She was too old to be Madonna. Maybe in her early 40's. But she sure looked like her.

"I'm an impersonator," she said, and now her Western inflection fully exposed her.

"Oh," said Andrew, more confused than ever. "I think I went through the wrong door. I was looking for the fortune teller."

"You got the right place, sweetheart, but the primary medium is out today."

Andrew almost walked out but instead tried, "Are you the secondary medium?"

"I guess you could say that," she said. "I don't do palms or cards or tea. I'm still learning."

"Oh," said Andrew, wondering if it was worth whatever she was going to charge.

"But I'm good with the crystal ball."

"Really?" he said. He thought the crystal ball was just something they did in movies.

"Yeah," she said. "I have the gift, but Nancy hasn't taught me how to use my natural talents yet except on the ball. I'm good though. It speaks to me."

Andrew decided he was going to try this if he had enough money, but he had to ask, "What's with the Madonna outfit?"

"I told you," she said. "I'm an impersonator."

"I understand that," said Andrew. "But why are you wearing all that for *this* job?"

"You think I make enough as an apprentice medium to afford rent?" she said. "I have a gig later tonight, and it takes a long time to get ready. So, I got ready early, but I can still do the crystal ball if you want."

"How much?"

"How much you got?"

"Ten bucks."

"That'll do for this first reading," she said. "But we don't always get to all the answers the first time, and when you come back, I gotta charge you twenty. You cool with that?"

"Cool," he said.

"Well, sit down," she said and pointed to the loveseat next to her chair. Then she got up and walked into another room. She dimmed the lights and then came out holding the ball in one hand and a candle in the other.

"I thought it would be bigger," said Andrew.

"The crystal ball?"

"Yeah."

"Did you also think it would have a magic fog inside that would turn into images of your future life?"

Andrew smiled. "Something like that," he said.

"Like the one the Wicked Witch of the West used?"

"I guess so," he said. In fact, she was right. He thought the crystal ball was going to be the size of a basketball and have moving pictures inside. But this ball was no bigger than a cantaloupe, and it wasn't completely transparent. It looked almost like a big white marble.

She sat down next to him on the loveseat. Then she lit the candle and placed it behind the crystal ball, which she'd balanced on a small stand. As the flame danced in the background, the ball revealed different shapes.

"Okay," she said. "We need to talk first, so I know what to look for." She adjusted herself in her seat so that she was almost facing Andrew, but he wasn't uncomfortable. Now that it was shadowy in the little room, he really felt like he was talking to Madonna. This lady had very similar features, and she had the makeup and clothes just right. Andrew had no problem relaxing and talking to Madonna about whatever she wanted.

"Do you ask me questions," he said. "Or do I just start talking? "

"Why did you come in today?" she said.

"I was just walking by and decided to come in."

"Why did you come in today?" she repeated.

"Seriously," he said. "I didn't even know this place was here."

"Why did you come in?"

Andrew was about to snap at her. He thought she was suggesting that he'd lied to her, but now that he was really thinking about the question, he paused to consider it. Although he didn't plan to see a medium today, he did choose to ring that bell. Although he felt like it was on a whim, he wasn't there to simply hear his fortune told. He didn't know his purpose when he rang the bell. It must have come from somewhere deep in his subconscious. But now, sitting here with the clairvoyant Queen of Pop, he knew exactly why he was there.

"I lost something valuable," he said.

"Now we're getting somewhere," she said and adjusted the candle behind the crystal ball. "How long have you been looking?"

"Months," he said and thought about all the closets and crawl spaces and blind spots into which he'd run his hand through cobwebs and dust in the hope of finding his cards somewhere in the giant old house.

"Is it valuable for sentimental reasons or financial?" she said, keeping her eyes on the magic sphere.

"Both," he said, and for the first time, he thought about his uncle and how disappointed he'd be that Andrew had traded the cards for weed and a secret.

"I'm seeing something here," she said. "Did you lose this item, or was it stolen?"

Andrew had to think about this answer. It wasn't so cut and dry. He'd lost the cards because of his own stupidity and carelessness, but they were stolen in the sense that Sawyer scammed him. "Both," he said again.

"C'mon," she said. "You need to be honest, or we're never gonna get anywhere." Then she looked away from the ball and made eye contact. She pointed at the ball and said, "This thing is saying that it was stolen."

"In a way, it was," he said. "I got tricked. I didn't know how valuable it was and basically gave it away."

She nodded and looked back at the ball.

"How did you know that?" he asked.

"What?" she said and kept adjusting the ball.

"That it was stolen."

"The ball shows pictures, and the pictures tell me stories," she said. "Tea leaves work the same way, but I haven't worked with tea yet."

"Well, what was the picture?"

"This might sound silly," she said. "But I saw what looked to me like a hand in a cookie jar, and that made me think that your item was stolen."

"I guess it was in a way," he said. "What else?"

"I assume you want me to tell you how to get it back? Is that why we're here?"

"I think that's why I came in," he said and was slightly embarrassed that it took him this long to say it.

"This part is a little confusing," she said. "It seems like the thief is a family member but not a family member?" She looked over at him again. "I'm still learning how to do this. Trees usually represent family, but the tree I'm seeing," she looked back at the ball, "it looks like the person has fallen from the tree. Does that mean anything to you?"

"It's my stepbrother," said Andrew and realized that he was whispering. He wasn't an idiot. He was very skeptical of psychics, especially ones dressed up like Madonna. But this was very convincing. "Can you show me the picture?"

She pointed to a small shadow on the ball that looked like the letter *T*.

"That's a tree?" he said.

"Yes," she said, a little annoyed. "And you see this here?" She pointed to what looked like a tiny lollipop next to the tree. "That's the family member who deserted the family. Do you know where he is?"

The lollipop didn't look like a person to Andrew, but he answered, "In jail."

"Then why can't you get your stuff back?"

"He hid it."

Madonna stood up and went into the back room again. She brought out a second candle. She lit it and put it near the other candle behind the ball, and the pictures—the little blobs and dots and lines—changed again. "And you want me to help you find it."

It wasn't a question, but Andrew responded with a question of his own. "Can you help me?"

"I'm going to need more details," she said. "But yes. I can help you."

10

If Edgar was telling the truth about the easy heist they'd be committing later tonight, then Carolyn felt she had nothing to worry about. She was very much forcing herself to believe Edgar because the rest of her plan for the day was coming together nicely. She was sitting next to Jerry in the back seat of Dan Harlan's car, and they'd made plans to go to a party a little later before picking up Edgar's friend's baseball cards.

After not hearing from Jerry for those weeks after the accident, this was beyond what she'd imagined possible when she set out for the game this afternoon. But the stars seemed aligned. She didn't want to be stuck in her school uniform for the rest of the night, so she'd asked Harlan to stop by her house on 41st Avenue for a quick change. He was very accommodating.

She ran up her front stairs and traded out her plaid skirt and white blouse for a jean skirt, an off the shoulder Esprit sweatshirt, and a pair of topsiders. She wasn't completely happy with her look, but her dad would have no objections, and the boys didn't have to wait too long for her to get ready. She didn't want to seem high maintenance, so she just put on the easiest combination and ran back down to the car. Jerry was holding the door for her, and she wished she'd taken the time to brush her teeth.

She sat in the middle between Jerry and the keg. It wasn't bad being squished back there because it meant she got to lean into Jerry, who didn't seem to mind.

"Thanks for waiting," she said when she'd climbed in. "You guys are saints."

"Becoming a saint these days," said Edgar, "is quite improbable."

"Oh, yeah," she said. "I forgot." Then she laughed and said, "Thanks for waiting. You guys are sinners."

Harlan looked at her in the rearview mirror. "What are you guys talking about?" he said, not really smiling, but not frowning either. He had the look of a guy reviewing a menu written in French. He couldn't understand any of the words, but he knew there was something interesting in there somewhere.

Jerry said, "Stricker said it when he was talking to us at the tennis courts."

"Said what?"

"Just that it's tough to be a saint these days."

With his finger and thumb, Harlan smoothed the wispy beginnings of an orange mustache and said, "Hasn't it always been tough?"

"Yeah," said Jerry, shaking his head. "Maybe that's what he said. Either way, we have no chance now that Stricker knows about the keg. I think he has a direct line to the Pope."

"I think John Paul would forgive us for beer," said Edgar. "It's all the other stuff."

Harlan was driving east on Taraval. "Pirro's or Round Table?" he said as they passed by Pirro's and the 7-11.

"I guess we're going up to Round Table?" said Jerry and stretched his neck to look at Pirro's through the back window. "I love Pirro's."

"It's a little greasy, isn't it?" said Carolyn.

"That's flavor liquid," said Edgar. "But apparently Harlan wants Round Table anyway."

"It'll give us time for a beer," said Harlan.

Jerry nodded, pumped the keg once, and started pouring beers into the extra 31 Flavors' cups. After he passed beers up to Edgar and Harlan, he looked over at Carolyn and raised his eyebrows. She nodded and indicated, by forming a C with her fingers, that she would take just a bit. He handed her half a cup and poured himself a full cup.

Carolyn watched him take a long swallow, wipe the foam off his upper lip and say, "What sin keeps you from being a saint, Harlan?"

Harlan was holding his cup in his right hand and steering the car by resting his left forearm at twelve o'clock on the wheel as he maneuvered around the L Taraval streetcar, rattling to the stop on 28th Avenue. "A little early for confessions, isn't it?"

"Just play along," said Carolyn. She watched Harlan take a sip and let his face rest in the uncommitted half-smile again.

"Okay," he said. "How about this? Last week, I walked by Fr. Dodd's desk and saw the passage he was going to use for our midterm exam."

When Harlan paused for a moment, Edgar said, "And…"

"Well," he said. "I'm terrible at Latin, but I saw that it was a specific passage from Cicero. So, I went to the library and looked up a translation of the passage, so I could pass the test."

"That's not so bad," said Carolyn. "At least you had to memorize something."

Harlan took another sip and turned right on 17th Avenue. "Not really," he said. "Fr. Dodd lets us use our Latin to English dictionary when we have to translate long passages, so I just copied the whole translation into different pages of the dictionary and then, during the test, I just transcribed the text into the blue book."

"Oh," said Carolyn and couldn't help giggling. "That's kind of ingenious."

"Except now Fr. Dodd thinks I'm some kind of Latin scholar, but I don't know jack."

Jerry was halfway through another swallow and snorted some of the beer back into his cup as he burst out laughing. "What are you going to do for the rest of the year?" he said and wiped at his face with the sleeve of his jacket.

"I haven't planned that out yet," he said. "But right now, I have an A, and Fr. Dodd wants to recommend me for some classics program at Holy Cross."

Carolyn put her hand on Edgar's shoulder and said, "How about you, Ed?"

"I actually went to jail," he said, looking over his shoulder at Carolyn. "I think that answers the question."

"So did Joan of Arc," said Carolyn. "For heresy. She dressed like a man and received communion when it wasn't allowed for women."

Carolyn felt Jerry turn toward her, but she kept her eyes on Edgar.

"Really?" said Jerry. "Did that make her a drag *king*?"

"Just saying," said Carolyn. "She went to jail and still became a saint."

Edgar turned all the way around in his seat. "And then she was burned at the stake," he said. "I'm trying to avoid that if I can."

"How about you, Jerry," said Carolyn, leaning into him even more, feeling her ear on his shoulder. "What's your saint-breaker moment?"

"I think I'm still in the running for sainthood," he said and looked out the window, but Carolyn could tell he was smiling.

Harlan took his eyes off the road to glance back at him. "You've literally been in more fistfights than anyone I know," he said.

Jerry kept looking out the window. "They had it coming," he said, and Carolyn hit him in the shoulder.

"Is that true?" she said.

He looked at her now. "Yes, it's true," he said. "They had it coming."

"No," she said. "Is it true that you've been in a lot of fights?"

"Not many," he said. "But probably enough to keep me from sainthood." Then he bumped her with his shoulder and said, "How about you Saint Carolyn?"

"Wait," she said. "Can we finish this first? I can't believe you've been in a lot of fights. You don't seem the type."

"I'm not," he said.

"Well, you need to stop. You're too old to be getting into fistfights."

"I know it," he said and put his arm around her. "I'm done with all that."

"Good," she said and rested her head back on his shoulder.

"Those guys really did deserve it though," he said. "But here's one that might keep me out of heaven, and it wasn't even a fight."

When he paused for a moment, Harlan glanced back at him again in the rearview mirror and then looked forward before turning on the headlights.

"A few weeks ago," said Jerry, "we were playing pick-up on the outdoor courts, and I was stinking it up. Couldn't hit a shot to save my life. Then Todd Erikson picked me clean out around halfcourt, and I stuck my foot out and tripped him."

"Did he fall?" asked Edgar, turning around in his seat.

"Cut up his hands and ripped his pants," said Jerry. "And then I made a big show about saying sorry for getting tangled up, and I helped him to his feet. But I did it on purpose. I mean, it was at least part instinctual. Like a reflex. I didn't really have time to think about it, but when I was helping him up, I knew that I'd done it on purpose."

"Like Gene and Finny," said Edgar.

"Exactly," said Jerry.

"Who're Gene and Finny?" said Carolyn.

Edgar said, "These characters in *A Separate Peace.* Sophomore English."

"Gene jounces a tree limb," said Jerry. "And makes his best friend fall and break his leg."

"We never read that one," said Carolyn. "Sounds like a boy book with boys doing boy things."

"I guess it is," said Jerry. "I don't remember any girls in that story." Then he squeezed her shoulder and said, "Okay. What's your girl sin that keeps you from sainthood? Enquiring minds want to know."

She couldn't help smirking. She knew she'd eventually tell them, but she didn't think it would be tonight. It seemed to have just worked its way into the conversation. "You know how I work at the St. Gabe's rectory a couple of days a week?" she said.

"I didn't know that," said Jerry. "But go ahead. That sounds like something that might help you avoid some time in purgatory."

"I just answer the door and the phone and do some cooking," she said. "But a couple of months ago. Right before the accident. I stole a blank baptismal certificate with an official seal."

Harlan had turned onto Vicente. They were about a block away from West Portal and Round Table Pizza, so everyone was rushing through the last of their beers. "What were you going to do with a baptismal certificate?" asked Harlan.

"Get one of these," she said and pulled a driver's license out of her purse. She held it up at Jerry's eye level. Jerry looked at it and then leaned back and blinked it into focus.

Harlan looked at her in the rearview mirror and said, "Why did you steal something from church just to get a driver's license?" he said. "I thought you already had your license."

"Tell 'em, Jerry."

Jerry took the license out of her hand and smiled. "You look good in this," he said. "Older."

"Thank you," she said and laughed.

"I don't get it," said Harlan.

Jerry's smile grew, and he said, "This authentic license issued by the California Department of Motor Vehicles has a beautiful picture of Carolyn, but the name is Marion Ravenwood, and it says she was born in 1964, which makes Marion twenty-one years old."

"Oh, shit," said Harlan. "You have a real fake ID?"

"I do," she said with pride. "And 'real fake' is an oxymoron."

"I think I actually know a Marion Ravenwood," said Edgar.

"You do," she said. Then she laughed and said, "*Raiders of the Lost Ark.*"

It was quiet for a moment as they pulled up in front of Round Table. Then Edgar said, "Oh ... Marion." Then he laughed and said, "Why her?"

"Cause she's a badass," said Jerry.

"Exactly," said Carolyn.

11

Helen didn't have the gift. Neither did her aunt, Nancy, who was in charge of the Haight Street operation. But people who came in for readings heard what they wanted to hear, so the two fake psychics somehow managed to pay the bills each month.

Helen had moved out to San Francisco from Montana. She was named after the city of Helena. But ever since she was about ten years old, she wanted out. She waited tables when she was young and then worked as a receptionist at a funeral home owned by her husband. She'd always thought he was a weird man, but after several years of marriage, when she eventually caught him one night doing some truly perverted acts in the reposing room, she took off without saying goodbye. Grabbed what little money she could get her hands on and hopped on a Greyhound to San Francisco.

For the last three months, she'd been living in the tiny apartment behind the reading room while she was trained by Nancy a couple of nights a week. Most other nights she worked as a cocktail waitress at The Backlot, a club that featured celebrity impersonators. The good ones performed on stage. The others waited tables.

Helen had tried out as a Marilyn Monroe, but they already had a Marilyn, so they asked her to try Madonna, and she did pretty well. She was a bit old for Madonna, or for Marilyn, but with all the makeup and the outfits, she made it work, and the owner liked her, said she'd give Helen a chance on stage if she improved her act, developed the dance moves and learned the songs from the new album.

So, she was practicing every day, simultaneously learning two trades. She wasn't saving any money, but as soon as she could, she'd move out of the apartment on Haight, find a nicer spot, and take one more chance at finding a man.

Aunt Nancy had taken a trip to Mendocino, so Helen was looking after the shop. Nancy told her it was okay to work the crystal ball, but that was it. She still had a lot to learn before she tried anything else. And it was okay if she had to turn away a patron if he or she wanted tea leaves or palms read. The business relied on return customers, and one inauthentic reading could cost them weeks of regular revenue.

So, when the kid came in today, Helen was upfront with him. Crystal ball readings only. That's all she had to offer. He didn't have much money, but she had time to kill before heading down to The

Backlot, so she decided to take the kid's cash and use this reading as practice for a bigger fish.

But as she talked to the kid—Andrew was his name—she found out that he was looking for something valuable. And now Helen wanted to help him find it. There'd definitely be something in it for her. Maybe enough to get her into a new place.

"Can the crystal ball help with a specific location?" he asked.

"It depends," she said. "We can try, but I might actually have to go to the location where you think the item is hidden."

"Really?" he said and scratched at his ear. She'd made him nervous. And now she had to get him back.

"I don't think the crystal ball will work that way, but there's a couple other tools that I've used for this kind of thing before."

"What kind of tool?" he said.

"I have tools whose capability drastically improves if I use them at the site where we're trying to find answers," she said.

"Yeah," he said and looked around the room, maybe trying to see if the devices were in plain sight. "But what are they?"

"They're both based on ideomotor movements," she said, trying to throw out as much terminology as she could. This strategy seemed to work with the general public. They usually didn't want to look ignorant, so they just went along with whatever she was saying. But Andrew was searching for something very serious, so he asked serious questions.

"Ideomotor movements?" he said.

"Yeah," she said and leaned over to look into his eyes. "It's nothing really spiritual. It's more psychological." Nancy didn't use an ideomotor, but Helen had done some reading on the topic and figured anyone could fake this stuff.

"Okay," he said. "In what way?"

She sighed softly and said, "The idea is that you already have the answers somewhere locked in your subconscious, but in the right circumstances with the right tools, we can open that portal and collect the desired information."

"I don't want to be hypnotized," he said and stood up.

Helen laughed. "I'm no hypnotist," she said. "But what do you have against hypnosis?"

"I don't want to go under and then have you making me act like a chicken or something."

She laughed again. "Yeah, I don't think it works like that," she said and motioned for him to sit back down. "And I can't do it anyway."

"So, how do you get these ideomonitor vibrations then?"

"Ideomotor movements," she said.

"Whatever," he said, sounding a little frustrated now. "How do you get these movements you're talking about?"

"We could either do a spirit board or Chevreul's Pendulum," she said. "Or we could try both. They might be helpful in finding a lost item. As I said, I've seen it work before."

"Can you tell me what these things are before I decide to take you to somebody else's house to run a séance?"

"It would hardly be a séance," she said and smiled reassuringly. She felt her fake mole above her lip move just slightly, but she didn't reach to secure it. She'd lost about twenty of them since she began her Madonna routine. "Chevreul's Pendulum is totally simple. It's really just a string with a weight on it."

"How is that going to find the cards?" he said.

"What cards?" she said, always looking for information that she could use later.

"Nothing," he said. "My item. How will a string help me find my item?"

"If we're in the house where the item is hidden," she said, "I will have you close your eyes and hold the pendulum out in front of you. Then I'll ask you some yes or no questions."

"And ..." he said, acting a bit petulant now.

"If the answer is yes," she said, "the weight will move clockwise. And if the answer is no, it will move counterclockwise."

"That's it?" he said.

"Yes," she answered. "That's the whole point of ideomotor movements. We're gonna get in that house, and you'll start thinking about all the places you've already looked, and you're gonna think about everything you know about your stepbrother. And then your subconscious is going to answer the questions for us."

"So, it can only do yes or no, I guess?"

"Correct."

"But we can eliminate rooms and other areas and maybe we'll bump into the hiding place because it's there in the back of my mind somewhere."

"That's the idea," she said. This was getting close now, and Helen knew that if she could get in that house, she'd be able to cash in on the kid. But she wanted to know what he meant by *cards*. She didn't want to spook him by pressing him on it, but she was confident he'd eventually spill the beans.

"And what if the pendulum doesn't work?"

"Then at least we tried," she said.

"And how about this spirit board?" he asked. "Can that give us something more specific? How does that work?"

"It's just a Ouija board," she said and tried to remember where Nancy kept it.

12

Jerry was feeling the change. It had crept up on him like a new friendship, and now it was here. After weeks of being effectively quarantined from each other, tonight had a different vibe. People were out. Girls were out. Carolyn and Edgar and Harlan were with him. And it all seemed normal again. Their parents' collective obsession about protecting their children from potential, unforeseen cataclysm had clearly waned, and Jerry felt a tingling throughout his body. Mostly in his fingertips. He could see that the lights had turned on behind his friends' eyes. They were feeling it too.

He allowed himself to also experience a swift pang of sadness or guilt or shame because Chrissy would not be with them tonight. But he forced himself to let it go as quickly as it came. The warm keg beer was probably helping modulate his emotions, but he knew it could work the other way as well. Maybe the beer is what made him think of Chrissy in the first place.

Carolyn was the one who'd gotten the address to the party in Pac Heights, so they'd sent her up the stairs to see if she could get them in.

The house was huge—three stories—and had wild decorative embellishments on every possible surface the architect could utilize for his artistic flourishes. Eaves, cornices, cresting, fluting. Everything he'd learned in his Art & Architecture class had been thrown onto this structure.

He'd grown up in the Sunset, where the houses mostly looked the same. He was certain there was no other house like this one anywhere in the world. It had to be worth millions, which explained why Jerry didn't know these people. Kids with this kind of wealth didn't go to parochial schools in the city even if they were Catholic. There were private, independent schools for these kids. Tuition at twice the rate of the Catholic schools. Twelve kids per classroom. College counselors, who were expected to get each student an Ivy League offer. Country club facilities. Still not east coast prep schools, but close.

The Catholics among all this privilege went to St. Ignatius Church on the hilltop for Easter and Christmas but otherwise had no affiliation with the parishes. St. Ignatius Parish was not affiliated with a school. In fact, kids like Jerry and his friends almost never had any contact with the elite kids. Until recently, Jerry didn't even know their schools existed. He'd heard of some of them but never met any of the kids because they played in different leagues and had different hangouts. And Jerry's whole house could fit inside this guy's garage.

The windows all had the shades pulled down, but Jerry could see the silhouettes of kids moving around in the rooms on the first floor. When the door opened for Carolyn, a tall, skinny boy with pants that tapered around the ankles opened the door and then leaned on the frame, his arms folded across his chest. His sneakers were impossibly white. They made Jerry glance down at his dirty Chuck Taylors.

It looked like Carolyn was making their case for an invitation, and the kid was listening attentively. After she finished, he shook his head and said something before he shrugged, stepped back inside, and closed the door.

"I guess that was a *no*," said Harlan when Carolyn walked up to the car and pantomimed the wiping of tears from her cheeks.

Jerry, Edgar, and Harlan were leaning against the car and drinking beer out of their paper cups, which were beginning to collapse from overuse.

"Apparently," she said, "it's a cast party for the fall play at The Brigham School, and they're not even drinking. He said his parents would kill him if they got caught with booze."

"So, why did Cheese tell us about this party?" said Jerry. "And I use the word *party* loosely.

Carolyn walked over and stood close to Jerry. "I don't know," she said. "Someone must have told him about it, and he thought it would be," she paused and then said, "different from this," and then waved a hand toward the big house.

Jerry put his arm around her. "Was Cheese even in there?" he said.

"I didn't see him," she said. "A couple of girls in really weird clothes peeked around the door, but I didn't see anyone else."

"This place is amazing," said Harlan and pointed up at the top floor. "I wonder if it has a big backyard."

"I'm sure it does," said Carolyn. "They might even have a tennis court."

"You sure there's no parents in there?"

"It didn't seem like it," she said.

"Grab the keg," Harlan said and nodded at Edgar.

"What do ya'mean?" he said.

Harlan pointed to the alley that ran along the side of the house. "We're gonna bring the keg into the backyard and *light* this candle."

"No," said Carolyn. "This guy said he'd get in big trouble.

Harlan smiled at her. "We'll make it the best night of his life," he said. "They're probably playing *Clue* in there or bobbing for apples."

"Were the girls cute?" said Edgar.

"Really pretty," said Carolyn. "But I don't want to get this guy in trouble." She looked up at Jerry with pleading eyes. "And we need to do Edgar's job in a while anyway…."

Jerry pulled her close. "Let's bring the keg back there and see what happens. If the guy starts crying, we'll leave."

***

The backyard was beautiful. Flat stones with moss between them made up a large patio with wrought iron furniture that matched the railings and roof cresting. A small guest cottage made out of aged bricks and covered in ivy sat at the back of the space near a tall wooden fence that sheltered this yard from the one next door. The cottage looked like something from a Disney movie—like it would be inhabited by dwarves or elves or fairies. There were trees and shrubs lining the walkways, and lattices with different types of climbing plants anchored to the fences.

Harlan and Edgar placed the keg in the middle of the patio. Edgar poured beers for everyone, and they sat in the chairs. For a moment, no one said anything. Then Harlan smiled, and they all laughed.

"Should we spark one?" said Edgar and put his hand into the pocket of his jacket.

"Absolutely not," said Carolyn. Jerry thought she was still concerned about getting the kid in trouble, but then she followed up saying, "No weed until we get your baseball cards. I don't want you guys high when we're doing the job."

"You're right," said Edgar. "It just seems weird sitting here in someone else's backyard drinking beer."

Jerry took a sip of his beer and then said, "Are you saying it would be less weird if we were smoking weed back here?"

"I don't know," he said, smiling. "I guess I'm just saying this is weird."

It was a full moon, and streetlights shined on both sides of the yard. And it took only about fifteen minutes of talking and laughing before someone looked out the back window and saw them.

The kid in the tapered pants, followed by a strange assembly of soldiers, sailors, hula girls, 1940's bathing beauties, and nurses, scampered down the back steps. The pageant looked like something from a strange dream. Jerry's group didn't move.

The kid who'd opened the door for Carolyn stepped onto the patio, pointed at the keg, and said, "What the fuck is happening?"

"We heard there was a party?" said Edgar.

A heavy-set kid in a sailor's outfit, complete with the hat tilted at a jaunty angle, stepped up close to Edgar and said, "You need to get the hell outta here."

Edgar was slouched in the patio chair and glanced over at Jerry. Jerry did not want to fight anyone. He'd told Carolyn he wasn't going to do that anymore, but here he was in a situation that was definitely escalating.

"You," said the kid in the tapered pants, the only one not in some kind of costume. He was pointing at Carolyn. "I told you there wasn't any booze here. I told you I'd get in tons of trouble if my parents found out I had a party."

Jerry didn't like the way the kid had pointed at Carolyn.

"I'm sorry," she said. "I misunderstood. I thought you said it wasn't really a party *because* you didn't have any beer. So we brought some." She pointed at the keg. Jerry was impressed with how she'd been quick on her feet.

Harlan started to pass out cups to anyone who would take one. He spent extra time trying to convince one of the hula girls that it would be in her best interest to try one cup.

"Stop," shouted the leader. "This can't be happening."

"Okay," said Jerry. "We'll pack up and hit the road, but can you tell us why everyone's dressed like this?" Jerry was genuinely curious.

"It's a tradition at The Brigham School for the cast of the musical to have a party in costume—"

"And in character," interrupted a pretty girl dressed in an old-fashioned swimsuit .

"Yes," said the leader. "And in character before opening night, which is tomorrow."

"Fun," said Carolyn, and she appeared to be a hundred percent sincere.

"How come you're not in costume?" said Jerry.

"I'm the stage manager," he said. "And I don't know why I'm talking to you people. It's time for you to go."

But it was too late. Half the cast already had beers in their hands or were waiting in line. The stage manager had lost control. When he looked around the patio and saw that there was an actual party in his yard, he looked like he might cry. "I can't," he said in a low whisper, and Jerry actually felt sorry for him. He was fine getting the keg back in the car and letting these people finish whatever it was they were doing.

"What's the show?" said Edgar, who was up now and standing near the stage manager.

"*South Pacific*," he said.

"I like that one," said Edgar, then held up a tightly rolled joint for the stage manager to see. "You want to try a little of this?"

"Oh great," he said. "Now there's drugs in my house." He shook his head and curled his lips inward. His face was pink. "Who are you guys?"

"We go to St. X," said Edgar.

The stage manager's face seemed to deflate and return to its natural color. "The waterslide school?" he said.

Edgar nodded.

"Holy crap," said the stage manager. "Were any of you guys there?"

"We were all there," said Edgar.

"Jesus."

By now, someone had gone into the guest house, turned on the stereo, and propped an old speaker up in the window. A strange kind of music jumped out into the yard. Loud horns and a quick reggae beat: *Party at ground zero. A B-movie starring you. And the world will turn to flowing pink vapor stew.*

All the drama kids were either dancing now or bobbing their heads.

"What is this?" said Jerry.

In unison, Edgar and the stage manager said, "Fishbone." Then they looked at each other, and Edgar held up the joint again.

"Why not?" said the stage manager.

***

Edgar had gotten a good percentage of the cast stoned. A girl dressed as a nurse was making out with a soldier. Before they both fell on a patch of grass near the coy pond, the two had looked like the sailor and nurse in the Times Square V-J Day photo that appeared in *Life Magazine.*

The hula girls were practicing their routine, and Harlan was critiquing the performance. They'd persuaded Carolyn to join, and she did pretty well.

When the dance was over, one of the girls reached into the waistband of her grass skirt and pulled out a silver cigarette case like you'd see from a lady in the movies. She removed a brown cigarette and waited for one of the other girls to light it for her. Once she'd taken a few drags, a strange aroma took over the backyard.

"Is that weed?" said Jerry.

The girl looked him up and down—elevator eyes. "Cloves, dude," she said and smiled.

Jerry nodded, had no idea what she was talking about. When she offered him one out of her little case, he politely declined. She offered one to Harlan, and he politely accepted.

The Sunset kids and the Pacific Heights kids were getting along swimmingly. They'd all danced to Fishbone, The Specials, Madness, Toots and the Maytals, The Clash, and the Mighty Mighty Bosstones. Jerry knew Toots and the Maytals. They were just straight Reggae. But he'd learned tonight that the rest of these bands would be considered ska. Rich kids apparently listened to different music than blue-collar kids. He hadn't known that, and it didn't make any sense to him. He wondered if they were familiar with the new Tom Petty album.

In between songs, Harlan declared that the keg was dry and memorialized this development by placing his cup over the pump. The stage manager, Kent, seemed moved by the declaration. He'd gotten into his parents' wine cellar and was carrying a half-drunk bottle with him when he climbed the trellis up to the roof of the guest house. Once he'd secured his feet, straddling the ridge of the pitched roof, he said, "The St. X kids went through a lot this summer." He sloshed the wine and slurred his words. Then he looked confused, as if he couldn't understand why he sounded the way he did—like an emcee puzzled by sudden reverb.

Jerry worried that he'd lose his balance, but Kent straightened up and continued, "But they stuck together like a family. They're the best people I know," he said and raised his bottle.

The other kids started to cheer, but when Kent shifted his feet to maintain balance, something caved, and he fell right through the roof. The last thing Jerry saw was the raised wine bottle. Otherwise, their host had simply disappeared mid-toast. If there'd been a smoke bomb to accompany the maneuver, it would have been a fantastic finale for an amateur magician.

But Kent was not an amateur magician. He was the stage manager, who finally got his moment in the spotlight and then disappeared almost immediately.

Jerry did appreciate the sentiments of the romanticized toast, but he was also uneasy about this development.

One of the nurses and a guy wearing his white sailor pants paired with one of the girls' bikini tops ran into the house to check on Kent's condition. Most of the other kids were either screaming in horror or laughing uncontrollably at the bizarre sight of Kent being swallowed by his parent's guest house.

Harlan caught Jerry's eye and said, "We need to get out of here."

Harlan grabbed the empty keg with the tap still attached and ran toward the alley. Jerry had seen Harlan do this before when cops showed up at parties. Harlan didn't want to lose his deposit. Jerry grabbed Carolyn's hand and ran. Edgar was right behind them when they hustled out to the car.

Before they crossed the street, a station wagon with wood paneling and a missing headlight stopped in front of the house. The windows were up, but they could almost feel the bass coming from the wagon's worn-out speakers. When the window slid down, a cloud of smoke cleared, and Jerry recognized Tony *Cheese* Chiesa squinting at them.

"Is this the party?" he said.

"It just ended," said Jerry. "And you guys better move out. I think the cops'll be here any minute."

Cheese looked confused. "What happened?" he said.

Carolyn said, "The host fell through the roof of the guest house."

"Kent?" said Cheese.

"You know him?" said Jerry.

"My dad works for his dad," said Cheese. "That's how I heard about the party."

"Jesus," said Jerry. "We should all get out of here."

"What are you listening to?" asked Edgar while Cheese was rolling up the window.

The back window came down. Their buddy, Dave, leaned out through the smoke and yelled, "Run D.M.C., homies," as the station wagon skidded away into the night. Dave's arm, still in a cast, was out the window, pumping in rhythm to the heavy baseline.

Once Jerry's group was in the Dodge, and Harlan had fired up the big engine, Jerry said, "Are we indirectly responsible for that roof collapse?"

"Did you tell him to go up there?" said Carolyn.

"Hell, no," said Jerry.

Edgar, who had partaken in too much of the weed, was giggling in the front seat. "No one in this car is innocent of the sins committed against the cast of *South Pacific*," he said. Then he went into a very quiet laugh, a low clicking coming from the back of his throat. Jerry thought he was going to pause and say something, but Edgar just took a deep breath, shook his head, and started laughing again.

13

Isaac was still learning the job.

But it didn't involve much expertise. He was 6'4" and weighed more than 250 pounds, so none of these kids was going to try to pull anything on him. If they did, it wouldn't end well.

The only one he worried about was Sawyer Puck, but that kid was also the most interesting.

Sawyer was actually in Juvenile Hall for attempted murder. That was a fact. Isaac had looked up the report. Sawyer had thrown a knife at his step-brother over some kind of dispute about baseball cards. Isaac couldn't imagine it. Fucking baseball cards. He knew some were valuable and that step-brothers didn't always get along, but you don't try to kill someone over cards.

Isaac didn't really take the charge seriously though. Sawyer wasn't some kind of knife-throwing expert like the guys on ESPN, who could hit targets from ten yards away. He was a scrawny kid. Even if he had a good arm, the chance of him hitting his brother with a fatal shot from even five yards away would not be likely. It would be equally probable that the handle, rather than the blade, would hit the step-brother and cause only minor bruising.

As it turned out, Sawyer was a pretty good shot. The blade had hit the other kid in the ear, which means Sawyer was probably aiming at his face. So, the mom called the police. She probably panicked when she saw the blood and didn't think they'd charge Sawyer the way they did. It seemed more like assault with a deadly weapon. And then things must have gone really badly in court. Isaac heard that Sawyer had taken the stand, but that's about all he knew from the trial. Though, in his mind, he could see Sawyer standing up there saying that he wished he'd killed the kid or that the kid deserved to die or something like that.

Sawyer was that kind of person. Really stubborn. He was smart too, but if he lost his temper, Isaac could see him doing some crazy stuff. The dude seemed like a brainy maniac to Isaac, but he'd heard one of the therapists use the term bipolar. Isaac had never heard of it before, but people who had it suffered from problems with mood swings that could last days or even weeks.

Isaac wasn't so sure that's what was going on with Sawyer, but he did like talking to him either way. Sawyer remembered everything he'd ever read. Seriously. He had a photographic memory. One time Isaac had said "photogenic mind" by accident, and Sawyer made fun of him for three days. Wouldn't let up. Kept asking if Isaac wanted to take a picture of his brain.

So, Isaac tried to be careful around him. If one of the other inmates tried to get physical with Isaac, that was easy. There'd be a quick and efficient beatdown. But Sawyer got you with his mind and his words. Made you feel stupid. And Isaac couldn't really take anyone down just for making fun of him. He could make the kid's time at the hall a little uncomfortable, but even that seemed unfair to someone who was just smart … and a little mean.

Just tonight, Isaac was practicing his handcuffing technique with Sawyer as a volunteer, and the kid had walked off while Isaac was pulling the handcuffs out of the case. Isaac wasn't sure if Sawyer did it to help him get better or to make him feel stupid. But maybe he was trying to make Isaac feel stupid so that he'd get better. That could definitely be it.

It was getting close to lights out when Sawyer said, "You know who Roberto Clemente is?"

"I was pretty young when he died," said Isaac. "But I remember him."

"Do you know how he died?"

"Plane crash," said Isaac. "Like Thurman Munson."

"Maybe," said Sawyer and looked at Isaac like he'd never understand.

"I'm just saying, they were both great ball players who died in plane crashes."

"I know what you're saying," said Sawyer. "But there's a difference."

"And I assume you're going to educate me."

Sawyer's girlish mouth turned down at the corners, like Isaac had hurt his feelings. "I'm just trying to have a conversation," he said. "But we need to get the facts right if we're going to get anywhere."

"Okay," said Isaac. "What facts do I need to know?"

"Since you brought up Munson," he said. "Let's start with him. The man was actually *flying* the plane. He learned to be a pilot so he could visit his family more in Ohio during the season. Then he crashed his own plane one day when he was practicing landings. So, he didn't really get to see his family more, did he?"

"Okay," said Isaac. "Dude died in a plane like Clemente, but Munson was the pilot of his own demise."

"Yes, he was," said Sawyer. "And I like how you put it: *pilot of his own demise.* Very poetic, Isaac."

"Thank you."

"Clemente was a little different."

"Okay."

"You know why Clemente was on the plane?"

"I don't."

"There was a big earthquake in Nicaragua," said Sawyer. "Clemente chartered a plane to bring supplies down there for the poor people of that country."

"I thought he was Puerto Rican," said Isaac, thinking he was maybe going to catch Sawyer Puck on his facts.

"He was," said Sawyer. "And he helped out that country all the time, but I guess he just couldn't ignore the Nicaraguans. The man thought he could save the world."

"Another reason why people admired him."

"True," said Sawyer. "But there's limits. One of the all-time greats who ever played the game thought it was a good idea to overload a broken-down old cargo plane controlled by a shady pilot, who earlier that day agreed to fly it for four grand."

Isaac hadn't heard any of those details. Or maybe he had but just blocked them out. He was a little kid when it happened. "It's easy to say all that in retrospect," said Isaac. He didn't like that Sawyer was trying to make a hero sound like an idiot.

"That plane never made it more than two hundred feet off the ground," he said. "It exploded over the water, and they never found the bodies."

"What they call a tragedy," said Isaac, not seeing the point here.

"Yes, it was," said Sawyer and then just sat there looking at Isaac like Isaac was supposed to have found some lesson in the story that he could preach back to Sawyer.

When Sawyer nodded at Isaac, apparently his cue to tell Sawyer what he'd learned from today's lesson, Isaac decided to take a stab at it. "Not sure what you're gettin' at with all this," he said. "Munson learned to fly so he could see his family, and Clemente got on that plane to help people."

Sawyer nodded and smiled. This little fucker could be annoying.

"Are you trying to tell me," said Isaac, "that we shouldn't want to spend time with our families or try to help people?" He shrugged and shook his head. "Because the penalty for that kind of thing is death? The whole *no good deed goes unpunished* philosophy?"

"Nah," said Sawyer. "I never thought that made any sense."

"Ya'mean, you don't think that people sometimes suffer for trying to help others?"

"No," he said. "I absolutely believe that's true. Didn't we just talk about two baseball greats who died because they were trying to do something good?"

"Yeah," said Isaac, feeling like he was falling into one of the kid's little debate traps. "So why don't you believe in the *no good deed* idea?"

Sawyer stood up and rubbed the sides of his smooth face with both hands like some college professor getting ready to enlighten his students. "The problem with the whole concept," he said, "is that it never acknowledges the meaning of *good deeds.* The term, by definition, suggests that if it's a good deed, it must involve some kind of sacrifice. Otherwise, it wouldn't be considered a good deed in the first place. Circulus in Probando."

Isaac thought about that but said nothing for a moment. He considered asking for a translation but didn't want to slow the dude down.

"It's like saying *Everyone likes Isaac because Isaac is really popular,*" said Sawyer.

"I am," said Isaac while he was trying to process what he'd just heard.

"Or *You shouldn't break the law because it's illegal to break the law.*"

Sawyer's engine was revved up now. He was frustrating, but Isaac liked to listen to him. At times, the kid could sound like a skilled lawyer, riffing during a closing argument. "Give me one example," he said, "of a good deed that didn't involve sacrifice or suffering of some sort. Otherwise, that phrase is just a circular statement that says nothing."

Isaac knew he shouldn't bite, but he was interested in seeing where Sawyer was going with this, so he said, "How about a rich guy who gives ten bucks to a bum?"

Sawyer smiled. "That's a good one," he said. "Kudos, Isaac. That's definitely a good one. But let me ask you a question. If the guy is rich … that is to say, ten bucks will have zero effect on his well-being … is his gift of ten bucks really a good deed, or did he just do it to make himself feel better?"

"Ha," said Isaac. "I think I just got you, and now you're trying to change the original thing, the premise."

Sawyer smiled again. "This is truth. To say less would dishonor the respect for truth, Grasshopper."

"Huh?"

"Kung Fu?"

"What?"

"David Carradine? Reruns on Channel 44?"

Isaac was not familiar with the show but was realizing that Sawyer Puck was trying to get him off-topic now that Isaac had won this latest duel. "Never saw it," he said, wondering if it was a show for white people, even though it sounded like a show for Chinese.

"Never mind," said Sawyer.

"How about a guy who helps an old lady carry her groceries?" said Isaac, excited that he'd thought of a second example in such a short period of time.

"How about that guy?" said Sawyer.

"Same thing as the rich guy," he said. "Good deed with no sacrifice."

"No, no," said Sawyer. "That one doesn't work. First of all, it takes time to help the lady. Time is money. Also, he uses some of his energy. That's a sacrifice. But there's also the risk involved. What if he slips going up the stairs or drops the groceries and the lady makes him pay for 'em? Or what if he asks her if she needs help, but she takes it as an insult? That's risk, and risk is sacrifice. So even if everything turns out okay for all parties involved, I think that example supports my assertion that the original idiom is nothing more than a circular statement."

"Okay," said Isaac. "I'll stick with the first example. How did we get on this topic in the first place?"

"Roberto Clemente," said Sawyer.

"Oh, yeah," said Isaac. "So, the difference between Munson and Clemente is that Munson was the pilot of his own demise?"

"Weren't they both?" said Sawyer.

"Shit," said Isaac. "I don't even know anymore." Then he looked at his watch and said, "But why did you bring up baseball in the first place?"

"I was going to tell you about my Roberto Clemente rookie card."

"You got one of those?"

"I do," he said and raised his eyebrows like a Groucho Marx impersonator. "Remember when I said I was glad that Edgar got out?"

14

After Helen got the address from the kid, she told him she'd meet him at the house at ten o'clock. If Paul would let her do a half-shift at The Backlot, and she helped the kid find his valuable item—his *cards*—this could turn into a very profitable night.

"I have a chance to make enough money to pay for a whole month's rent," she said. "Maybe more."

Paul was the perfect Billy Idol. The hair, the clothes, the attitude … even the Idol scowl, which was just an angry parody of Elvis's lip curl. Paul had the mouth for this move and used it the same way people who can lift one eyebrow might—to express a wide range of emotions. It worked for him, so he used it often.

When Paul performed, it would always end in a standing ovation and sometimes several women's undergarments on the stage, scattered around his feet like religious offerings. But while the owner Mrs. Wang was back in China, Paul didn't perform because he was the acting manager and took his job very seriously. Though he still worked in full costume.

Paul stayed in character once he entered the building, so he used a British accent when he said, "Helen, love, you have a job to do."

"I know," she said. "But I have a newbie with some money, and the only way to see if he's a serious prospect is to meet him tonight. There's a deadline for this score, and then it's gonna disappear."

"Hun," he said and employed the scowl. "What if we have a load of blokes come in at ten looking to get pissed, and you're off doing your little thing?"

"Paul," she said, "there's five other servers tonight. That's plenty."

"Yeah," he said, "but there'll be four without you, won't there?" He was looking at the stage, where they were setting up for Thomas, an Eddie Murphy impersonator, who tried his own jokes while looking and sounding like Eddie. The only problem was that Thomas wasn't funny. Not at all. He walked around on stage like he was going to be funny, but he needed to hire someone better to write the material for him. Helen cringed every time he was up there. "And we'll have uneven gender representation between the lads and the birds," said Paul, pointing around the room at the other servers.

Helen thought for a moment, trying hard to take this man seriously while he waved his bangled arm around. "Not really," she said, her eyes on his five bulky rings as he ran his fingers over the black roots and through his bleach blonde spikes.

"Do you want me to count for you, love?" he said.

"Boy George," she said, and nodded in the direction of the impersonator, whose fedora was pushed back on his head to reveal heavily made-up eyes and long, colorful braids.

Paul paused and kept his eyes on the stage. "Right … right," he said and broke character for just a moment when he smirked like Paul instead of Billy. "Bollocks," he said under his breath. He forced his smirk into a half-assed version of the scowl and said, "Let's see how things look after the second set."

***

At around 9:30, a group of eight sat down at Helen's station. There was no way Paul was going to let her cut out early with a group this large just sitting down. But when Helen walked over to take their drink orders, she heard one of them say, "I can't believe that's a man," and pointed up to Autumn, who was on stage as Cyndi Lauper, doing *Girls Just Want to Have Fun.*

Helen figured she might have just caught a break.

"Are you guys looking for a drag show?" she said to the woman who'd been pointing at Autumn.

"Oh, boy," said the woman. "Are we in the wrong place?"

"You are if you're looking for a drag show," she said. "But if you're just looking for celebrity impersonators, this is the best show in the city."

The woman looked sheepish. She turned to her friends, who were pretending not to hear the exchange. "We're from Arizona," she said. "We kinda wanted to see something we don't have in Scottsdale."

"I hear you," said Helen. "You all are looking for Finocchio's. It's all drag. You can walk from here. It's just up on Stockton. They go pretty late, so you still might be able to catch a show."

The lady's friends gathered up their purses and pushed back their chairs. "Thank you for being so helpful," she said. "You're actually better looking than her."

Helen must have looked confused because the woman said, "Madonna, I mean. You're prettier."

"Thank you," said Helen and looked over at Paul who mouthed, *What the fuck?*

Autumn was really belting out *They justa wanna … they justa wanna …*, and the women in the front row were singing along. It wasn't full tonight, but it was a fun crowd.

Paul made his way over to her, and before he could say anything, Helen said, "I know what that looked like."

"Yeah," he said. "It looked like you just told those lovely ladies to take off so you could leave early to do your thing."

"They thought they were in Finocchio's and that Autumn was a man," she said. "They're from out of town and were looking to see a drag show. What was I supposed to do?"

"Take their bloody drink orders," he said and turned toward Autumn as she finished her finale and ran off stage. "She's damn good," he said.

"I like her," said Helen. "She's a bit of a nut, but so is Cyndi, so it works for her."

"Yeah, well you're not a bloody nutter," he said. "You're a normal person, so I expect that you can do your job like a normal person and not tell customers to go to other clubs."

He was pissed. Helen was feeling like she probably should just stay and finish her shift. She needed this job, and she needed Paul to respect her work ethic. She could apologize to Andrew if he ever came back to get a reading. But she would feel bad standing him up.

It was probably wishful thinking on her part that she'd be able to not only find the stash for him but also get something out of it. She couldn't take the whole thing from him because he knew where she lived and worked, but she had a feeling that she could get something big out of it. The kid seemed pretty naïve.

"Sorry, Paul," she said. "I won't ask you to split early."

"Now that your station is empty, what's the use in staying?" he said. "You might as well go ahead and do your fiddle as planned."

"Fiddle?"

"Your scam," he said. "Your swindle."

"I'm trying to help the kid," she said.

"Come into the office," he said.

She followed him to the back, and when he flopped down into the soft chair by the desk, he wasn't Billy Idol anymore. He still looked almost exactly like him, but he dropped the attitude when he slouched into the chair. "Can you tell me about this thing before you go?" he said, smiling and replacing the British accent with his more natural southern California surf gab.

"I'm doing a psychic reading for him in his old house to help him find something valuable."

"Something valuable?" said Paul. "Old house?"

"Yeah," she said. "He knows it's in there, but it's hidden, and his family has moved out."

"Ducats?" he said.

"The kid said something about cards."

Paul paused for a moment. "Stolen credit cards?"

Helen thought about this. It actually made some sense. "Maybe," she said. "He just mentioned cards."

"I can help with those," he said.

She brushed her hair out of her eyes and said, "Oh, you want in on this now?"

"I'm just saying I know how to do it."

"Is credit card fraud complicated?" she said.

"If you don't want to get caught."

"Okay," she said. "If I get access to credit cards tonight, you're in."

"Smart girl," he said.

"I didn't know you came from a crime background," she said, smiling at Paul as she stood up and grabbed her bag from a hook behind the door.

"Nothing big," he said. "Pushed a little weed. Boosted a few cars. The credit card stuff. Mostly victimless crimes."

She thought about his job at The Backlot. "Well, the fraud part has helped you here," she said and raised her eyebrows.

"Fraud?" he said. "Bullshit. I'm an entertainer."

"You are," she conceded and reached for the doorknob.

"Hold it," he said and opened the bottom drawer of Mrs. Wang's desk. "I think you should bring this just in case." He held up a pistol. The kind you'd use for Russian roulette with the thing that spins.

"Um," she said. "Andrew's just a kid. I don't think I need a gun for the job."

"Last words of people who needed a gun for a job."

"I'm trying to think of something that could go sideways on this," she said. "And I really can't."

"How are you going to get him to pay you?" said Paul.

Helen didn't answer. She really didn't think the kid would try to screw her if she helped him find the money. "I'll ask for a percentage of the take before I give him a reading," she said.

"That's not what I asked," he said.

She thought about it again. "I guess I'm kinda putting my trust in him that he'll appreciate my work and compensate me fairly."

"I thought you said you might try to take the whole thing from the kid."

"That was my original thought," she said. "But I never figured out a plan to get it off him, and he knows where I live. I guess I was just going to improvise."

Paul walked over to her, too close, invading her space—his cheek close to hers. He dropped the gun in her bag, and she felt the weight of it. Then he spoke softly in her ear, back to the Billy Idol voice again. "Use it if you have to, love. Then bring back those cards, and we'll have a nice party together, won't we?"

15

Jerry thought it was still too early to go to the house—too many people still walking around the neighborhood—so they drove north past Lombard and Chestnut and found a parking spot on Lyon, across the street from the Palace of Fine Arts. It wasn't really their turf, but it was a nice spot, and there was an empty bench looking out across the pond at the lighted Rotunda.

They sat four across on the bench. The only sound came from the spout, shooting water straight up in the middle of the pond.

"Those kids thought we were some kinda heroes," said Edgar.

"They'd probably never seen a keg before," said Harlan.

"No," said Edgar. "Not because we brought beer. They thought we were heroes because we didn't die at the waterslide."

They listened to the splashing fountain for a few beats before Jerry said, "Yeah, I don't really feel good about that."

Carolyn put her hand on his knee. "I don't think *heroes* is the right word for what they thought about us," she said but didn't provide a replacement. And then they were right back to listening to the fountain again.

"Victims?" offered Edgar.

"Not that either," said Carolyn. "They weren't treating us like victims. It was more …" Her words trailed off, and they heard voices behind them.

When Jerry turned his head, he saw a couple guys he knew from Sacred Heart walking with their girls toward another bench. He nodded at them, and they nodded back. The SH hangout was the Marina Greens just a few blocks away, and Jerry hoped they didn't see this as some kind of challenge—Saint X guys sitting quietly in enemy territory.

Edgar said, "You know those guys?"

"I know who they are," said Jerry.

"The girls are cool," said Carolyn, and Edgar shrugged.

"Survivors," said Harlan.

"The girls?" said Carolyn.

"No," said Harlan, shaking his head. "Us. That's the word for us. It's how those drama kids were treating us. Like survivors. Like we'd gone off to war or something and come back with some scars but, otherwise, okay."

Jerry thought that was probably right, but it still bothered him. "Yeah," he said. "But soldiers don't cause wars. They just go fight and hope to make it home when it's over."

It was quiet again, and Jerry spotted some movement in the shadows at the edge of the pond. He pointed, and they all watched as a swan led a group of other swans past the fountain, through the ripples of water, to a sheltered area under an overgrown tree near the arches of the Rotunda. There was enough light coming from under the dome to illuminate the swans as they huddled together under the low branches.

Jerry heard Carolyn's sigh under the sounds of the splashing water and the distant, muted din of traffic on Lombard.

"I hope you don't somehow blame yourself for the accident," said Harlan. "I was on that slide. I blame the guy who built it." Harlan leaned over, his elbows on his knees, and looked across Edgar and Carolyn at Jerry. "Or the architect or whatever. But I don't blame a bunch of teenagers who did what thousands of other kids have done before them."

"You're right," said Jerry. "But I feel like I was one of the people who organized it or helped pull it off or something, and that bugs me. Is that all right?"

The girls with the Sacred Heart guys a few benches down giggled, and Jerry looked over but realized they were too far away to be listening to the conversation.

"No," said Edgar. "It's not all right."

Jerry didn't say anything. He thought about all his friends who got hurt that day. He thought about Dave. He thought about Chrissy.

"I was there," said Edgar. "Remember?"

"Not on the slide," said Jerry, not trying to demean Edgar. Just wanting him to understand that it was different up there.

"I know," said Edgar. "I was sitting with you when Chrissy came up to us. You weren't going anywhere until she asked you to go, so I don't think you're supposed to think of yourself as one of the ringleaders or something because I watched you following the others."

Jerry knew Edgar was right. And he was a little embarrassed to be sitting next to Carolyn and having to rehash his walking away from her to follow Chrissy. But he also felt like there might be a flaw in Harlan's argument about the architect or the builders being at fault.

"How about this?" said Jerry. "Let's say we're at the zoo, and one of those SH guys over there is taunting the tigers and throwing stuff at 'em."

"Okay," said Edgar. "Not sure where you're going with this."

"And these guys keep at it for a long time," he said. "Until finally, one of the tigers jumps over the moat."

"And does what?" said Edgar.

"Climbs the fence and mauls the guys who were throwing stuff at him."

"First of all," said Edgar. "That's the most ridiculous hypothetical I've ever heard. They build those things so the wild animals can never get out. Otherwise, no one would ever go to the zoo."

"I'm just trying to make a point here," said Jerry. "Let's say the guys who made the tiger cage underestimated how far a tiger could jump if it was mad enough. In that situation, is it the fault of the tiger cage builder or the assholes who provoked the tiger, when a tiger can get so infuriated that it jumps out of its cage and goes on a rampage?"

Jerry felt like he was arguing against himself now. He was feeling that the cage-builders in his stupid hypothetical were, indeed, morons and responsible for the carnage he'd described. Jerry had unwittingly punched a hole in his own logic, but he was okay with that. It made him feel better about his own role in the waterslide accident. This was a foreign emotion for him—he didn't like to lose debates of any kind. But this was soothing. And he liked that his friends were being thoughtful in their case against his premise, which was, in fact, a case *for* his character.

Carolyn said, "There's an expectation when you go to the zoo that the tigers can't get out and eat you."

Jerry put up a half-assed fight just to see where it would go. "But isn't there also an expectation that people won't try to provoke a tiger?" he said.

"No!" said Harlan. "No such expectation. People are assholes. Of course, they'll try to provoke a tiger."

Edgar was smiling. "And of course, they'll try to stuff as many kids as they can on a waterslide."

"And of course," said Carolyn, "the designers should build a slide able to hold a hundred fat kids at the same time. Kids do stupid things."

Jerry knew they were right now. Maybe when he made up the tiger analogy, he already knew. But it helped him to talk through it. He still didn't feel like himself. He didn't feel the way he did before the accident. But he was starting to come around. He knew he'd lost the argument and was happy about it, so he was ready to move in a different direction.

"Are we ready to go get Edgar's cards?" he said and leaned forward on the bench so that he could see all of them.

"You guys," said Harlan, his voice sounding thick, labored. "The drama kids know we go to Saint X." He stood up and took a step away from the bench so that the Rotunda was in his background. "When they get in trouble for the party we just orchestrated, someone's going to call Fr. Stricker." He squatted down now in a catcher's stance so that he was seeing them at eye level. "McNaughton saw us holding beers before the game. He saw a keg in my back seat. And now we're headed up to a house in Pacific Heights to participate in a breaking and entering or trespassing or burglary or whatever it is that Edgar's supposed to do. ...." Harlan took a moment to look at all three of them individually. "I can't do this, you guys. I could get lucky and get away with some of the stuff we've done so far today, but not everything. And Carolyn, you don't know this, but these guys do. My dad will literally beat the crap out of me if he finds out about any of this. I don't know what the hell I was thinking today."

Carolyn didn't miss a beat. "Just drop us off a block away, Danny. We don't want you in any trouble with your dad."

"I don't want *any* of you guys to do it," he said. "I'm trying to tell you to quit this." He had a look of desperation that Jerry had never seen in him before. "Ya'know how our lockers are conveniently located across the hall from Stricker's office?" he asked.

Jerry shrugged at him. It was true, but he didn't know why it was relevant to the discussion.

"That's so Stricker can have Fr. Gilligan spy on us," he said. Fr. Gilligan was about ninety years old, and his reception desk was about five feet from Jerry's locker. Jerry wondered why his locker and Harlan's and a handful of other senior troublemakers' lockers were out of alphabetical order and all clustered next to Fr. Gilligan's window. The priest was old, but he wasn't stupid. Harlan was making a decent argument.

"My brother," said Harlan, "said they did the same thing to his class."

"Pretty smart," said Jerry, trying to think of anything he'd said in front of Fr. Gilligan's window.

"Yeah," he said. "And I think Stricker can actually listen in on our conversations in the hallways too. He just turns on the PA for a certain hallway and listens."

"That sounds a little far-fetched," said Jerry. "But the locker stuff seems real."

"I'm just saying they're watching us."

"Harlan," said Edgar. "Just drop me off and take everyone else home." He leaned back behind Carolyn's head and looked at Jerry. "Actually," he said. "I can walk from here."

Harlan came out of his squat and put his hands in the pockets of his corduroys. He shook his head and then turned around and looked out toward the swans, but they weren't huddled under the low branches anymore. The flock had broken up. They were either in pairs or singletons drifting off into the shadows beyond the illumination of the Rotunda lights.

"We'll be fine," said Carolyn. "Drop us off, and if anything looks fishy, we'll abort the mission and take the bus back to The Sunset."

Harlan turned back toward his friends but kept his head down. "Why do I somehow feel like the bad guy here," he said, "for *not* wanting to participate in the commission of a crime?"

Jerry laughed. "Harlan," he said. "No one blames you for not wanting to do this. I just keep thinking that if this kid knows where his cards are hidden, then they must be his cards, and Edgar's just picking them up for him."

Harlan kept his hands in his pockets but looked up at his friends. "So, you guys are okay with me just dropping you near the house?"

***

They stood on the corner under a streetlight a block away from the destination. Edgar's map of the house seemed pretty clear.

"There's apparently a door in the alley that leads to a boiler room," said Edgar.

"What's a boiler room?" said Jerry, knowing that he'd heard the term before but never knew exactly what it was.

"In a steam ship or a train," said Edgar, "it's the place where they shovel the coal to make steam to run the engine."

Jerry smiled. "And ...?"

"I think it's just the place where the heat gets sent to the radiators."

"Okay," said Jerry. "What's next?"

Edgar looked down at the paper. "I walk past the boiler," he said, "and there's a tilted ceiling."

Carolyn had been quiet since Harlan abandoned the crew. "What does that mean?" she said.

Edgar said, "It's the underside of the stairs." Then he paused and presented a forty-five-degree angle with his hand. "And on the wall connected to that ceiling, there's a ventilation grate near the ground."

"It's in there?" asked Jerry.

"So, I'm told," said Edgar.

Carolyn was shaking her head. "Why couldn't anyone else find it?" she said. "That doesn't sound so hidden to me."

"This is just the information given to me," said Edgar. "The bag is pushed back in the shaft, so after I unscrew the grille, I'm supposed to reach in there until I feel it and then pull it out."

"That part sounds scary," said Carolyn.

Jerry felt like the whole thing should take only a few minutes. "So then," he said, "you just screw the grate back on and sneak out of there?"

"That's it," said Edgar.

"Okay," said Jerry. "Then give me the screwdriver."

Carolyn and Edgar both said *What?* at the same time. High pitched. Like a junior high school choir warm-up.

"If Edgar gets caught," said Jerry. "He's going back to jail. So, give me the screwdriver."

16

In the old house with only a single candle flickering in the front room, Helen thought Andrew looked even younger than he had on Haight Street. He didn't blink. In the shadowy, trembling half-glow, he stared at Helen, waiting for her to help him find his treasure but unaware that Helen was angling to secure a substantial share of the take if she could orchestrate the evening just right.

She knew that neither the spirit board nor Chevreul's Pendulum was going to provide much help. Helen didn't believe in her aunt's powers, and she didn't believe in any of these tools designed to deliver a glimpse into the spirit world. She didn't mind learning how to use the tools. And she appreciated getting paid to let people *think* they were stepping into another dimension. She further recognized that the readings—even fabricated—could help people. But she was under no illusion that she was a soothsayer, a mystic, a fortune teller, a psychic, a clairvoyant, or a medium of any kind.

She only knew that she was naturally good at finding things, and she intended to help Andrew find what he was looking for. And when they retrieved the cards tonight, she was confident that he'd compensate her for her efforts, especially if the stash was as valuable as he'd led her to believe it was.

While Andrew was pulling the curtains closed to isolate the two of them from the outside world and prevent the neighbors from seeing inside the house, Helen said, "Let's start with the pendulum."

She was squatting on the hardwood floor in front of the candle, and he joined her. "I'm ready for anything," he said. "This is literally a last-ditch effort for me."

"Is there a chance your brother already came and got it?" she asked. She didn't want to waste time on this if there was a possibility that the cards weren't even in the house."

"Impossible," he said. "He's incarcerated. And he's my *step*-brother, by the way."

"He couldn't have grabbed the stuff before he was put in jail?"

"He didn't have time," said Andrew. "Unless he pre-planned to throw the knife at me that particular night, and he knew his mom would call the police, and he knew they would immediately take him into custody, there's just no way he would have had the opportunity."

"Could he have asked someone else to pick it up for him?"

"Can we just start?" he said.

"We have," she said. "This is part of the process." She tilted her head and looked at him as if he were a puppy learning his first trick. "I need you to be thinking about all that has happened so that when we get to the pendulum, we can extract information from your subconscious. I told you this."

"Yeah," he said. "But I don't get it."

She knew she looked ridiculous, still in her Madonna getup. And she probably sounded a bit ridiculous as well. But she needed him to keep talking. The more he told her about the situation, the better chance she'd have of helping him find it, despite the fact that she wouldn't be using telepathy or anything else except common sense.

"We need to get as much information from your subconscious as close as we can to your actual consciousness before you even get to the pendulum."

"Okay," he said, frustrated now, like she was ruining his Friday night. "Fire away."

"Did your family pack up all your stuff together before you moved out?"

"Not Sawyer," said Andrew. "He was already locked up."

"Sawyer?" she said. "That's your step-brother?"

"Yeah," he said. "Sawyer Puck."

"Well, that's a name," she said, looking past Andrew at closets and built-in cabinets and floorboards and vents. "Is there a basement or an attic?" she asked.

"Both," he said.

She nodded. "Is there a chance that the cards were hidden in a piece of furniture that the movers took to your new house?"

He shook his head like someone trying to snap out of a daze. "I hadn't thought of that," he said.

"Inside the box springs of a bed or behind a false back in a bureau?"

"A bureau?"

"Like a dresser," she said.

"Yeah," he said. "I didn't think of that. I guess Sawyer could have done something like that." His eyes shifted away from Helen's to the candle and his hands tightened into fists.

"It's okay," she said. "If we can't find it here, you can always check the furniture at your new place." She needed him to stay positive and focused. The mention of the step-brother was affecting his emotions. She wanted him to be dialed in to the process. When people are emotional, they aren't focused. She had to get him back now. "Let's try the Chevreul's Pendulum," she said. "I think we've done some work unearthing some buried memories and getting them closer to your present consciousness."

"I don't think so," he said.

"Why not?"

"I don't feel anything," he said and put his chin in his hands like a little boy denied a Vanilla Wafer after finishing his homework.

"You're not going to," she said. "The mind is complex. All we're trying to do is take the blurry memories that you've filed away and clean up the edges. Convert them into clear pictures. We don't even know what kind of question might spark the right memory."

"But how can I remember something that I never saw," he said, raising his chin now like he'd somehow stumped her.

She smiled. "You might not have seen him hide the cards," she said. "But maybe you saw him come out of the attic one day, or maybe you saw an entry to a crawl space somewhere when you were sweeping or something. We won't know until we try."

He nodded. "Okay," he said. "Let's give it a try and see what happens."

"Positive energy," she said.

He nodded again.

Helen reached into her bag and retrieved her pendulum, which was a length of sewing thread tied to a house key on one end and a dresser drawer handle on the other side. Both were from her old house in Montana.

"It works better if you stand up," she said and placed the handle end in his hand. Then she pulled a square card out of her bag. It was about the size of a formal dinner napkin. On the card, a circle was drawn with a cross inside. The ends of the cross touched the circle and had letters above the intersections: A and C on the top and bottom; B and D on the left and right.

She placed the card near his feet and said, "When I ask the questions, if the key moves vertically, from A to C, the answer is yes. If it moves horizontally, from B to D, the answer is no. And if it moves in a circle or oval, that means we can't bring it to the surface. We don't know."

Andrew nodded. He was holding the handle, the key, and the string all balled up in his hand. He looked scared.

"There's nothing spiritual about this," she said. "No need to be nervous. This is all generated by your own mind. Just be open to it, and we might get something."

He nodded again, and Helen crawled over and put her hands around his.

"Okay," she said. "Hold onto the handle and drop the key."

Andrew did as he was told, and Helen reached out to hold the key between two fingers.

"I'm going to let go of the weight in one moment," she said. "And then I'll ask you to close your eyes. But for now, look down and view the card. Memorize it. You got it?"

"Yes," he said and tried to hold his hand steady out in front of him.

"Close your eyes now," she said and let go of the key.

He closed his eyes and sniffed once. He didn't seem to know what to do with his other hand, so he pushed it into his jacket pocket.

The pendulum hovered over the diagram, just barely swaying.

"First question," she said. "Is the bag in this room?"

She waited a moment and watched the key settle and then begin to swing from B to D.

"That's a no," she said. "Does that seem right?"

"It can't be in here," he said, his eyes open now. "I even checked up the chimney."

Helen looked over at the enormous chimney bordered in old brick. The screen was still in place, and the charcoal black accessories stood at attention in their caddy on the hearth. The house had been cleaned out entirely, but Andrew's family had apparently left these items even though, to Helen, the little brush, the shovel, and the poker looked like expensive antiques with opulent designs on the handles.

She looked back at Andrew. "Okay," she said. "Let's try again. Close your eyes." He squinted at her and then complied. She steadied the key and then let go. "Could the bag be in the kitchen?" she asked.

The key immediately moved from B to D again.

"The pendulum says it's not in the kitchen," she said.

Then they went through a lot of spaces and got the same result. The answer was *no* for the bedrooms, the attic, the backyard, and the garage. Helen went through everything that came to mind, and then Andrew said, "There's a boiler room."

"Is it in the boiler room?" she asked and released the key.

She looked at Andrew's face, his eyes closed. He reminded her of a Christmas figurine her mom used to put on the mantle during the holidays. It was a choir boy holding a songbook, his eyes closed as he let the spirit of Christmas take over his soul. There was a wind-up key on his back, and when you twisted it, a music box version of *Silent Night* played out of the tiny holes on the front of his plastic robe.

The pendulum was doing little ovals now, and Andrew said, "Is it doing anything? It feels like it's doing something."

"Give it a second," said Helen. "Maybe it wants to change course."

She waited for it to shift to a vertical pattern, a steady movement from A to C, but it changed only from ovals to circles. "It doesn't know on this one," she said. "Ovals. I guess that's better than no."

Andrew opened his eyes and handed the mechanism back to Helen.

She said, "Maybe there's a reason it said no to every other space except the boiler room."

"I will admit," he said. "I checked down there, but I didn't tear the place apart like I did with every other room."

"Why not?" she said.

"Because I hate it down there," he said.

"But you did at least a cursory search?"

"Yeah."

"Do you want to ask the spirit board something specific about that room?" she said. "Maybe it'll tell us where to look."

Andrew nodded.

Helen reached into her satchel and pulled out the board. She placed it on the floor near the pendulum diagram. Then she reached back in to grab the wooden planchette and felt her hand brush up against the hard metal of Paul's revolver.

17

The side door was easy. Jerry just jiggled the knob, and the battered stub of a latch released. Once inside, he took out the map to double-check his next move, but it was dark, and he couldn't find a light switch. He'd memorized the directions, so he turned left and felt along the wall until he came to the door of the boiler room.

Near the door, there was a high narrow window that provided some light from either the moon or a streetlight. Jerry couldn't tell from his angle. It was enough illumination to make out the door, which was not a normal door. It was smaller and metal. The frame came up off the floor so that a person had to actually step over the thin metal footing in order to enter the room. To Jerry, it looked like a door you might see in a submarine. He pushed through and let his eyes adjust. The door was equipped with a spring, and it clicked closed immediately after Jerry let go of the handle.

Once he stepped into the room, he could see that there were exposed, low-hanging pipes attached to brackets on the ceiling. He also saw several fuse boxes along the far wall. Snaking out of one of the boxes were wires that looked to be about a hundred years old. And everything was covered in a layer of thick dust and heavy cobwebs. This room had the same high, narrow window as the first room, and the dim light reflecting off the cobwebs gave Jerry the impression that a dense fog had settled into the small space.

It took him only a moment to recognize the slanted ceiling, follow it with his eyes to the wall, and then locate the ventilation grate near the floor. There was just enough light for Jerry to see the four screws he needed to remove before he could detach the vent cover.

He dropped down onto his knees and took less than a minute to take out the screws. He put them in his pocket and removed the cover, which he leaned up against the wall next to the opening. There was a low whistling sound coming from the duct, not unlike what you'd hear if you put your ear up to a seashell.

He didn't like the idea of sticking his arm in there, but he wanted to get it over quickly, so he didn't spend more than a few seconds looking into the black hole before he let his backside drop down to the point where it was resting on calves. He stuck his arm in but couldn't feel anything. He swore quietly and thought for a moment that the whole thing might be a hoax. He put the side of his face flush against the wall so that his arm could reach even deeper into the vent.

Then he felt it.

The duffle bag took up the whole area of the duct, and Jerry struggled to find something to grab. Eventually, he felt a zipper and gripped that between two fingers. He was able to pull the bag a few inches. He pushed down on top of the bag and got a fist full of a nylon material that was slick in his fingers. Jerry wanted to get his arm out of there badly, and he jerked wildly a couple of times and lost his grip before he finally pulled it out and fell back onto the dirty concrete floor.

He was so happy that his arm was safe from the boiler room creatures he'd imagined living in the vent that he didn't mind falling. He jumped back on his knees and replaced the cover quickly before he took a deep breath and stood up with the grips of the duffle bag in his right hand.

The next thing he needed to do was get out of that house and around the corner to where Carolyn and Edgar were waiting. He planned to creep out of the alley and peek around the shrubs to make sure all was clear before he jogged down the street to find his friends and look through the contents of the bag.

But when he got to the submarine door, he saw that it had no handle from the boiler room side. There was no way to pull it open. He tried to put his fingernails in the seam and pull back, but the door was sealed. He cursed himself for not sticking something in the door to prevent it from locking. But he also cursed Edgar for not telling him to stick something in the door to prevent it from locking.

The window was too high and too small. So, he walked to the end of the room and saw that there was a right-angle turn down a narrow hallway. It got darker the farther he went, and by the time he got about fifteen feet in, he couldn't see his hand in front of his face. He considered turning back and waiting for Edgar to come see what was taking him so long, but at the end of the hall, while Jerry was feeling for a light switch, he touched a smooth wooden railing.

He realized that it was going up, so he kicked out in front of him and found stairs. He looked up and blinked. He couldn't tell how many steps were in front of him, but he saw the door at the top was open a crack, and a dim, flickering light was glowing orange in the room up there.

He knew what he had to do. He would climb these stairs, walk through the room, and exit the house by means of the front door. It wasn't the original plan, but there was no other way at this point, so he held onto the railing and took the stairs one at a time. He didn't know what to make of that light. It was the same color as the sky during a forest fire, but it didn't make any sense in a vacant house. So, he stepped lightly and hoped it would be an easy walk from the opening at the top of the stairs to the front door.

But when he got about halfway up those stairs, he heard voices. The plan was now garbage. He was trapped in the boiler room unless these people left. He wondered if they were the new owners. And when he reached the top of the stairs, he had to push the door open a bit wider so that he could peer down the short hallway into the big living room, which was lit by a small candle resting on the floor between a man and a woman.

He'd stopped drinking over an hour ago and didn't smoke any weed, but what he saw in that living room made him feel immediately drunk again. He pulled the door back to its original small crack and considered what he'd seen. The man looked young, maybe early twenties or even younger. It was hard to tell in the dim light. The man wasn't making him feel drunk though.

It was the woman.

He was almost positive it was Madonna.

He sat down on the stairs and pondered this development. He couldn't think of a reason Madonna would be in an old house in Pacific Heights. He wondered if she could be scouting a location for a music video, or maybe she was the new owner. The house needed work, but it was on a beautiful street.

He pushed the door open enough to take a second look, and, yes, it was Madonna.

When the man spoke, Jerry could tell he was younger than Jerry's initial estimate. He sounded more like a high school kid when he said, "I don't know if this thing is gonna help."

Jerry pushed the door open a crack to see what the *thing* was.

"You never know, Andrew," she said, and Jerry saw that they were doing a Ouija board. He'd walked into a damn séance.

"It hasn't told us anything the pendulum didn't already tell us," he said.

"Well, let's keep trying," she said, and it clicked for Jerry that this wasn't Madonna. Jerry had heard Madonna talk in an interview on MTV, and this gal didn't sound anything like her. In fact, she didn't sound like she was from San Francisco either. Something about her voice made Jerry think of cowgirls. She was also prettier than the real Madonna.

"Should I ask another question?" this guy, Andrew, said.

"Go for it," she said.

"Um." The guy was staring down at the viewfinder thing. From where Jerry sat on the stairs, it looked like the guy's knuckles were touching hers. "If it's downstairs, could it be behind a trap door or a false wall or something?" he said and waited.

Jerry didn't like Ouija boards. A babysitter had messed with him once when he was little and made him think he could be possessed by the devil because he'd played with a Ouija board at a sleepover. For years, he believed that he'd opened some kind of portal and that a demon would come through it one day and take over his body. He was so sure that it would happen that he was resigned to the fact that he would end up like Linda Blair, and there was nothing he could do about it.

He couldn't see much of the board from where he was, but he heard the Madonna lady say, "It says *no*" and then shake her head. "What else?" she said.

"Could it be in the boiler room?" he asked, and Jerry felt a tingling behind his ears. His saliva tasted like metal.

The viewfinder moved again, and Jerry saw the woman smile. "Yes," she said. "The boiler room. What else?"

"Holy shit," he said. "Why didn't I look better down there?"

"Ask it something else," she said.

"Is it in the ceiling?" he said and shook his head. "I don't know what to ask. It's a small room."

Madonna didn't say anything. She was waiting for the Ouija board to tell them.

The house went completely silent, and Jerry let himself fall into a trance. He should have been strategizing an exit plan, but he was mesmerized by the séance and stared at their hands lightly touching the view-finder.

He thought he heard a distant click above his head or somehow beneath him. The sound came from nowhere and everywhere, but he ignored it and remained focused on Andrew and Madonna and the board, like he was looking through a telescope at the scene playing out in front of him in the flickering orange light.

"There he is," he heard in a stage whisper that broke him from his trance.

He turned around and saw Edgar and Carolyn just a few steps below him. When he turned back to the séance, Andrew and Madonna were both standing and looking at the door.

18

Helen wasn't moving the planchette. She didn't believe in any of this stuff, so she assumed Andrew was moving it. Or his subconscious was taking over. Either way, it looked like they were going to search the boiler room. But she wanted to narrow it down because Andrew had already searched it once. He must have information stored in some small section of his brain that could help with the process. It could give them a more precise spot to search so that they didn't have to rip everything down to the studs like Hackman in *The Conversation*.

"Ask it something else," she said, thinking about that movie and the things paranoia can do to a person.

"Is it in the ceiling?" he said and then shrugged. "I don't know what to ask. It's a small room."

He looked hopeless. At this point, Helen didn't care what the spirit board told them. She was ready to go full-Hackman and get after the walls with a sledgehammer if they had to. But she decided to give Andrew a silent moment to search through his mental files and see if the lost material was in some secret, long-forgotten drawer in his mind's file cabinet.

He had his eyes closed, but Helen's were open when she heard a muffled click.

She'd heard the same sound while they were working with the pendulum a while ago, and she'd dismissed it as a car door shutting somewhere down the street. But this wasn't a car door. And it wasn't down the street. It was closer. She was losing focus now, trying to define the click. It had a crisp finality, like fingers snapping, but she knew that wasn't it because there was also something metallic involved. C-3PO snapping his fingers?

She was starting to lose it now and was ready to dismiss the sound for a second time, but then she saw shadow movement behind the partially open door in the hallway and almost immediately heard someone whisper something.

She stood up.

"Who's there?" she said.

Andrew stood.

"We can see you," he said and sounded scared, ready to run if he had to.

They waited a few beats, and then a nice-looking kid stepped into the hallway. He was holding a duffle bag over his shoulder.

Helen almost gasped at the sight of it.

He held it casually, like a lawyer who'd just won a big case might carry his sport coat into a bar to brag to his friends. The kid was about Andrew's height, but he had a sturdier frame. His sweatshirt sleeve was stretched tight over his bicep. On the front of the sweatshirt, in simple print, it said COLLEGE, right out of Belushi's wardrobe in *Animal House*. But this kid was in better shape than Belushi. Looked like he might have played some football.

He was followed by a skinny Mexican kid with messy hair. If they had to use him at The Back Lot, they'd throw a fake mustache on him, strap a guitar over his shoulder, and make him a teenaged Carlos Santana.

Finally, a lovely, wide-eyed young woman poked her head through the doorway and then stepped into the hall. In this light, she was a dead ringer for Diane Lane. They could do her up at The Lot in a tight sweater and a little preppy skirt, and she could be a fantastic Cherry Valance from *The Outsiders.* She'd make a killing in tips.

"We're sorry to bother you guys," said the kid with the bag. "We got locked in, and we're just gonna go out through the front." He took a couple of steps toward the door with the other two following him, but Andrew stepped past the spirit board, crossed in front of Helen, and stopped in front of the door.

"Who the hell are you?" said Andrew.

"Nobody," said the kid with the duffle bag.

Then little Santana said, "I'm a friend of Sawyer."

Andrew looked over at Helen and then back at Santana. "So what?" he said, keeping his head on a swivel, looking back at Helen, shifting his eyes to the bag, and then back to Santana again.

"Oh," said Santana, looking very innocent for a kid who'd broken into a house to pilfer a trove of stolen credit cards. "Sawyer asked me to pick up his stuff for him." He pointed at the duffle bag, and the kid holding it pulled it off his shoulder and held it in front of him like he was going to drop it down a well.

"This is a joke," said Andrew, his emotions leaking into his words. "That's not Sawyer's."

"It isn't?" said the kid holding the bag.

"It's mine," said Andrew and walked toward the kid with the bag.

Andrew extended his arm like he was offering to shake hands but then he turned his wrist so that his hand was palm up, and he indicated with his fingers that he wanted the bag right now.

When he got within a few feet, the bag man put out his free hand like a traffic cop. "Hold on," he said, and Andrew stopped. "If it's yours, why were you asking that board to help you find it?"

Andrew looked stumped. "I don't need to explain myself to you," he said finally. "This is my house, and that's my fucking bag." He shot a quick look at Helen, but she had nothing to add. They were outnumbered, and this kid in the COLLEGE sweatshirt was right. The ownership of the bag was ambiguous at best.

The bag man wasn't satisfied with Andrew's answer. "Where's all your furniture, man?" he said. He wasn't smiling or sneering or frowning or scowling. He was just laying out questions that Andrew couldn't answer.

"Screw this," said Andrew and took two steps closer.

The next part was hard for Helen to process.

She must have blinked while it was happening because she felt like she'd missed something. From her perspective, standing in front of the fireplace and squinting through the dimness of the big room, she saw only pieces of the action in front of her.

The best she could tell was that, without dropping the bag, the kid uncoiled.

From her angle, it looked more like a flinch than anything else—a muscle spasm. When Andrew reached for the duffle bag, the other kid rolled his shoulders slightly. It was so quick that it was only a blur to Helen.

But then she heard the sickening crack and knew it had to be the sound of knuckles crushing through soft tissue, getting all the way down to bone. It wasn't the sound she would have anticipated if she'd had time to process what was happening. She would have expected some version of a thud. But this was nothing like that. The impact from this short, compact strike, sounded like the explosion in the air caused by the sudden, extreme heat of lightning or maybe the crack of a bullwhip. It was a sound she'd never heard before.

Andrew took one step backward. Then he stepped back toward the bag man, so Helen thought Andrew was going to retaliate. But she was wrong. Andrew was out. Dead on his feet and simply falling forward.

Despite the bag man's attempt to catch Andrew before he fell, the reverberating smack was followed by the thud of Andrew hitting the floor.

Helen didn't hesitate. While the bag man was checking on Andrew, she dropped to her knees and crawled to her own bag. She reached in and grabbed Paul's pistol. Without standing up, she pointed it at the bag man and said, "That's enough, College. Step away." She was surprised to hear the authority in her voice. She used the gun to point to where Cherry Valance and Santana were both standing near the arch between the living room and the hallway. Both of their mouths were agape. The girl turned her head and looked behind her as if she were developing an escape plan. Then she looked at the bag man, who had his hands raised now, the bag still in his right hand, as if this were a bank robbery, and he was ready to provide her with the loot. He walked over and stood in line next to his friends.

Andrew wasn't moving, but he was making a low, gurgling sound, or else Helen would have thought he was dead.

"I think you guys got mixed up in something here," she said. "But it's all cool now." She didn't want anyone to panic and do something stupid. Although she knew the gun was loaded, she had no intention of ever pulling the trigger. No matter what treasure was in that bag, it wasn't worth hurting one of these kids just to find out if there was a big payday for her. And if there was, it should be bigger now. She'd saved the day. Andrew owed her.

"That bag isn't his," said Santana, pointing at Andrew. "He must have lied to you."

"It doesn't really matter now," she said. "All this just happened." She motioned toward Andrew, who was lying on his stomach, taking thick heavy breaths. "Now you guys are gonna go, but we're keeping the bag."

"What am I supposed to tell Sawyer about his cards?"

"Tell him Madonna's got 'em now."

Cherry Valance walked away from the lineup and pointed down at the spirit board. "What about this stuff?" she said.

"What about it?" said Helen.

"Were you really using it to try to find the bag?" she said and leaned over near the candle to get a better look.

Helen turned to look at Andrew, who still had his eyes closed. Then she looked at Cherry. "This stuff is all bullshit," she whispered and waved a dismissive hand at her tools of the trade. "But he doesn't know that." She gestured with her chin toward her hapless partner.

"So, you were never going to find the bag?" said Santana.

"You never know," she said. "Was it in the boiler room?"

"You're helping a thief," said Santana.

"Or maybe *you're* the thief," she said.

"Possession is nine-tenths of the law," said Cherry Valance.

Helen considered this. "Is that true?" she said.

Cherry said, "I don't know. I heard it somewhere."

"Hey College," said Helen "Bring that duffle bag over here."

The kid with the cattle prod left hook, hands still in the air, took slow, careful steps toward Helen and placed the bag at her feet. Helen picked it up in her free hand while she kept the gun pointed in the general direction of the kids.

"There you go," she said to Cherry. "Now I have the nine-tenths thing goin' for me."

19

The sight of the gun flipped a switch for Jerry. He wanted out.

He was surprised that Edgar and Carolyn were still challenging the lady, despite the fact that she was casually waving the gun around. Edgar was still trying to convince her that the kid lying on the floor was a thief, and Carolyn was trying to explain to her something about the law.

When Madonna asked for the bag, Jerry gladly gave it to her. He didn't want anything to do with it anymore. He suddenly wondered what the hell he was doing in this house in the first place.

The earlier encounter with Fr. Stricker in the school tennis courts seemed like it could have happened a month ago, but, for some reason, the water park incident felt like it happened this afternoon. His mind was playing tricks on him.

After Jerry dropped the bag on the floor next to Madonna, he walked back over to where Edgar and Carolyn were standing. He should have been planning an escape strategy, but disparate thoughts were strobing through his mind in double-time. The images were bouncing back and forth between fuzzy longshots of Fr. Stricker and clear close-ups of Chrissy. Saints and curses were blending with blood and water until they coalesced and became one thing in his mind, separate but somehow connected to his current predicament of being held at gunpoint by a Madonna impersonator.

He could sense that there was still talking in the room, but he couldn't concentrate on the words until he caught the end of something Madonna was saying in her almost-cowgirl twang.

"… Andrew'll explain it to him," she was saying.

"That won't help me," said Edgar. "Do you even know Sawyer Puck?"

"I sure don't," she said. "You scared of him?"

"Yes," said Edgar.

"But he's stuck in jail," she said. "What can he do?"

"Again," said Edgar, "you don't know this guy."

"Well," she said. "I don't know what to tell you." The gun must have been getting heavy because she switched hands and then extended it again in a lazy way, still pointing it toward Jerry and his friends.

Carolyn must have disapproved of the gun aimed in her general direction, so she walked over toward the Ouija board and started asking questions. Jerry wished she'd just stop. It was time to go.

He tried to shake away the water and the blood that had pooled together in his mind. He wanted to focus on the present, but something kept pulling him back to the waterslides. Maybe he was having some kind of biological reaction—a mini-stroke—brought on by the stress he'd experienced the day of the accident combined with today's tension, triggering something in his brain that was making him want to jump over the railing again, despite what he knew he'd see at the bottom. The sandy landing. Chrissy's head. Her body. The water everywhere.

Softer versions of this stress-trance had occurred over the past several weeks. Those were more like daydreams though. Tonight's version was different. It was sensory. He could smell the suntan lotion and the chlorine. Feel the hot metal of the railing. And, as usual, the water was overwhelming, though somehow internal. While he could hear it, as he had that day, splattering off the destroyed slide, the sensation of the water came from within. He felt as if his internal plumbing had expanded and the water, which had been dammed up in his head was draining down through his arteries, getting ready to spill out and splash across the hardwood.

The real voices around him were still active, but he was incapable of grasping any meaning. He sensed movement to his right and watched Carolyn rise out of her squatting position in front of the Ouija board.

Then he heard from behind, "What the hell?"

It was Andrew. He was sitting up and pressing lightly on the welt that had developed above his eyebrow. It was about the size of a walnut, and it pulled the skin tight on his forehead and the side of his face. "What's happening?" he said, and his voice sounded like a confused child.

"Oh, damn," said Madonna. "That doesn't look too good."

"What is it?" he said, still with his fingers testing the bump for size or density.

"You tried to tangle with College," she said. "And it did *not* go well."

"Tangle with college?" he said.

"Don't worry about it, Andrew," she said. "We got the goodies, and these folks were just leaving."

"What about my head?" he said and turned his eyes upward. "I think I can see the thing."

"We're going out for some frozen peas," she said, "as soon as the three amigos are on their way."

"Say no more," said Jerry. "Good luck in all your future endeavors." Then he looked down at Andrew and said, "Sorry about the bump."

Andrew was sitting on the floor with his knees pulled up to his chest. He wouldn't look up as Jerry passed by him to get to the door.

Edgar was right behind Jerry, but Carolyn was over by the Ouija board, so she had to step around the candle, then pass in front of the fireplace and Madonna to get to the door.

Madonna's arm was still outstretched because she had the gun trained on Jerry. When Carolyn got close, she stopped as if Madonna were a crossing guard. Madonna glanced at her and then lowered the gun for a moment to let Carolyn pass.

Jerry felt bad that Edgar wasn't going to obtain Sawyer's baseball card collection, but he was relieved that this episode was coming to end. He was literally inches from the door when Carolyn moved to step past Madonna.

But when Madonna let down her guard for that split second, Carolyn, with both hands, clutched the woman's forearm and then bent over like some creature from a zombie movie and chomped down hard.

Jerry's eyes met Madonna's for a brief moment before hers bugged out and her sharp yelp ricocheted off the walls of the empty house. Her cry was immediately followed by a cherry bomb blast that disoriented Jerry and left him momentarily deaf as he watched Madonna fall to the floor.

Jerry was crouched and holding his ringing ears, but Edgar was not affected. In fact, he sprung forward as if the gunshot signaled the start of a race. He took three quick steps and then executed the most athletic maneuver Jerry had ever seen him achieve: Edgar performed a perfect baseball slide across the hardwood. He snatched up the gun with one hand and continued to skid past Madonna, who didn't seem to want the gun anymore.

Carolyn was on her knees next to Madonna, who was in the fetal position. Madonna was moaning, her eyes shut tight but with a steady stream of tears leaking through the seams and rolling in indiscriminate tracks down her face. The tear routes changed direction every time she altered the angle of her head as she writhed in pain.

While Carolyn tried to comfort her, Jerry felt the need to get some control of the situation. "Carolyn," he said. "Get away from her."

"She's hurt," she said.

"She was pointing a gun at you a couple of seconds ago," he said. "And by the way, you bit her."

"I'm so sorry," said Carolyn to Madonna as Carolyn got to her feet and stepped backward toward the fireplace.

"Go into her bag," said Jerry, "and try to find something to help stop the bleeding." Jerry had only glanced at her foot but saw the hole the bullet had produced before it made its way through the hardwood floor. Jerry saw blood bubbling out of the hole. The pool growing on the floor looked black in the dim room.

Andrew wept silently.

Edgar aimed the gun at him.

Carolyn pulled items out of the bag. First, she held up some long, lacy gloves. She dropped them on the floor. Then she retrieved a pair of black stockings and placed them next to the gloves. Finally, she extracted a black cropped t-shirt. She held it up to her chest as if she were going to try it on. It said *HEALTHY* in sparkly letters.

"Yep," said Jerry. "We'll use that."

Carolyn walked toward Madonna.

"No," said Jerry. "*He's* gonna do it." Jerry pointed at Andrew and said, "Let's go." Jerry was surprised at his voice. He sounded like his old football coach barking at the players to line up for sprints.

Andrew looked frightened. He wiped the tears from his face and crawled over to Madonna. Carolyn tossed him the t-shirt, and he immediately began to attend to Madonna's wound, wrapping the t-shirt tightly around her foot as she wailed and slapped her hand on the floor.

Jerry pointed at the door, and Edgar and Carolyn knew what to do. They hustled past Jerry and stepped into the night as Jerry reached for the duffle bag. He gripped the handle and turned back to check on Madonna, but his eyes focused on Andrew, who stood up, took one step, and kicked the candle across the room. The flame was extinguished, and the room went black.

Jerry froze for a heartbeat and then ran for the door. Just before he crossed the threshold, he heard a whoosh—like golf club whipping through the air. Then he might have felt something brush the hair on the back of his head. And finally, as he jumped down the front stairs, he felt something at the base of his skull that felt like someone had smeared Bengay in a horizontal line just above his collar—icy hot.

Carolyn and Edgar were about halfway down the street when Jerry ran across the driveway. He was happy to be outside—the house had been running out of oxygen. He took a deep breath, glanced one more time over his shoulder, and saw Andrew's shadow in the doorway.

Jerry felt something wet on the back of his neck and prayed to God that the water memories weren't flooding his consciousness again and seeping through his pores.

Deep down, he knew the memories would never stop completely, but he felt that, after all they'd been through, he'd earned a break. Like the song in the commercial: *You've been going strong all day. You deserve a break today. At MacDonald's!*

20

When Sawyer Puck said, "One more thing …" Isaac knew it would be something juicy. It always was.

"It's lights out, little buddy," Isaac said and laughed to himself, sounding like the Skipper on *Gilligan's Island*.

"There's more in the bag," he said.

"Sweet dreams," said Isaac, reaching for his key ring but knowing the kid was dying to tell him more.

"Wait," said Sawyer before Isaac had the door closed all the way.

"Don't let the bed bugs bite," said Isaac and winked.

"Can you wait a second?" said Sawyer.

"What, man?" said Isaac. "I got other doors to lock."

"There's more in the bag," he said.

"What bag?"

"The one I asked Edgar to retrieve for me."

"The baseball cards?" asked Isaac, even though he knew exactly what Sawyer was talking about.

Sawyer grinned. "It's not just baseball cards," he said. "There's more in there under a false bottom."

"Why you telling me this?" said Isaac, pretending he wasn't interested. Doing his best to look impatient, fiddling with his keys again.

"'Cause I'm not fully confident Edgar's gonna pick up my stuff tonight," he said. "And it'll be extremely difficult to get it once the new people move in."

"Again," said Isaac, sounding like the vice-principal at his middle school now. "Why you telling me this?"

"We gotta get it tonight."

"*We* ain't doing nothing," said Isaac. "You forget about your incarceration?"

"That bag is worth way more than just the baseball cards," he said.

Isaac stepped into the cell and closed the heavy door behind him. "I thought the baseball cards were worth tens of thousands?" he said.

"They are," said Sawyer. "But I've got something else in there."

Isaac didn't like the way the kid was being coy. "Let's get to it, Sawyer," he said. "I've got shit I gotta do right now."

"I understand that," said Sawyer. "Go finish up. Then come back and get me, and we'll go pick up the bag." He was nodding confidently and gesturing at the door, as if they'd already decided that Isaac was going to break this kid out of jail for the night to go run some errands.

"What's in the bag?" said Isaac. If it were straight cash, the kid would have said it already. So, it had to be something valuable but also had to fit in a duffle bag. It wasn't a Lamborghini. Jewelry or drugs came to mind. If it was jewelry, Isaac didn't know how to fence it, so it wasn't worth much to him—pennies on the dollar at a pawn shop. If it was drugs, that was a different story. He knew people. But he also knew how ugly things could get in that particular industry.

Sawyer was still nodding. "Yeah, yeah," he said. "The thing is, I think you'd prefer not knowing what was in the bag. Plausible deniability if something goes sideways."

The fact that there was even a chance that things could go sideways didn't sit well with Isaac. Unlike most of his friends, Isaac was employed. He was earning steady income. It wasn't much, but he put money in the bank every two weeks.

"Not gonna happen, Sawyer," he said.

The kid took a couple of steps toward Issac, and Isaac leaned forward. Sawyer put his hands in front of him, like he was getting ready to brace himself against an oncoming train. "Hear me out," he said.

"You already been heard."

"This is an easy job," he said. "We'll be in and out."

"This is at your old house?" said Isaac. "The one you were living in when you got busted?"

"The same one," he said.

"Where's your stuff stashed?"

"Boiler room," he said. "And the lock on the side door to the house is broken. We'll walk right in."

"And it's just sittin' on the floor in the boiler room?"

"No," he said. "But it'll only take a few seconds to remove the grill over the ventilation duct."

"You got all that valuable property in a ventilation duct?"

"I had limited locations in which to store my valuables," he said.

Isaac stared at the kid. Sawyer had probably talked his way into and out of so much shit in his short time on the planet that he was lucky to be alive. "What neighborhood?" said Isaac, though he knew all he had to do was check Sawyer's file for his former home address.

"Pacific Heights," he said and looked at Isaac with hopeful eyes.

"If we got caught with the contraband in that bag, I assume we'd be doing considerable time?"

"We would."

"And what makes you think Edgar didn't already get it for you?"

"Edgar's not a criminal."

"Does he know there's something in that bag besides baseball cards?"

"He does not."

"Then maybe he already picked it up, not thinking he was committing a felony."

"And maybe not."

"Either way," said Isaac. "You did your boy wrong, youngblood."

"I told him I'd pay him to do it."

"But you didn't tell him about the contraband," said Isaac. "That's like slipping a gun in your buddy's carry-on before he goes through the security check. It ain't right."

"It's actually nothing like that," he said. Then he put his hands together as if in prayer and looked Isaac in the eyes. "So, are we gonna do this or not?" he said, still sounding confident that he'd convinced Isaac that sneaking him out of juvie tonight was a smart thing to do. But it wasn't. It was a crazy ass wish from a desperate, spoiled kid.

"Fuck no," said Isaac. "Go to bed."

***

When Isaac finished his rounds, he made sure the main office was empty. Then he grabbed Sawyer's file and went in to make a phone call.

His old buddy, Ronnie, was the right guy for this job. Ronnie and Isaac played on the offensive line together at McAteer High in '79. They were both big boys back then and ready for almost everything.

Isaac's grandma helped him get the position with the city, but Ronnie didn't have a grandma who cared about him, so he ended up doing odd jobs for his nasty uncle Norris, who was some kind of pimp or a pimp's associate. It wasn't really clear. Ronnie never got involved with the girls or anything, but Norris would send him out on stupid fast-money assignments, and Ronnie did them all.

He needed the money. He was always just a few wrong turns away from getting popped. Isaac was thinking maybe his old homie could help him with this easy job lifting some baseball cards and whatever else. Then Isaac would split the cut with Ronnie, and his old buddy could separate himself from Norris, maybe get out of the city altogether. Try LA or Reno.

This kid, Sawyer Puck, living up in Pacific Heights, throwing knives at people, and trying to con Isaac into breaking him out. Fuck that dude. Grew up with a silver spoon and ended up in jail. Isaac liked talking to the kid because he was like a TV character, but he didn't feel sorry for him.

Isaac was hoping the other kid, Edgar, chickened out, and the bag was still sitting in that boiler room. And if it was, Ronnie was going to get it for him. For both of them. And when little Sawyer Puck got out, it wouldn't matter what Isaac and Ronnie had done. The little psychopath was going to blame Edgar. Isaac liked Edgar, so he did not feel great about this part of the plan. But all the cards were falling into place. He wasn't in a position to pass this up.

Splashdown: The Pirate's Plank Disaster 25 Years Later

A Six-Part Documentary Series

Produced by NorCal Newsreel. Presented by Small Town Consortia in association with The Joint Center for Civic Review and The Sonoma County Film Institute

2010

Episode Four: Invisible
TRT 29 min

[Transcript]

Narrator: What was the extent of your injuries?

Samantha Dunleavy (St. Mary's '86): I was the fourth person on the slide, so I wasn't as high up as a lot of the others when it collapsed. I tore some ligaments in my ankle and broke a bunch of teeth when my knee smashed into my mouth. My lip was pretty bad too. But I couldn't complain after I saw what happened to everyone else.

Narrator: What was it like when you got back to school?

Samantha: I just thought it was kind of funny how many people said they were Chrissy's best friend. I loved her. She was my best friend. But then people were coming out of the woodwork to say how close they were. I was, like, did Chrissy even know you? Chrissy and I were like sisters. I think people were definitely shook by what happened, and they were mourning the loss of a really great girl. But there were a lot of girls I barely knew who were crying their eyes out at the funeral. They made me feel like I should be crying more.

Narrator: Why do you think they acted that way?

Samantha: I don't think they were bad people or anything. But there was a certain amount of celebrity that went along with being friends with the girl who died on the waterslide. To be totally honest, I got caught up in it too. But I really was her friend. I had a reason to be screwed up. And I felt horrible for her family. And then at the height of all the craziness around the funeral, I kind of made myself invisible.

Narrator: What do you mean by invisible?

Samantha: I went over once a couple weeks after the funeral to talk to Chrissy's parents and her older sister, Jill. My jaw was wired, so I couldn't say much. It was just all very difficult. They were such awesome people. But we sat out in their living room, where Chrissy and I would do our sleepovers, you know? When we were little, we'd stay up late and watch Benny Hill. Well, on the day of the visit, I could really feel her missing. I'm not even sure what I'm saying. Maybe it was this—I always thought I could see little parts of Chrissy in her parents and in Jill. But when I sat with them that day, it was gone. For some reason, I couldn't see it anymore, and after that, I went invisible too for a while. I could walk into rooms and no one would notice me. If I didn't talk to anyone, I wasn't there. And I kind of liked it. Don't use that. I don't even know what I'm saying.

21

They ran downhill toward the bay.

They wanted to create as much space as possible, as fast as they could, between themselves and the house. When they finally got to Lombard, they turned east. No one said anything. Carolyn felt relieved to be walking on a busy street with plenty of traffic. If Andrew decided to come after them, there would be a lot of witnesses.

"Where are we headed?" she said.

Jerry just pointed in front of him and kept moving forward. He was carrying the duffle bag at his side.

Carolyn decided to drop back so that she could check in with Edgar. She could hear his heavy breathing behind her. When he caught up, he was holding his side, apparently cramped up from all the running.

"What did you do with the gun?" she said, surprised that she wasn't as winded as Edgar, but she figured adrenaline must have carried her down the hill.

He licked his lips and said, "I wiped my prints off with my shirt and threw it in some bushes when we were still on Steiner."

"You threw your shirt in the bushes?" she said, messing with him but then immediately realizing this wasn't a good time for jokes.

"Huh?" he said.

"Never mind."

"But now I'm worried," he said.

"That you didn't get your prints off?"

"No," he said. "I'm worried some little kid'll find it and kill someone."

"Oh," she said, concerned now that he had a point.

"I couldn't see it after I dumped it," he said, still pausing to take in big gulps of air in between thoughts. "But when it gets light out, it might be in plain sight."

"Okay," she said. "Well, we can come back and get it at some point and drop it off the bridge or something. Okay?"

He reserved his breath and just nodded. But he looked satisfied with this plan.

When Carolyn looked forward, something didn't look right with Jerry. They were passing under the awnings of storefronts, which were mostly closed and dark at this hour, so the sidewalk was shadowy. But Carolyn didn't like what she was seeing. At first, she thought Jerry's hair looked longer in the back, like he'd grown one of those stupid mullets. But when she squinted him into focus as he moved with purpose down the middle of the sidewalk, she realized that it wasn't hair at all. There was something dark smeared on the back of Jerry's neck. And it also appeared that his sweatshirt, down to about the middle of his back, was stained with either sweat or something else.

"Jerry," she said and jogged a few steps to close the gap. "Stop for a second." When he didn't slow down, she put her hand on his shoulder and said, "Jerry."

He stopped, but before he turned around, Carolyn felt the stickiness on her hand and saw the blood. "What happened?" she said and felt a tingling, like antifreeze shooting up through the veins in her legs all the way to her shoulders.

"What?" he said.

"Dude," said Edgar.

"Turn around," said Carolyn. "How did you not notice this?" She held him by the back of his belt and pulled him close. He stumbled a bit, and when he steadied, she put her face near the back of his neck to try to examine the source.

"I guess I noticed something while we were running," he said. "But I didn't want to stop."

"What did you think it was?" said Carolyn.

"Water?" he said.

"From where?" she said, frustrated that Jerry was all of a sudden acting mental.

"It doesn't matter," he said.

"Well," she said, "we gotta get a towel to clean this off so we can see what the cut looks like."

"Damn, dude," said Edgar.

"Let's keep walking," she said. "We can cross and go to the Jack-in-the-Box."

"I heard something right before I was out the door," said Jerry. "Andrew kicked over the candle and came after me, I think."

"What did you hear?" said Edgar, as he pulled the duffle bag from Jerry. Jerry held tight for a moment and then appeared to realize what he was doing and released the bag to Edgar's care.

"Like a whoosh," he said.

"That's a lot of blood," said Edgar. "Do you think Andrew had a knife?"

"I don't think it would have made that sound," he said.

"Finger nails?" said Carolyn, not fully believing that nails could do this much damage but also not having a clue what else Andrew had available. "It couldn't have been the Ouija board?" she said and took

Jerry's hand as they crossed Lombard toward the lights of the Jack in the Box.

"I've heard people say that Ouija boards can be dangerous," said Jerry and squeezed Carolyn's hand.

"Ha ha," she said. "Does it hurt?"

"Not at all," he said. "It just feels a little cold on the back of my neck."

"What did you mean by a *whoosh*?" said Edgar.

Jerry paused when they reached the sidewalk on the westbound side of Lombard. "Like the sound Bruce Lee's hands make when he's karate chopping people in the movies," he said. "But slower. Like if he had a really long arm."

When they got to a lamppost in front of the Jack in the Box, Carolyn said, "Stop here, so we can look at it in some light."

It wasn't ideal, but it was better than trying to see it in the shadows. Carolyn told Jerry to turn around, and she grabbed his belt again. When she did this a few minutes ago across the street, it was in a panic after seeing the blood. This time it was different. It was intimate. She was holding the back of his belt, and Jerry was doing what she was telling him. "Bend your knees a little bit," she said so that her eyes would be at his neckline.

Their bodies were touching.

Because of their experience at the water park and now this strange day that started at the football game and involved so much chaos afterward, she felt like they were boyfriend and girlfriend. Like they'd been dating for a long time. She'd had a couple of boyfriends during the past few years, but those were different.

First of all, Jerry wasn't her boyfriend. It just felt that way. And also, with those other boys, it was more that they just wanted to have a girlfriend. It didn't matter who. They wanted to grope around in the dark and learn about the mysteries of girls and perhaps try to discover something about themselves. And maybe Carolyn just wanted to have a boyfriend to figure out what kind of strange command she might have over boys who were confused and needy and scared and stupid.

The situation with Jerry was nothing like that. She just wanted to be with him and knew that she would not be able to stop thinking of him after tonight. She was almost giddy to be so close to him, but also almost sad that he might not be feeling the same way about her. And even though she was looking at his bloody neck and smelling him—the musk of his sweat and blood and beer—she wanted to kiss him.

She wanted to tell him how excited she was when he'd knocked out Andrew. She didn't like violence. She didn't like it at all. But she'd definitely been awakened by the potency of his actions. His power in that split second. The force that he was able to generate with his body, through his core, up into his shoulders and out to his fist.

But also, his strange kindness, trying to catch the kid as he fell forward, as if the punch were obligatory, but afterward there was no reason to duck his responsibilities regarding the consequences of the blow. She knew there was something important about that.

She'd never seen anything like it. And he was also handsome and funny and a little weird, too. And everyone liked him. And she felt like he'd picked her. Even though she was the one who'd approached him at the game, he'd made it known to her in subtle ways that there was a connection.

The light still wasn't good, and a lot of the blood had already started to coagulate, but she could tell the cut was at the base of his skull, right at his hairline. And it looked deep. She let her mind wander back to the living room of that big house: the thick curtains, the dusty floor, the Ouija board, the candle, the fireplace, Madonna's foot, the feeling of her teeth breaking the skin on that woman's forearm.

The fireplace. The fireplace tools. The poker.

"The poker," she shouted, too close to Jerry's ear.

He jumped forward and looked back at her. "What?"

"He must have hit you with the fireplace poker," she said.

Jerry nodded. "The top of that thing was probably pretty sharp."

Edgar said, "Shouldn't it hurt more?"

22

Edgar desperately wanted to look through the duffle bag to see if the Roberto Clemente was in there. But Jerry was hurt because he was helping Edgar, and Edgar felt really lousy about that. However, he would have felt even worse if they had to leave without the bag.

He put his fingers on the zipper but didn't pull it.

He knew they had to focus, at least for the moment, on Jerry's head. To Edgar's mind, the wound could have been much worse. It seemed like Andrew must have swung when Jerry was running for the door. From the look of the cut, the tip of the poker just grazed Jerry's head and sliced his scalp.

"I guess it could've been the shovel," said Jerry. "That was probably pretty sharp too."

Carolyn got some wet paper towels from the Jack in the Box bathroom, and she tended to the wound. Once she'd cleaned off most of the blood, she separated Jerry's hair and looked at the clean slash that ran in a perfect three-inch, horizontal line at the base of Jerry's skull.

"This is pretty deep," she said and threw another bloody paper towel into the garbage bin by the door.

"Hey," said a guy in a paper hat behind the counter. "This isn't a M.A.S.H. unit. Take it outside, or I'm gonna call the cops." He was leaning out over the register. His eyebrows were slanted in a sharp V, maybe trying to intimidate them. It looked like Jerry was staring right back at him, not budging, so the guy changed his tone. "There's people trying to eat in here," he said, kind of whining now.

Jerry stood up and saluted the man.

Carolyn took Jerry's hand and said to the manager, "You're a dick, dude."

Edgar grabbed a bunch of napkins from the dispenser near the door, and the three of them walked out into the parking lot. Before Jerry pushed the door open, Edgar could feel the music vibrations coming from the parking lot. And when the door swung open, he heard a funky train engine rhythm and then the lyrics. It was the Talking Heads' *Road to Nowhere*:

We're on a ride to nowhere
Come on inside
Takin' that ride to nowhere
We'll take that ride

When they got to the bottom of the steps, Edgar saw Cheese's station wagon parked in the corner of the lot. The tailgate was down, and Cheese and Dave were sitting in the back with their legs over the bumper and their feet hovering just inches above the pavement. They were devouring their Jumbo Jacks like two guys coming out of a hunger strike.

Bags, napkins, greasy wrappers, and bottle caps were spread across the back seats. Both guys clenched Lucky Lager bottles between their thighs as they took enormous bites from their burgers and jammed handfuls of fries into their mouths. Cheese licked his fingers after every bite.

Saint X's starting power forward, Marcus Moore, was leaning up against the side of the wagon. He wasn't eating. He was working on something, using his long finger like a screwdriver and swearing quietly to himself.

"What happened to Run-D.M.C.?" said Edgar as he approached their camp.

Cheese and Dave looked up, but only Marcus spoke while the others continued to chew. "This dude's car ate my tape," he said and pointed at Cheese.

The tip of a fry was sticking out of Cheese's mouth when he said, "I think there was something wrong with that tape."

"Bullshit," said Marcus as he continued to wind the ribbon back into the plastic cassette.

"We're listening to KFOG for now," said Cheese. "Because Marcus put a damaged tape into my new Blaupunkt."

"Bullshit," said Marcus again, still concentrating on his work, studying the twisted ribbon and delicately cranking the wheels like an apprentice watchmaker.

Dave lifted himself off the car and flicked an onion off his cast. "How did you guys get here?" he said and looked around the parking lot.

"We walked," said Carolyn.

Edgar hoped these guys wouldn't ask why it took so long to get from the Pacific Heights party down to Jack in the Box. The crew hadn't really discussed creating a story about their adventure and Jerry's injury, so they were going to have to wing it. Edgar didn't want these guys to know about the baseball cards or Sawyer Puck or Andrew or the Madonna impersonator.

Cheese finished his burger and crumbled up the last wrapper. He took a long pull on his Lucky Lager, then looked like he was going to burp but merely let his cheeks fill with gas before closing his eyes and swallowing it, maybe because Carolyn was looking at him. He picked up a beer cap, brought it up near his ear, and then snapped it across the parking lot. It whizzed past Edgar and spun to a stop under a Chevy Nova.

"Was that a Lucky Lager cap?" asked Carolyn.

"Yeah," he said and looked guilty.

"You didn't even do the riddle," she said and started to walk toward the Chevy.

Before she got far, Cheese said, "Here, you can do this one." He moved some napkins around and picked up a cap. He tossed it underhand, and she caught it with one hand.

She studied it for a moment, then squinted and pulled a pair of reading glasses out of her jacket pocket. Edgar liked the way she looked in the glasses. She could really pull it off, like the girl in Adam Ant's *Goody Two Shoes* video—both she and Carolyn had good faces for specs.

"Okay," she said. "There's the letter *U*. And then a beer can + the letter *T*." She looked up to the sky. *You Can't,"* she said, then smiled and nodded.

"Bravo," said Marcus. "That's it?"

"No," she said. "Then there's a symbol I can't read." She wiped at the cap with her thumb, then said, "Forget that one. Then it just says *IT*."

Marcus was involved now. "All right," he said. "So, we got *You Can't blank It?"*

"Yeah," she said and then turned the cap upside-down for a moment before righting it again. "Then it looks like there's a picture of a witch and another picture of a shoe."

Marcus scratched his head. "You Can't blank It Witch Shoe?" he said.

"You can't take it with you," she said. Then she kicked up one leg and clapped her hands underneath like a cheerleader. She laughed and ran in a little circle with her hands behind her back. She kicked her feet up high behind her, almost touching her butt with her heels as she bounced around the parking lot. She still had her glasses on and looked like a nerd-cheerleader. She was just clowning around, but she looked good. And Edgar thought she might've been one of those girls who didn't even know it.

"Where's your car, Jerry?" asked Dave.

"I didn't tell you?" he said, not taking his eyes off Carolyn, who tried to snap the cap like Cheese had done, but it shot straight down to her feet, and she kicked it.

"We haven't really been hanging out," Dave said and raised his eyebrows.

"I guess we haven't," said Jerry.

"So, what happened?"

"To the car?" asked Jerry.

Dave paused for a beat. "Yeah," he said. "Did you total it?"

"Not exactly," said Jerry, and Edgar could tell Jerry didn't really want to get into this in front of Carolyn.

"Your blue Comet's gone?" she said.

Jerry reached out to Edgar with one hand. Edgar gave him the napkins, and Jerry put the whole stack on the back of his head before he said, "One night I brought it home with a big dent on the front bumper."

"How did it happen?" asked Carolyn.

"That's the problem," he said. "I have no idea."

Edgar felt bad for Jerry. Carolyn was hearing a lot of bad stuff about a really good guy. All in the same day.

Carolyn tilted her head. "You can't remember?" she asked.

"Either I can't remember," he said. "Or somebody hit my car while it was parked." He shrugged but didn't take his eyes off Carolyn. Like he'd just confessed to her and was waiting for his penance. Not proud of his sins but willing to accept however many *Hail Marys* were prescribed.

"But if it's just the bumper, the car should be okay, right?" she said and put her hands up in a little kid's shrug. "So, what happened?"

"My dad sold it," he said.

Marcus had finished repairing his Run-D.M.C. tape and was putting it in the pocket of his jacket when he said, "Oh, that's cold, Jer." Then he walked over and put his arm around Jerry's shoulder. "Didn't you buy that car with your own money?"

"A whole summer working at Mr. Liquor," said Jerry and then dug into his own pocket. He pulled out a set of keys and held it up for Marcus to see.

"Are those the keys to the Comet?" asked Marcus. "Your pride and joy?"

"One and the same," said Jerry and put the keys back in his pocket. "My dad sold it and gave the new owner the other set of keys without even telling me. I just came home one day, and it was gone."

"Ice cold," said Marcus and laughed. "Your old man doesn't play."

"He does not."

"Why you holdin' on to the keys?" Marcus asked.

"They're on the same ring as my house key."

"Don't have the will to separate yourself?"

"Something like that."

Marcus stepped away from Jerry and looked at his hand. "What the hell?" he said and rubbed his fingers like he'd touched tree sap.

Edgar saw the blood and said, "Jerry cut himself."

"Damn," said Marcus.

Jerry pulled the napkins from the back of his head and presented the evidence to the group.

"Can we have a ride to the emergency room?" said Carolyn. "Jerry needs to get his head examined." Then she paused and looked up at Jerry. "He needs stitches too."

23

Ronnie spent a lot of time at Shanley's on Valencia. Not because he loved it there, but because Norris wanted him in the neighborhood in case Ronnie was needed for a job. Technically, he was on-call.

The pub was in the Mission District, where Norris did most of his business, and people around the horseshoe-shaped bar generally left Ronnie alone to drink his gimlets and take calls on Shanley's direct line. This was pretty much his office.

Tonight, he was sitting next to Sid DiPiu. As a district manager for the Chronicle, Sid was usually a mid-day drinker. He got up at four o'clock in the morning and drove his truck around the neighborhood, dropping bundles on corners for the paperboys to deliver. Then he'd spend the rest of his day dealing with complaints before heading over to Shanley's.

But Ronnie hadn't seen him in weeks.

"So, where you been?" he asked.

"I'm cuttin' back on the drinking," said Sid.

"You pregnant?" said Ronnie.

Sid laughed and took a long drag from his cigarette. "Trying to stay sharp for my classes."

"Driver's ed?" said Ronnie, picturing Sid in his Chronicle truck skidding into tight turns on the busy, narrow streets of The Mission.

"I started law school," he said with a shy grin.

"Bullshit," said Ronnie, not so much surprised as impressed. Sid read the paper cover-to-cover every day and had opinions on everything. Not in-your-face. Just thoughtful ideas about what was happening in the world and in the city—informed, like a good lawyer would be. Apparently, Sid also had the wherewithal to know that he didn't want to drive that truck for the rest of his life. "That's a feather in your cap, Sid," said Ronnie and nodded, wondering if Sid cared if this young punk was impressed.

"Well…" he said but went back to his beer without finishing the sentence.

"I'm proud of you," said Ronnie and held his gimlet out for a toast. Because Ronnie spent hours upon hours of time in Shanley's, he'd mastered the art of sipping. Once he'd achieved a buzz, all he wanted to do was maintain that buzz until he'd get a call and have go to work.

Sid clinked glasses with Ronnie and said, "Nothing to be proud of unless I finish."

"You'll finish," said Ronnie and then looked over at the door, which opened slowly. Uncle Norris swaggered in and leaned against the cigarette machine. Then he wrinkled his nose and checked the bottoms of both leather boots before walking over and standing next to Sid.

Norris's boots were the only slick part of his outfit. Otherwise, his charcoal, three-piece suit looked like a banker's.

"Nice threads," said Sid and looked Norris up and down.

"Aren't you usually in bed by now?" said Norris.

"I'm off tomorrow."

Ronnie said, "What are y'all drinking?"

"Let me get it," said Norris. "Sid'll be my personal attorney someday, so I'm gonna take care of him in the meantime."

"So, you heard about law school?" asked Ronnie.

Norris didn't smile, but he clutched Sid's shoulder and shook it lightly, "Word gets around."

"What kind of law you looking at?" said Ronnie.

Sid shook his head. "I just started," he said.

"Yeah," said Ronnie. "But you probably got something in mind."

"I'm actually thinking about becoming a prosecutor," he said and bent his head to drain his pint. He kept his eyes down—looked like he was reading the cocktail napkin that had the same logo that it always had, at least since Ronnie started showing up there as a nineteen-year-old kid: Shanley's in green handwriting with a shamrock acting as the apostrophe.

Ronnie wanted to laugh about the possibility of Sid someday putting both him and Norris in jail, but Ronnie didn't think Norris found any of this amusing.

Norris looked across the bar and held a hundred dollar bill up for the bartender to see. "Olive," he said. "Please bring these gentlemen another round."

Ronnie was pretty sure that Olive looked good about twenty years ago, but she didn't anymore. Everything about her was drooping. She wasn't fat, but her skin looked too heavy for her bones. Ronnie could imagine her years ago, when her young frame was still sturdy enough to hold everything in place. She probably did all right. These days, she made a living being a wiseass who understood not to cross the line with the wrong people. Ronnie felt like there was an art to that.

"Same?" she said to Ronnie and Sid.

They both nodded.

All three of them watched Olive make the drinks. Ronnie was waiting for Norris to say why he was at the bar. He came in once or twice a week to check in, but he usually had some information to share or a new job assignment. Tonight, he just looked like he was bored.

When Olive placed the drinks in front of Ronnie and Sid, she said, "Anything for you, Norris?"

"No, thank you," he said and placed the hundred-dollar bill back in his pocket.

Olive didn't blink, but she made eye contact with Ronnie before she took away the empties and turned back toward the two heavy-set Filipinos, wearing number sixteen Niners' jerseys and nursing their beers on the other side of the horseshoe.

Norris was standing behind Sid and Ronnie. There was an empty stool next to Sid, but Norris didn't move to take it. He stood back there for a long time before Ronnie turned on his stool to face him. Sid kept his eyes on his drink.

Norris looked back at Ronnie for several beats before he said, "Slow night, Ronnie?"

"Slower than most," said Ronnie.

"Olive," Norris shouted across the bar. "Did Ronnie get any calls tonight?"

Olive looked at Ronnie with her sad eyes before she turned back to Norris. "Not yet," she said.

"Slower than most," said Norris and checked his watch. "Keep up the good work, Ronnie." Then he touched Sid's forearm and walked toward the door. Before he pushed it open, he looked over his shoulder at Ronnie. His face looked like a reptile's as he slithered out onto the sidewalk.

"What's it like working for him?" said Sid after the door swung closed.

"I do what I'm told, and he pays me to do it."

"Not what I asked," said Sid.

"Yeah," said Ronnie, "but that's my answer anyway."

"Why don't you—?"

"Let's just leave it," he said.

Ronnie could feel Sid looking at him, but he kept his eyes on the old TV propped up on a shelf behind the bar. The news was on. They were showing footage of an earthquake that shook up Mexico City. Then Ronnie heard the phone. The ringer was broken, so it didn't sound normal. It was more like a buzzing vibration, like the sound from one of those novelty prank buzzers that shocks a person when he shakes hands.

Olive brought the phone down to the end of the horseshoe and nodded at Ronnie.

"That can't be Norris already," he said.

She shook her head and said, "Someone named Isaac?"

Ronnie hadn't heard from his old friend in months. After Isaac passed the civil service exam and finished the sheriff's academy, Ronnie thought it would be best if the two of them took a bit of a break until Isaac figured out if they could still hang or not. Ronnie didn't want to get in the way of Isaac's career. Isaac was a kid from the neighborhood, just like Ronnie, but Isaac was doing something with his life.

Ronnie was stuck. He got in with the wrong fools, and the situation was now his only source of income. The money was coming in steady, and it was a cash arrangement, but he felt like he wasn't building anything. He had no resume if he ever wanted to get out. He had no defined skills. He'd turned into the kind of adult all his teachers had warned him about in high school.

Isaac was never going to be rich in that job at juvie, but he could finance a car right now if he wanted to. Maybe save up and get season tickets for the Niners or even buy a house someday. If Ronnie wanted to try something like that, Uncle Norris would intervene. So, if Ronnie wanted to try something like that, he'd either have to leave the city or get rid of Uncle Norris. Neither seemed possible.

Ronnie picked up the receiver, turned his back to Sid and the rest of the regulars sitting around the bar. "Hey, hey," he said. "You lock yourself in a cell or something?"

He heard Isaac's slow, easy laugh. "Nah, dude," he said. "I got something you might want to consider."

"Lay it on me," said Ronnie, hoping Isaac might have some opportunity to get Ronnie away from Shanley's Pub and watery gimlets and Uncle Norris.

But Isaac was pushing more of the same old crap Ronnie'd been doing for Norris.

Isaac's dance involved baseball cards and maybe something else. Tens of thousands of dollars' worth of something. He kept saying that if the bag was still in this Pacific Heights boiler room, Ronnie could pick it up, and someone else would take the fall for the burglary.

"It's the perfect job," said Isaac. "No risk."

"That's funny," said Ronnie. "Norris told me the same thing when he brought me in on my first gig."

"This is me talking," said Isaac. "You know me, bro."

Ronnie and Isaac grew up in the Bayview. When they were teenagers, they went to war together during football season every year. They blew open big holes for running backs to waltz through on their way to glory. Ronnie and Isaac didn't get as much credit as the backs, but people knew who they were. Opposing teams had to strategize just to slow them down.

And now Isaac was saying that the hole had already been blown open. All Ronnie had to do was strut on through and grab that trophy.

Unless the bag was already gone.

In that case, no harm, no foul. Isaac would take Ronnie out for Chinese food.

"Gimme the details again," Ronnie said.

24

To Carolyn, the inside of Cheese's station wagon smelled like weed, teenage-boy-body-odor, and, well, cheese—the food, not the driver. In fact, the gorgonzola fumes were more powerful than the weed and the B.O. combined. Carolyn and Jerry were sitting in the back seat with Marcus. Edgar was in the way back. There was an assortment of junk at their feet. Carolyn used her foot to clear away the garbage on the floorboards. She wanted to make room for her feet. After she kicked away some fast-food wrappers, she saw the source of the odor: a single dirty sock that had been hidden under a tired old pee-chee folder.

"It's pretty disgusting back here, Cheese," said Carolyn. She was tempted to snatch up the sock and hold it under his nose, but she thought the jolt might cause him to drive off the road. There was also no way she was going to touch that sock. It was so stiff, it looked like a cast for a broken foot.

"I just cleaned this car," he said and turned off Lombard onto Gough. "St. Francis emergency room, right?"

"That's the closest one," said Jerry. "I got stitches there before."

"Do I even want to know?" asked Carolyn.

"PAL soccer," he said. "I went up for a head ball and so did the guy from Holy Name." He pointed to a fine line that ran in an inch-long diagonal through his eyebrow.

Carolyn had seen it before but hadn't thought about it. To her, the scar looked like it was supposed to be there. She reached up and touched it. Jerry averted his eyes, a shy little boy now. She was very close to him. It felt like an intimate moment even though they were in the car with four other boys. "This isn't from a fight?" she said and smoothed his eyebrow.

"No," he said. "This was a hundred percent from the kid's head smashing into my face." He put his hand over hers and brought it down on her lap. "Though I did punch him afterward."

"Jerry," she said. "What's wrong with you?"

"I was there," said Marcus. "Dude had it coming."

"See?" said Jerry.

"When did it happen?" said Carolyn.

"I think I was twelve," he said. "And, seriously, I'm not fighting anymore."

Carolyn thought back to Jerry's knockout punch at the house. She couldn't decide how it made her feel. She knew she didn't like violence.

But she also knew that she enjoyed roller derby and football. There was something exhilarating about seeing someone get flattened during competition. And if her dad was watching Friday Night Fights on the television, she'd sit with him. She'd decide which fighter was her favorite and then cheer for him, clenching her fists and feeling the electricity every time her guy landed a punch.

Maybe she was just against *senseless* violence but appreciated other kinds of violence. She knew this internal line of reasoning didn't make sense. But she also knew how she felt when Jerry put Andrew on the floor. Once she'd realized what had happened, she felt a tingling in her chest. Maybe she liked that Jerry seemed to be a guy who could protect her. Before that exact moment in the house, Carolyn was feeling vulnerable. She was scared. They were doing something unfamiliar and probably illegal. After being under house arrest on 41st Avenue since the waterslide collapse, the baseball card adventure was a big leap, and she was having trouble evaluating her emotions. And her actions.

She bit that lady's arm. Carolyn was still surprised she'd done it. As soon as she saw the lady with the gun, she tried to formulate an exit plan. She'd thought about running back down the stairs, but she remembered the door to the boiler room had locked behind them. She measured the distance to the front door and calculated how many steps it would take to get out. But that didn't make sense either. The Madonna lady seemed like she was going to let them go. She just wanted the bag.

Carolyn pulled her skirt up slightly and pointed at the jagged scar on her thigh, just above her knee. "German Shepherd," she said. "St. Gabriel's school yard, circa 1978."

"Oh, man," said Jerry. "Fifth grade?"

"Fourth," she said and pulled her skirt over the evidence that she too was tough. "Didn't even cry," she lied.

Marcus pulled his pant leg up and lowered his sock to reveal a long vertical scar on his shin. "Took a metal baseball spike against St. Francis, JV year," he said and let his pant leg fall back into place. "Dude slid into third spikes up."

"Ow," said Carolyn.

"Jerry came running over from shortstop," said Marcus, "and beat the guy up."

"What?" said Carolyn, her face getting hot.

"Joking," said Marcus. "Nineteen stitches though, and I missed a couple of games."

Carolyn looked over at Jerry, who was grinning but not looking at her. The moment seemed odd, suddenly, that they were sitting around joking when they were headed to the emergency room after being involved in a shooting. That's the way she would refer to this if she ever had to talk about it. *Involved in a shooting.* She didn't shoot anyone, but she felt that she was certainly the cause of a woman being shot. But those were two different things. In fact, Madonna had actually fulfilled the qualifications of the old idiom. She had literally shot herself in the foot.

And now they'd all survived and were telling their scar stories.

Carolyn wasn't sure if their situation at the house would be considered a near-death experience, but something in her core was telling her that they should all be taking it more seriously and thanking God that no one was killed.

Last year, she was driving in the rain back to the city from Marin. On the Waldo Grade, she hit her brakes too hard and started to spin on the slick highway. Somehow, she stayed in her lane and eventually bumped gently into a guardrail with the car facing nearly in the correct direction. When she steered back into traffic, her hands were shaking. She could barely keep the car on the road. It lasted all the way back to her house.

Yet, somehow, tonight, she and her friends didn't seem to be rattled.

Now Edgar was leaning forward between Jerry and Carolyn. He was holding his long hair back from his forehead and pointing at his own scar. "Me and my cousin were little kids," he said. "And we doing one of those forts you do in your house, you know?" He waited for everyone to say *yeah* before he said, "And most of it was couch cushions, but part of the roof was a blanket that my cousin stuck under my grandma's sewing machine to hold it in place on the dresser."

Edgar took a break and closed his eyes like he was trying to picture it. He was probably imagining a time when forts were important. Then he said, "Well, I was inside the fort, and I must've pulled the blanket or something, and the sewing machine fell on my head." He laughed and said, "I think I might have even been knocked out for a second. I can still feel the feeling if I concentrate. Like my brain was exploding."

"Good thing you were protected by the fort," said Dave. Then he held up his cast. "Remember when you first saw my wrist after the fall, Jerry?"

"It's all kind of a blur," said Jerry, and his voice sounded shaky, like he was already in Stricker's office, having to explain why he was drinking beer before the game.

Dave turned all the way around in his seat. "First you looked like you were gonna throw up," he said. "And then you were in a daze, like you were hypnotized or something."

Jerry nodded. "I think I might have lost my mind for a few minutes," he said.

"You did," said Dave. "And remember how I wasn't really hurt. I mean, I was scared because it made a terrible sound, and I could see the bone and everything. But I couldn't feel it until later."

Jerry didn't say anything. Carolyn put her hand on his knee and gave it a squeeze.

"You were in shock," said Cheese. "It happened to me when I fell off my bike and knocked out all my front teeth." He flashed a Pan Am smile into the rearview mirror. "Dentures," he said, and turned left onto Bush. "And when I ran home holding my teeth in my hand, it didn't hurt at all. I was bleeding all over the place, but I was numb."

"How you holding up, Jer?" said Marcus.

"A dull sting?" said Jerry. "I mean, I feel it, but I wouldn't say it hurts."

Carolyn couldn't tell if he was being a tough guy or telling the truth. She didn't know if a cut this clean was painless. It couldn't have hurt that bad because they'd run several blocks before he even noticed it.

They passed over Van Ness, and a couple blocks later, Cheese pulled the station wagon into the emergency lot on Hyde.

Before Jerry opened the door, Cheese said, "Where you guys going after?"

Carolyn was about to say, "Home," but before she got it out, Edgar said, "Where you guys going?"

"Either the Grove or the Boathouse," said Cheese. "Whichever one the cops haven't hit yet."

"Isn't it getting a little late?" said Carolyn, trying to make eye contact with Jerry, but he was looking out the window at an ambulance pulling in front of the glass doors.

"Carolyn," said Cheese. "Don't be a killjoy. We're just getting started."

"Drive safe," she said and reached over Jerry to open the door.

When Jerry noticed what she was doing, he said, "Oh, sorry," and stepped out into the parking lot. "Maybe we'll catch you guys later," he said, and his face was blinking red and white to the alternating colors of the beacon on top of the ambulance. He was beautiful in the washed-out illumination of the white light, his features softened by the glow, his scar invisible.

During the red flashes, he looked like he could be in a rage even though he stood with his hands in his pockets, stooped over slightly to look into the passenger side window at Dave and Cheese. The permanent half smile was still on his face when he said, "Good to see you guys."

Dave said nothing.

Cheese leaned over and said, "Good to be seen."

25

Jerry waved to the station wagon as it pulled out of the lot.

He heard Edgar say, "Well, shit," and then take a quick step as if he were going to chase down the car. But Edgar stopped short and sighed. Jerry watched the wood side-panel pass under a streetlight and then move out of view down Hyde.

"What?" said Jerry.

"I forgot the bag in the back seat."

Carolyn had Jerry's hand and was pulling him toward the automatic doors, but she let go and turned to face Edgar. "The bag we just risked our lives to get?" she said.

Jerry looked over the top of Carolyn's head and gave Edgar a *you're busted* look.

"That's the one," said Edgar and looked out toward the exit as if Cheese was going to make a U-turn and bring the bag back to Edgar for safe keeping.

Jerry saw the hint of distress on Edgar's face. The guy was usually unflappable, so Jerry tried to lighten the mood. "Cheese has probably already traded your Orlando Cepeda card for a twelve pack of Olympia," he said and reached over for Carolyn's hand.

"Roberto Clemente," said Edgar. "Do you think they'll notice the bag back there?"

"What else was in the back?" said Carolyn.

"Nothin'"

"So, they have no reason to even look?" she said.

"Only if they pick up more people and need passenger space."

"Hey," said Jerry, thinking they should haul ass out of there and find a way to get that bag back. "This thing's starting to heal up." He pulled out the Jack-in-the-box napkins from his pocket and tapped the back of his head. "I don't think I need to get the stitches anymore." He pulled the napkin back and held it in front of his face. Squinting in the flashing lights, he saw a straight red stripe in the middle of the white napkin, like Mr. McNaughton had drawn a line through one of his stupid ideas.

"Jerry," said Carolyn. "Will you please go inside and get the stitches?"

Edgar said, "We can track those guys down later."

Jerry nodded and walked toward the glass doors. They passed the ambulance, where two paramedics were taking their time pulling a drunk lady out of the ambulance. The guy who'd been driving was smoking a cigarette and swearing under his breath.

The lady refused a wheelchair.

When they got her to her feet, they held her under each of her arms like an injured athlete and escorted her to the entrance.

"You two pervs trying to feel me up?" she said.

The driver threw his cigarette on the ground and turned to the other paramedic. "There's probably *real* emergencies out there right now," he said and let his sentence drift away with the smoke.

"I'm a *fake* emergency," she said and then went into a coughing cackle that made her sound like a Disney villain.

When they crossed the lot toward the lobby, Jerry thought the woman looked like she might be pregnant, but she simultaneously seemed too old.

"That was something," said Carolyn. "Can we let them get a little ahead of us?"

"Sure," said Jerry and guided her over to a bench on the concrete slab in front of the automatic doors. "She's the reason I don't like emergency rooms."

"Is she pregnant?" said Edgar.

"That's what I thought, too," said Jerry. "But she sounds like an old lady.

"Elizabeth," said Carolyn.

"You know her?" said Edgar.

Carolyn laughed. "No," she said. "Elizabeth from the Bible. John the Baptist's mom."

Edgar shrugged.

"I thought you were good at the Bible stuff," she said.

"I guess they only teach us about the men," he said. "But I think I know about Elizabeth."

"She was really old, right?" said Jerry. "And wasn't she related to St. Anne?"

"Let me think," she said and closed her eyes. "Anne was Mary's mom. And I'm pretty sure Elizabeth was Anne's aunt? Something like that."

"Stricker would be proud," said Jerry. "Can we go in now?"

He stood up and walked through the glass doors toward the elevator. They were quiet as they waited for the doors to open. Jerry thought he could hear the drunk somewhere, still yelling at the paramedics, bringing their moms into it now.

Once inside the elevator, Carolyn said, "How are we going to find those guys?"

"They're either at the Grove or the Boathouse," said Edgar, pressing the button marked EMERGENCY.

The quiet came into the small space again while they felt the elevator start to rise. Then Jerry said, "While I'm getting stitched up, you guys figure out a plan to get us there." The doors opened, and he continued, "I'll pay for a taxi, and if it's gonna be a long wait in the ER, you two should go without me and try to find Cheese before something happens to the cards."

"Edgar can go," said Carolyn. "I'll stick with you."

"Let's see if there's a big crowd," said Edgar.

When they pushed the doors open to the waiting room, it was almost full, and the pregnant drunk had been liberated from the paramedics. She was yelling at a scruffy-looking man in a Hawaiian shirt. "You're a little baby bitch," she cackled.

"I got a hernia," he said and doubled over. Then he pointed at the reception window and said, "And these assholes won't let me see a doctor." He sat down and curled up into himself. "It feels like someone's got a vice on my balls."

Jerry looked over at the pregnant drunk and realized right away that she wasn't pregnant at all. The skin on her face looked like the fake leather in Cheese's car—brown and cracked. She must have been at least sixty years old. She was wearing a loose-fitting, knee-length dress that was sticking out in the front. That's why Jerry initially thought she was with child.

She pointed at the guy in the Hawaiian shirt and said, "You think you got a hernia …" She pulled her dress up to her chin and said, "This is a hernia."

Once she raised the dress, Jerry knew he should have looked away, but he couldn't help himself. He pulled Carolyn's head to his chest so that she wouldn't be able to see the fleshy protrusion sticking straight out of the woman's abdomen.

"No," Jerry heard Edgar whisper and then gag.

The bulge looked like the thing that came out of that dude's chest in the movie *Alien*. Jerry only looked at it for a second before turning away. When his eyes met Edgar's, Edgar shook his head and gagged a second time.

"I'll never be able to forget that," said Edgar.

The drunk lady pulled her dress back down and took up two seats when she sat down and pulled her feet up under her. The thing was still poking her dress out so that it looked like a tent, and she had a look on her face like she was proud of it, like it really was her baby.

The guy in the Hawaiian shirt yelled to the entire waiting room, "The hell with this place," and he limped out the door clutching his crotch and whimpering like a wounded animal.

Jerry watched him leave and then realized he had his own arms stretched out behind him, shielding Carolyn, whose face was buried in the back of his sweatshirt. He pulled her around so that she was next to him again, but she kept her face pressed against his shoulder. He guessed that she had her eyes closed so that she wouldn't have to see who else might be in this particular ER.

Jerry looked around the room, and a couple of things caught his eye. First, there was a dead ringer for Billy Idol, sitting in the corner, chewing gum and scowling. There was something just slightly off about the impersonation. His eyes were too far apart, or there was too much space between his nose and his mouth. Something off. But really close.

The seat next to him was empty, but sitting in the next one over was a guy Jerry didn't immediately recognize. He had a plain face and looked about Jerry's age. For a moment, he thought it was someone from the South Pacific cast party. But this guy had a huge lump over his eye—like the size of a golf ball.

"You should put some ice on that," said Jerry.

"Where's my bag?" said Andrew. He was trying to sound tough, but there was very little crack in his whip.

"You sliced my head open with the poker," said Jerry.

"It was the shovel," he said. "I thought I missed."

"You could have killed me."

"Where's my bag?" he said.

Then Billy Idol looked around to see if anyone was listening.

An elderly Asian couple was moving away from the hernia lady. A middle-aged guy with an angry rash on his neck and cheek was watching the Asian couple and trying not to scratch. And a young Hispanic guy was crouching like a catcher near the door. He was wearing a plaid shirt, only the top button fastened, and a pair of thin sunglasses. He was taking deep, crackling breaths like the oxygen was fighting to get through molasses. His black, upside-down horseshoe mustache looked like the luck was running out of it.

Billy Idol looked back at Jerry and whispered in an English accent, "Where's my gun, Mate?"

Jerry pulled Carolyn closer but said nothing.

The door to the examination rooms opened, and a nurse pushed a wheelchair into the room. The nurse said, "You'll have to wait out here until an examination room opens up."

Madonna's eye makeup was all over her face. She had a compress on her forearm. And her foot was wrapped with so many bandages it looked like something out of a low budget war movie.

She looked around the room and said something that sounded to Jerry like, "Star Wars Cantina." Then she looked over in Andrew's direction and said to no one in particular, "I thought you were gonna bring ice for this kid?"

The nurse left her and walked back through the doors.

Madonna looked into Jerry's eyes and said, "Oh … *you* little punks."

26

The doctor shot something into her foot and gave her two valiums. Helen felt like she was in a warm bath. She knew there was a foot attached to the bottom of her leg. She knew the foot had a hole in it. And she also understood that she was going to need surgery to repair the shattered metatarsals.

But she couldn't feel anything when the nurse wheeled her back into the waiting room, where Paul and Andrew were sitting patiently.

They still hadn't given Andrew any ice, and the lump over his eye was a nasty looking thing that was starting to take on color now—different shades of pink and blue.

"I thought you were gonna bring ice for this kid," she said, but she already heard the nurse walking back through the swinging doors. Then she looked at a different kid standing in front of her. It was the slugger with the atomic left hook. "Oh," she said, "*you* little punks."

She wasn't mad at them anymore. She was almost void of emotions. The air in the waiting room was warm and dry. She could feel it brushing against her eyelashes. But when she reached up to fan the air away from her face, her hands were still on the armrests of the wheelchair.

Then the girl—the young Diane Lane—was walking toward her.

"I'm so sorry," she said, as she drifted toward Helen. "I don't know what happened to me. I panicked."

The girl was talking too fast, and Helen's mouth was dry. Her brain sent a message to her voice, but the words came out slow and labored. "It's okay, sugar," she said. "They're gonna fix me up. You didn't mean it." It was as if Helen were listening to her mother speak. She couldn't figure out when she'd gotten so old. She actually felt like she was going to cry because she missed her mom. Then she thought she might fall asleep. She forced her eyes open and said to the girl, "The bite was totally uncalled for though."

The girl nodded and walked back to her guy. He put his arm around her. They looked good together. They'd probably been dating since junior high.

"Where's the bag?" Helen said, and her voice sounded more like her own.

The room went quiet. The Latino near the door stood up and cleared his throat but said nothing. And even the older lady with the hernia popping out of her dress seemed to be listening.

Finally, the young Santana said, "In a safe place."

When he said it, the girlfriend and boyfriend looked like they were holding back laughter.

Paul had been quiet, sitting in one of the chairs and fidgeting with a Time Magazine. He rolled it up and drummed the top of the coffee table. Then he unrolled it and was smoothing the corners when he said to Helen, "How are you feeling, love?"

"Like I had a lobotomy," she said. "But a good one. I can't feel anything."

"Well," he said. "I think you're gonna be off your feet for a while." He dropped the English accent, and Helen noticed the kids looking at each other, a little confused now.

"I might have to say so-long to San Francisco," she said. "This isn't really working out the way I'd imagined."

Paul looked upset and shot a look over at the girl.

"No, no," said Helen. "She's got fire, this one. I like her." She nodded over at the girl and felt herself smiling at her through the fog.

Paul lowered his voice to an angry whisper and said, "Which one of you has my property?"

Quiet again.

"I don't even care about the cards at this point," he said. "But I need my property."

"I still want the bag," said Andrew. "It's mine."

Helen thought back to their discussion about possession being nine-tenths of the law, but her mind went off the rails with thoughts about fractions and decimals, so she didn't say anything. Andrew seemed like an innocent kid, but she didn't know if the bag was his or not. All these kids seemed like they were in over their heads.

And then a massive Black man walked into the waiting room. He looked like he could be a professional football player, and he moved that way. He was wearing a nice leather jacket and all the parts of him were moving in coordination. He seemed light enough on his feet to win a dance contest but also powerful enough to crush all the other dancers with his bare hands.

He walked around the room looking at everyone. He knelt down and peaked under the chairs. Then he looked at the young Santana and said, "You Edgar?"

Edgar's eyes went wide. He looked over at his buddy, but the slugger had nothing to say.

The big Black guy looked at the slugger and then over at Andrew. "Which one of you two is Andrew?" he said. He had a smile on his face that made him look tired, but Helen sensed he was ready for action if it presented itself.

Andrew sat up straight in his chair as if a teacher had caught him hiding a MAD Magazine behind his science book.

The Black guy kept his eyes on Andrew. "And where's the bag?" he said.

No one spoke up. Helen didn't know why she was doing it, but she decided to answer the man's questions. "Andrew's the guy sitting over there," she said to the big guy and pointed at Andrew, who opened his mouth to say something but closed it almost immediately. "And, yes, that's Edgar, I believe. But as far as the bag goes, these guys have it hidden somewhere."

The Black guy nodded and paused to think for a moment. Then he said without emotion, "I need that bag, fellas."

"They have it," said Andrew and pointed at the kid who'd given him the lump.

"Okay," said the big guy. "Now we're getting somewhere."

Helen felt like she was watching a TV show playing out in front of her. "Why do *you* get the cards?" she said and was surprised to hear herself talking.

The Black guy looked at her and then let his eyes drop to her foot. He smiled. "I saw the hole in the floor and the blood," he said. "Did you shoot yourself in the foot?"

"You didn't answer my question," she said and thought about how, if she didn't have a hurt foot, she'd like to walk over there and kick him in the balls.

"What question?"

"Why do *you* get the prize?" she said. "You're just showing up now after we did all the work."

"Who's *we*?" he said.

Helen felt like she was making cartoon faces to show her emotions, and then she was caught up thinking about the fact that she was making cartoon faces, so she lost track of the conversation for a moment. Looking around the room at all the players helped her organize her thoughts. "Who's *we*?" she said after a long moment. "*We're* we." She gestured with her hands at the collection of nimrods, weirdos, and nutjobs loitering in the waiting room.

"So, you guys all in this together?" he said, laughing a little bit now.

"I'm just saying, we cleaned the stable, but you want to ride the horse." She felt herself shrug, thinking her metaphor sounded like some old Montana adage, but also feeling like she might have just made it up. "We went to war over that bag." She pointed at her foot. "You didn't do shit," she said. "And now you want to show up at the end and think you're about to walk off with the product of our labors."

The big guy let out a deep, slow laugh. "It's not what I *think*," he said, the smile flattening into a straight line under his wide nose. "It's what I *know*."

Helen was actually impressed with his confidence. She believed him.

Paul stood up in front of his seat and said in his normal voice, "This guy thinks *he's* the fortune teller in the room."

Andrew stood up next to Paul and said, "It's my stuff." His voice had the hints of a whimper coating every word.

The big dude's lips curved into a smile again. "The stuff is not yours, young man," he said. "It belongs to a kid named Sawyer, and I'm here to pick it up for him."

"That's a lie," said Andrew, sounding a little tougher than he did a moment before, but not much.

"Say what?" said the big dude and took one step in Andrew's direction. Andrew and Paul both sat back down in their seats.

Then the Black dude turned to Edgar, touched the kid's elbow, and said, "You and me need talk private."

27

Ronnie knew Edgar was scared, but the kid was holding up all right so far. He had his hands in his pockets and kept his head down. They took a silent elevator ride down to the main lobby, and Ronnie directed Edgar to a bank of chairs lined up against the wall on the opposite side of the lobby.

When Edgar slouched into the chair and had his arms folded over his chest, Ronnie smiled at him.

"Dude," said Ronnie. "We on the same team."

Edgar kept his head down but turned his eyes up toward Ronnie. "Huh?"

"Who you workin' for?"

"I don't work for anybody," said Edgar.

"You just breakin' into houses on your own?"

Edgar shook his head for a moment and looked away. "What are you asking?" he said.

Ronnie said, "Look at me."

Edgar's expression didn't change when he looked back at Ronnie. The kid's eyes made him look like he might be stoned.

"Sawyer Puck?" said Ronnie. "He your man?"

Edgar straightened himself in the chair. "What do you want?" he said, raising his voice a little bit like he was frustrated now.

"I want that bag," said Ronnie. "Sawyer has me on the job 'cause he thought you'd chicken out."

Edgar smiled a little bit on one side of his mouth, but it was gone as fast as it'd come.

"I give you credit for gettin' it done," said Ronnie. "And you're gonna get your share." He paused to see if he'd get a reaction, but the kid seemed lost in thought now, staring out at nothing, the little smile a distant memory. "Son, you need to tell me where you got that bag stashed."

Edgar nodded. "How am I gonna get my share?"

"What?" said Ronnie, not expecting the kid to challenge him.

"You said I'm gonna get my share," said Edgar. "How do we arrange that?"

Ronnie was losing his patience, but he figured he had to play nice until he had the bag in his possession. "Same as any transaction," he said. "You go get the bag and then hand it over." Ronnie hadn't thought this through. He paused for a moment to try to figure out how to convince the kid that he'd be compensated.

"That's only half a transaction," said Edgar.

Ronnie felt his stomach contract. Then he leaned down and grabbed the kid's skinny arm, just above the elbow. "The other half of the transaction is that I don't kill you."

Ronnie had the kid's attention now.

"Fine," said Edgar. "But I'm not exactly sure where it is."

"It's gettin' late," said Ronnie. "I don't have time for this shit."

The kid took a deep breath and then looked right into Ronnie's eyes like he was trying to prove that he wasn't lying. "I screwed up," he said. "I left the bag in someone's car, and I don't know where they are right now."

Ronnie could hear some kind of commotion going on behind him, but he stayed with Edgar. This was an important moment.

Edgar was looking over Ronnie's shoulder, but Ronnie kept staring at him until Edgar was back with him. "When will you know where the bag is?"

The kid took one more peek over Ronnie's shoulder and then started to shake his head slowly.

"Where's the bag, Edgar?"

"I have an idea where to look," he said. "But …."

The kid let the rest of his thought hang in the air between them and then directed his full attention to what was happening behind Ronnie.

When Ronnie turned around, he saw two cops talking to what appeared to be a set of angry parents and their son, who was in a wheelchair and had casts on both of his legs. The kid looked past Ronnie and then pointed.

"Edgar," he shouted across the lobby.

Ronnie looked down at Edgar, whose squinty little eyes were wide open. "What's this?" said Ronnie.

"Long story," said Edgar.

When Ronnie looked back over his shoulder, the whole group was stomping across the lobby. One of the cops was pushing the wheelchair, and the two parents were leading the parade, shouting, and pointing at Edgar.

The kid in the wheelchair yelled, "Sorry, Edgar," and then put his head in his hands.

Ronnie stepped to the side and watched the group approach. He knew both cops.

The two parents were both talking at the same time, so it was tough for Ronnie to make out what they were saying, but he was picking up a theme. It had to do with their house. Occasionally, one of them would say something about their son's legs, but it was mostly about the house.

Edgar didn't get up. He listened to them shout and took periodic glances at the cops.

While they were still yelling, the short, chubby cop—McFadden—said, "Hey, Ronnie."

Ronnie nodded but kept his mouth shut.

McFadden finally stopped the clamor. "Okay, okay," he said and stepped between the parents and Edgar. Finally, the mom turned around and remembered her son. She took over for the cop behind the wheelchair.

"You Edgar?" said the cop.

Edgar stood up. "Yeah," he said and seemed tired, like even that short word and his effort to rise from the bench were hard work.

McFadden nodded. "Did you bring a keg of beer into this family's backyard and host a party?"

Edgar blinked. "I'm on probation, officer," he said.

"That's not helping your cause, Edgar."

"Technically," said Edgar, "there was already a party." He looked over at the kid in the wheelchair. "Kent?"

Kent looked up at his mom. "Cast party," he said. Then he looked at his legs and said, "Oh … cast party … pun."

McFadden looked confused. "Edgar, did you bring a keg into the backyard?"

"Technically," said Edgar. "It wasn't my keg."

McFadden looked disappointed with the answer and looked over at his partner.

Edgar said again, "I'm on probation."

Kent said, "I'm sorry, Edgar."

McFadden looked at his partner and then back at Ronnie before he said, "You have anything to do with this, Ronnie?"

"Me?"

"Yeah," said McFadden. "You're sitting here in the lobby with this kid who's looking at a minimum of trespassing and contributing to the delinquency of minors."

"But he *is* a minor," said Ronnie.

"That don't matter," said McFadden.

Ronnie looked over at Edgar and said, "How did you get in the backyard?"

"We just walked right in."

Ronnie looked at McFadden, then back at Edgar. "Didn't you just say that the keg wasn't yours?"

Edgar showed that little half-smile and said, "Yes, sir."

Ronnie looked at McFadden again.

McFadden said, "What's your connection to this kid, Ronnie?"

"Just met him."

"Here?" said McFadden and gestured around the lobby with his hand. "What're you doin' here, Ronnie?"

"Visiting a friend," he said, getting ready to give up on Edgar and get away from these cops. The boss did not like Ronnie talking to the cops.

"Oh, yeah?" said McFadden. "Who?"

"I mean, I have an earache," he said. Tough to prove he didn't.

"Yeah, all right," said McFadden. "Why don't you go upstairs and get some antibiotics."

"You gonna take the kid in on these trumped-up charges?" he said, one last effort to keep Edgar out of jail tonight so that the kid could lead him to this goddamn elusive bag of baseball cards and whatever else.

McFadden directed his attention to Edgar and said, "Come here." The cop's eyes were narrowed in an annoyed glare now as he watched Edgar step up to him.

McFadden patted him down. He retrieved a doobie from Edgar's pocket, held it up for all to see, sniffed it, and then said, "C'mon, kid. You're gonna have to come with us."

"This is some bullshit," said Ronnie, mostly to himself.

"You say something, Ronnie?" said McFadden.

"Me?" said Ronnie.

"Go get your ear fixed," said McFadden, "Or head back to Shanley's. This isn't your neighborhood, son."

Ronnie nodded slowly at the fat cop, letting him know with his eyes that he didn't like being called *son* by a pink-faced tub of lard. "Good luck in all your future endeavors," Ronnie said to Edgar, who looked over his shoulder as he walked toward the exit. "Anything you want to tell me 'fore you head back to see your boy, Sawyer Puck?"

The kid shrugged, and the two cops looked back at Ronnie one last time before they stepped out into the night.

28

Dave had finished a twelve pack of Lucky Lagers on his own over the past four hours. He didn't really feel drunk, but he was bloated from all the beer and the Jack-in-the-Box burgers. When they drove into the Boat House parking lot, he belched, placed his hand on his stomach, and belched again. Then he almost felt like he was going to throw up, but he swallowed a mouthful of saliva and gulped in as much air as he could.

"You okay?" said Cheese.

"Just re-living the burger," said Dave.

Marcus was in the back and said, "Does it look like anyone's here?"

There was a cluster of cars parked facing the fishing pier. Cheese pulled the station wagon in next to a dented-up VW bug.

Dave looked out the window and squinted into the darkness. He could see there were fifteen or twenty kids standing in pods, shivering now that the fog was rolling in over Lake Merced and dropping the temperature down into the fifties. "You wanna get out and see who this is?" said Dave.

"We're out of beer," said Marcus and threw the cardboard packaging into the way back.

"You got any weed left?" said Cheese.

"First you ruin my Run DMC tape," he said. "Now you wanna smoke the rest of my ganja?"

"Good," said Cheese. "We won't have to walk out there empty-handed."

"*You'll* be empty handed," said Marcus. "If there's some honeys out there who wanna get high, you're shit outta luck, Cheese-man."

"I think those are sophomores," said Dave. "That girl with the braids is Amy. She goes to St. Mary's."

"How you know that?" said Cheese.

"I think our parents are friends."

"She's nice-looking," said Marcus. "I might take a run at that."

Dave sighed. "She's a sophomore," he said again.

"I'm not sure what that's supposed to mean," said Marcus, spraying some Binaca Blast into his mouth. "Ooh-wee," he said. "Sophomores. They're wise fools. Sounds like a perfect match for me."

"Please don't," said Dave and watched Marcus open the door.

Cheese looked over at Dave. "Does he think he's a perfect match for the *wise* part?"

"I assume he's talking about the *fool* part," said Dave and opened the door. "I need to try and stop this before something dumb happens."

By the time Dave walked over to the group, Marcus had his arms around Amy and her friend. The two girls were drinking Bartles & Jaymes wine coolers and laughing hysterically about whatever Marcus had said when he walked up to their group.

"These ladies didn't know that my nickname's Superfreak," said Marcus. "I'm super freaky."

The girls laughed again.

"When did that become your nickname?" said Dave. He'd never heard this before and wondered where Marcus had come up with this particular handle. Then he heard the staticky version of the Rick James song hiccupping from a mini-boombox sitting on top of the VW.

Marcus laughed. "Dave's just upset about his own nickname."

"What is it?" said Amy's friend.

"Marbles," said Marcus.

The girls laughed again.

"Hi, David," said Amy, and she looked less like a little girl than she did when he'd seen her at a barbeque during her freshman year.

"Hi, Amy," he said and tried to sound cool, but he was fully aware that he didn't. She was a sophomore, and he was embarrassed that she was having this effect on him. Dave glanced up at Marcus, who was smiling now, probably because he'd heard Dave's voice crack just slightly when he said hi to Amy.

"Wait a minute," said the other girl. "Why do they call you *Marbles*?"

Just as Dave was saying, "They don't," Marcus was saying much louder, "Tiny balls."

The girls laughed again.

Then five guys who'd been murmuring over near the garbage cans pimp-walked over to where Marcus had his arms around the girls. These guys were wearing dark jackets and baseball caps turned around backwards. Dave could sense some animosity. He recognized some of them from school, but he didn't know them. Sophomores and juniors. They had a different kind of energy than Dave's friends. They seemed fired up for no reason. Dave wished Hawk was with them. Jerry's reputation usually kept red-hots like these dudes from trying to start anything. And with the cast on, Dave didn't have any desire to get stuck in the kind of Boat House fight that seemed to break out without warning every time he was down there.

Cheese stepped around Marcus so that he was now standing next to Dave. The girls were looking at Marcus and then back at the other guys.

"Lighten up, boys," said Amy and gave Dave a look to reassure him that nobody was going to start anything, but Dave wasn't so sure. Amy walked over and stood next to the tallest kid. Dave could feel himself blushing. He had no idea what was happening in his head. He didn't have anything to be embarrassed about, but he was also feeling like he wanted to punch the tall kid in the mouth.

Instead, Marcus walked up to one of the smaller kids. Dave recognized him as a guard on the JV basketball team. He actually looked like a mini-Marcus.

"'Sup, Marcus," the kid said, trying to look tough, like they were choosing sides for a pick-up game.

The kid was holding a six pack of Lowenbrau with five left. Marcus reached down and pulled out three. "We'll let y'all get back to it," he said and walked away toward the boat dock.

Dave took a quick glance at Amy, who was looking at him. Dave wasn't sure what had just gone down. This kind of mental state was washing over him a lot lately. He felt like he'd been walking around just a little bit confused for the past month. He felt like he was misreading every situation. So, he was very comfortable just following Marcus, who was using his class ring to open a Lowenbrau, which he handed to Dave.

When they arrived at the dock, Cheese said, "Are we going out?"

"Of course," said Marcus. "Grab some oars."

"It's too foggy," said Dave. He shook his head at Marcus, who was untying the rowboat at the end of the dock. "Let's just sit here and have a beer, maybe smoke Marcus's J."

"Cheese, pass me my beer after I get in," said Marcus and tossed the rope over toward Dave. He climbed into the boat and took a moment to get his balance. You could tell he was an athlete as he straddled the little bench in the middle of the boat and controlled the rocking. "The oars, Dave," he said and put his hands out.

Dave looked over at Cheese, hoping to get some support in aborting the mission. But Cheese was high-stepping on the wet deck over to the boat, holding a beer in each hand and trying not to slip on the slick wood. He looked over his shoulder at Dave. "Let's go, dude."

"I'm not supposed to get my cast wet," said Dave and held it out in front of him, displaying the crusty thing as if it were a small, non-aquatic animal that required his protection.

"Then stay out of the water," said Marcus, gesturing with his hands now like a toddler who wanted his toy. "Gimme the oars."

Dave rested his beer on a flat part of the deck and brought the oars over to Marcus.

"Thank you, Dave," said Marcus and lowered himself onto his seat.

Cheese handed Marcus his beer, which Marcus balanced on the bench. Then Cheese climbed into the back, spilling his own beer down his forearm.

Dave stepped into the front. He got in low and avoided any rocking. He didn't spill a drop. "Not too far out," he said. "Last time, the wind picked up and the current made it a bitch to get back."

"Not for you," said Marcus. "You just sat in the front and complained."

Dave smiled. That was true. He took a long pull on his beer and said, "You guys notice anything weird about Hawk?"

"Jerry?" said Cheese, maybe struggling to hear Dave over the sound of Marcus's paddling.

"Yeah."

"I think everyone's been weird," said Cheese. "I know *I* am."

"I'm not," said Marcus. "Except that I'm rowing you two ladies around like a water chauffeur."

"You weren't there," said Dave and was surprised that the words had slipped through his filter.

"Are you saying Hawk's been weird because of the waterslide stuff?" said Marcus.

"I don't know," said Dave. "I was the first person he saw after he jumped off the platform." He corrected himself immediately. "The second person."

"And ...," said Marcus.

"And then I didn't see him outside school until tonight."

Marcus pulled up the oars and let the boat drift toward the fishing pier, just below where Amy's little party was still in session up near the cars.

"He seemed like himself tonight," said Cheese. "That chick Carolyn is cute."

"They going out?" said Marcus.

"I don't know," said Dave. "I told you I haven't talked to the guy."

"Maybe you remind him of that day," said Cheese, who leaned around Marcus to look at Dave.

The boat tilted to one side and Marcus said, "Cool it, Cheese." Then he put the oars back in the water and steered the boat so that they had a clean angle looking up at the lot. With all the fog, they could see only silhouettes moving in clumps and an occasional cigarette lighter.

"I don't like thinking I'm giving him flashbacks or something," said Dave.

Marcus patted Dave on the shoulder. "He saw your bone coming through your skin, dude."

Dave thought about that for a moment. "You know who else saw it, Marcus?

Marcus shrugged.

"*I* did," said Dave. "And I'm not having flashbacks."

"Watch this," said Marcus. Then he rested the oars on his lap and cupped his hands around his mouth. He was facing the parking lot and yelled, "Hey, Amy."

Dave looked up at the parking lot—still just shadows. "What the hell are you doing?" he whisper-yelled. "I think the big guy's her boyfriend."

Marcus nodded at Dave, cupped his hands again and yelled even louder, "Hey, Amy."

"What?" she yelled back. Then Dave heard her and her friend laughing.

"What are you doing?" Dave said to Marcus. He didn't like this. Amy was a family friend.

Marcus nodded again and yelled out across the water, "Dave's in love with you."

"Hi, David," she yelled back and laughed.

Marcus started to row the boat again.

Then they heard a guy's voice yell from the fishing pier. "Hi, Dave," he said. "I'll be waiting for you when you get back."

It was quiet for a moment. The only sound came from the oars cutting through the surface of the water. Dave suddenly felt drunk. He thought back to the sound of his voice when he'd asked Marcus what he was doing. And now, in his mind, the memory of the question sounded slurred. He was confused again.

Dave listened to the oars and the water for a few more strokes. "Why did you do that?" he asked Marcus.

Before Marcus could answer, Cheese burped and threw his empty bottle in the water. "Those guys already weren't happy with us. And now …" He let the words fade and then mix in with the fog.

"Dave likes her," said Marcus.

"We used to go to Pizza & Pipes together when we were little," said Dave.

Marcus laughed. "The place with the organ?" he said and finished the beer that he'd been holding between his legs.

"Yeah," said Dave. "Our dads played on the same softball team, and we'd go there after the games."

"I never got that place," said Marcus. "I mean, why did people want to listen to organ music when they ate their pizza?"

Cheese took a deep breath and then let it out. "How're we gonna get my car?" he said.

Splashdown: The Pirate's Plank Disaster 25 Years Later

A Six-Part Documentary Series

Produced by NorCal Newsreel. Presented by Small Town Consortia in association with The Joint Center for Civic Review and The Sonoma County Film Institute

2010

Episode Five: Abnormal
TRT 29 min

[Transcript]

David Kramer (St. Xavier '86): Of course, we stuck together after. I still see a lot of those guys. We meet up for reunions and Christmas lunches. We're pretty close.

Narrator: Do you think the accident played a role in your class's identity?

David: We were teenagers. Some of us have teenagers now. So, we know how resilient they are. We were too. It was awful what happened. It was definitely a mortality check for all of us. But we kept going and tried to have a normal senior year.

Narrator: Did you have a normal senior year?

David: No

Narrator: Can you elaborate?

David: Well, I missed football because of my wrist. I think that made things abnormal, at least for me. I ended up spending too much time drinking. And probably too much time pretending things were normal. Then, about a month after the accident at Pirate's Plank, I actually witnessed a shooting. I was literally ten feet away from a guy who got shot. And I guess I bounced back from that one too because I did a hundred more reckless things before graduation. We had short memories.

Narrator: A shooting?

David: Yeah

Narrator: So, you had two near-death experiences within a few weeks?

David: I didn't really think about it at the time. But when you say it like that, yeah, I guess I could have died in both of those situations.

Narrator: How did you end up in a situation where someone got shot?

David: I'm not the best one to answer that question.

Narrator: Who is?

David: Did you talk to Carolyn Roddy yet?

29

Paul listened to Helen rehash the entire night until she eventually started talking gibberish and fell asleep. The last thing she said before her head dropped down into her chest was "Santana."

A few minutes later, a nurse stepped into the room and called in the kid to get his stitches. Paul had heard the girl call him Jerry. But he didn't look like a Jerry. He looked like a *Frank*. Like an honest guy who'd be your buddy but wouldn't hesitate to kick your ass if the occasion arose.

The girl could be a TV star, her face on the cover of *Tiger Beat Magazine*. She was sitting across the room alone waiting for Jerry to get his head patched up so they could get that bag and drive off into the sunset together. Unless the big black guy already made the other kid, Edgar, get it for him. Then the adventure would be over for everyone.

Paul didn't even care about the bag anymore. The whole night was a disaster. Helen's injury was serious. It was time to cut their losses. He just wanted his gun back at this point. He didn't like the idea of it being out there where someone could pick it up, shoot a person, and then leave it for the cops to find. He was anxious about some random person dying because he was careless with his gun. Helen already had a hole in her foot. He should have never given it to her, and now he just wanted it back.

He walked across the room, feeling stupid in his Billy Idol getup. He sat down next to the girl. "I don't care about the bag," he said and looked back at Andrew, who was watching him, maybe still holding out hope that he'd end up the winner in this stupid game.

Paul had no such hope.

The girl allowed herself a thin smile.

"I really don't," he said. "That was between her and him and you guys." He pointed at Helen and Andrew and then squinted at her, making sure she believed him.

She smiled again, flashing a row of straight white teeth. "I like your earrings," she said.

"Oh, I wear them for the act," he said seriously and then realized she was making fun of him. She had the kind of face that could make a man momentarily lose his mind. He hadn't noticed that she was putting him in a trance with those eyes, so the earring crack felt like a sucker-punch, and he was embarrassed that he'd been caught sleeping. "I don't want the bag," he repeated. "But I need to get that gun back."

"So you can hold it on me and force me to take you to the cards?" she said and raised her eyebrows.

The old lady with the hernia was talking to Andrew, and he was looking up at the ceiling, his arms folded across his chest.

Paul felt himself sigh. "We're not criminals," he said. "You guys win. I don't give a shit about this kid." He pointed at Andrew, who wasn't looking at the ceiling anymore, but he had his eyes closed and was nodding at this lady's meandering diatribe about San Francisco history. She went from Patty Hearst to the Black Panthers to the Zebra Murders as if all the events had happened earlier that day, and she was somehow connected to all the players.

Paul continued, "Can you help me, so I can get out of this shithole and go home?"

"Edgar threw the gun in some bushes," she said.

"Do you know where?" he said.

"Somewhere between the house and the Jack-in-the-Box," she said and bit down on her bottom lip, probably trying to narrow down the parameters of his search. "It's only a few blocks, and not all the houses have bushes in front. Edgar'll tell you when he comes back."

Paul nodded and thought for a moment. "So, you think that dude's bringing your friend back here?"

She frowned, but on *her* face, it looked more like pouting. "Probably not," she said and turned toward the exit.

The big black dude had swung open the door and stepped in, his face like a statue—no indication of his current emotional state unless he was void of emotions. "I need to sit here," he said and pointed at Paul, who moved over one seat to make room. The dude gave him a look, so Paul moved down another seat and picked up a Sports Illustrated, the cover featuring twenty-year old Dwight Gooden in his Mets uniform. Paul couldn't help thinking about the young man's promise, his career spread out in front of him like a road paved in gold.

Paul was already thirty-one and still dressed up like Billy Idol. He opened the magazine and pretended to read as he strained to hear the conversation between the girl and the big guy, both of whom were speaking in hushed tones.

"Where's Edgar?" she said.

"Cops took him," he said.

"Cops?"

"Yeah," he said. "Some kid with two casts on his legs identified Edgar down in the lobby."

"Identified him as what?"

"As a person who brought a keg into a stranger's backyard."

"Kent," she whispered.

"In Kent's defense," he said, "I think he just wanted to say hi to Edgar, but the parents went nuts. They were in the middle of making the police report when me and Ed came out of the elevator."

"Edgar's on probation," she said.

"So I heard."

"They're gonna put him back in juvie."

"Yeah," he said. "The doobie in his pocket didn't help."

"Shit," she said and looked at the door to the examination rooms.

"Where's your guy?"

"He's back there now getting stitches."

"I should make you come with me now," he said. "But I don't want to make a scene."

"Come with you where?"

"I'll wait until your guy's ready to come with us."

"Where?" she said.

"To the cards."

"Why do *you* get 'em?"

He shook his head and folded his lips into themselves. "We workin' for the same guy," he said in his regular voice now. "Sawyer Puck hired me because he didn't think Edgar had the cajónes to do the job."

She sneered at him. "Well, he did have the cajónes, didn't he? Great big cajónes."

The big guy gave her that. He nodded and smiled a little bit.

"And now he's not just going to miss out on his payday," she said. "But he's also going back to jail with Sawyer Puck, the asshole that got him into this in the first place."

"When you put it that way …"

"Yeah," she said. "It's fucked up."

"He'll be compensated," he said but didn't look convincing.

"Bullshit," she said.

He nodded again and said, "Did y'all look through the bag?"

"It's baseball cards," she said. "Edgar took out one of the binders. It's just like Sawyer told him."

Paul felt like he got an electric shock. He was dizzy with the sensation. All this was over *baseball cards*. The misunderstanding about what kind of cards they were dealing with was like something out of an episode of *Three's Company*. He almost laughed, until he looked over at Helen in her wheelchair, snoozing and drooling slightly, her wrapped foot propped up in front of her like a flag of surrender. He wondered if she'd have a permanent limp.

His eyes were glazed over, staring at a Marlboro ad in the magazine and imagining Helen hobbling down the street like an old west cowgirl, who'd had an accident with an unruly mule.

His mind shot back to the waiting room when he heard the big guy say, "There's more in that bag."

Paul had enough self-control to keep his eyes on the Marlboro Man on page twenty-nine. If he were a wolf, his ears would be standing up in furry triangles. But he kept it cool, turning to page thirty now as if he were captivated by Boris Becker's latest winning streak.

"What do you mean?" she said.

Out of the corner of his eye, Paul could see that she'd adjusted herself in her chair so that she was facing the big guy.

"Sawyer didn't say what it was," he said. "But there's some kind of contraband in there worth more than all them baseball cards."

"So, my friends have illegal shit in their car?" she said.

The big guy paused for a moment. "The bag's in a *car*?"

"Darn," she said.

"I'll take it off your hands, little lady," he said. "No reason for you to get caught up in all this nonsense."

Paul realized that he'd turned away from the magazine. He was looking at the girl and thinking about twenty-year-old Dwight Gooden being a millionaire and thirty-one-year-old Paul being behind on rent.

"What do you want, Idol?" The girl's voice startled him.

"Me?" he said and realized how stupid that sounded. This chick was a killer.

"No," she said. "The real Billy Idol, standing behind you. I was about to ask him to sing *Hot in the City*."

Paul almost looked behind him but was able to catch himself. "I don't want anything," he said. "I'm just waiting for my friend." He looked at Helen and then back down at the magazine, though he couldn't see any words—they were all superimposed over one another. But he didn't blink away the blurriness. He let his eyes rest on the page in their fuzzy state until the big guy spoke again.

"Let me share your load, baby," he said in a soft voice, just north of a whisper but loud enough for Paul to hear.

"Isn't Edgar gonna get in trouble with Sawyer?" she said.

"Not sure why y'all don't get this," he said. "We on the *same team*." He was back to his normal speaking voice and sounding frustrated. "Sawyer gonna get his cards. Then we all cool, right?"

"And whatever else's in that bag" she said.

"Correct," he said. "Which is probably something you don't want to mess with."

"When Jerry comes out," she said, "I'll tell you where we think the bag is."

"What are their instructions?" he said.

"Huh?"

"What did you tell them to do with it?"

"Who?" she said.

"The dudes who have the bag in their car."

She rubbed her eyes with the heels of her hands. "They don't know they have the bag," she said.

"Yes, ma'am," he said. "That sounds about right."

"Edgar left it in the way back," she said.

"It's a station wagon?" he said and smiled a little bit again.

She nodded.

"I don't want to fight these boys," he said. "So, I need you and your boy to come with me and make sure we have a peaceful exchange."

The girl looked back at the door to the examination rooms. Then she looked across at Andrew. Finally, she looked sideways at Paul, who turned his eyes back to the magazine.

"We'll go with you," she said. "As soon as Jerry gets stitched up."

30

Isaac felt like he should have heard from Ronnie by now.

He didn't like the suspense. Once Ronnie agreed to help with the job, Isaac thought the whole thing would be done in an hour. The initial trip to the house wasn't bad, but this emergency room mission was taking longer than it should.

He pulled a legal pad from the top drawer of the desk and decided to write down the possible scenarios:

1. *Ronnie gets to ER, but no one's there.*
2. *Ronnie gets to ER, and Edgar or Andrew or someone else is there but unwilling to give up the bag.*
3. *Ronnie gets to ER, but cops are there.*
4. *Ronnie gets to ER, but—*

The phone rang, and Isaac dropped his ball-point pen and picked up the receiver. "Juvenile Hall," he said and was surprised at the breathless sound of his own voice.

"A few things," he heard Ronnie say. "Let's start with this. Is the butter worth the churn?"

"Say what?"

"Is the pirate's booty worth the risk of having to walk the plank?"

Isaac didn't like to hear Ronnie like this. The man sounded tired and a little pissed off. And he rarely spoke in weird-ass puzzles.

"Hell yeah," said Isaac, knowing he had to be convincing. "It's valuable, and we're not dealing with dangerous people here. These are kids. So, there's no plank?"

"Not for *you*," said Ronnie. "You're sitting in your office. Probably got your feet up. Sipping coffee and listening to KMEL. I missed dinner, and this is already more than you said it'd be."

"The hell you talkin' 'bout, Ronnie," he said. "Been staring at the phone, waiting to hear back from you."

"So, you worried?"

Isaac smelled the trap and avoided it. "Excited," he said. "This gets you out of the hole." He was sitting up in his chair and looking across the office at a *Just Say No To Drugs* poster that was hanging next to a former inmate's pencil sketch of Isaac's face—not bad for a kid who'd been locked up for assaulting his own grandpa on a Muni bus.

"I don't want to end up in jail for this shit, Isaac."

"You won't," he said and believed it.

There was a long pause and Ronnie said, "What else is in the bag?"

Isaac took a moment. It hit him that he had no idea if Ronnie had made any progress. "Where you at?" he said.

"ER," said Ronnie.

"You got Edgar?"

"I lost Edgar."

"Shit," said Isaac. "So, what's up? You got a line on the bag?"

"What's in it?"

"Do you know how to get it?" said Isaac.

"What's in it?"

"Baseball cards," he said.

"What else?" said Ronnie. "You said there's something else. And before I continue with this job, I need to know."

"You got a line on it?"

"Yes."

"How?"

"I got Edgar's friends here with me," he said. "They gonna take me to the bag."

"Okay," said Isaac. "That's good."

"What else is in there, Isaac?"

"I don't know," he said. "I'd tell you, but Sawyer won't give it up."

There was another long pause. Then Ronnie said, "C'mon, man."

"What does it matter?"

Another long pause. "Here's the thing," he said. "If it's stacks of cash or drugs, I can work with that. But this whole thing's been weird. I'm hangin' out with teeny-boppers at the ER. We're dealing with baseball cards and …" Ronnie let the words trail off.

"So what?" said Isaac.

"So I'm thinkin' that maybe this other valuable thing is some kind of antique or heirloom that might be worth something to someone, but we won't know how to fence it, which makes it worth nothin' to us."

Isaac considered this. If it was something like that, Ronnie was right. And then maybe the butter wouldn't be worth the churn. The baseball cards had potential. Isaac knew there were conventions and trade shows where they could make some deals. But there was still some doubt. "You don't think the cards are enough?" he said.

"I don't know," said Ronnie. "I'm in deep now. Talked to some cops in the lobby."

"Cops?" said Isaac, feeling like this was slipping away. "Does that kill it?"

"They saw me with Edgar," he said. "I feel like that could come back on me."

"Did they know you?" asked Isaac.

"It was McFadden."

Isaac didn't like it, but it was still a stretch that anyone would go down for this. Everyone involved was doing something illegal. They would all be smart to keep their mouths shut—mutually assured destruction. "What do you want to do?" he said.

"I want you to find out what else is in the bag," he said.

Isaac didn't want to talk to Sawyer anymore, but if that's what Ronnie needed, Isaac would take one more shot at the kid, see if he'd give it up. Nothing to lose at this point. "I'll go squeeze it out of him," he said.

"We gonna get on the road," said Ronnie. "The bag's in a car on the other side of town. I'll call you from a pay phone when we're close. If everything looks good, and the contents seem worth it, I'll make it happen."

Isaac looked at the sketch of himself hanging on the wall. The inmate had drawn Isaac's chin a little weak but got the eyes right. The sketch made Isaac look like he was a thoughtful person—someone who could make sound decisions. "We got this," he said and hung up.

***

Sawyer was wide awake.

When Isaac opened the door, the kid said, "I assume you're ready to take me to get my belongings?"

"Yeah," said Isaac. "But I need to know what's in there and what's my cut."

Sawyer tried to hide it, but he was smiling. Not with his teeth and barely with his lips, but something was going on with his face that told Isaac the kid thought he was going on a field trip tonight.

"What do you *want* your cut to be?"

"We gonna play this game?"

"It's not a game," said Sawyer. "I need to know what you're thinking."

"I can't tell you what I'm thinkin' 'less I know the value," he said.

Isaac could never tell if Sawyer thought he was just a little smarter than Isaac or a lot. But Isaac calculated that it was only a little. The kid knew how to structure an argument. And he knew a lot of facts that could help you on *Jeopardy*, but he was a kid. A rich kid. He didn't really have time to develop instincts for this kind of thing.

"It looks like we have a stalemate," said Sawyer, scratching his head like a character in a stage play trying to make the audience believe he was thinking deep thoughts.

"It's not," said Isaac. "The sensible thing would be for you to give me the information I need so we can get over to that house and retrieve your shit."

"If it's still there," said the kid.

Isaac nodded, wondering if Sawyer somehow sensed that Isaac had sent someone out to steal Sawyer's bag. "If Edgar didn't get it done," said Isaac.

"So, you won't get me out of here unless I divulge the contents?" he said.

"That's our current situation," said Isaac.

"I'm trying to protect you," said Sawyer.

"How's that?"

"Let's say there's illegal contraband in that bag."

"Yeah?"

"As a peace officer," he said, "you would be in a compromising position."

"But I wouldn't be in a compromising position by sneaking you outta here to get the illegal contraband?"

"Point taken," said Sawyer. "But there's some nuance to this." He looked up at the ceiling and pinched the bridge of his nose. "If we somehow get caught, and we were simply recovering my valuable baseball cards, that would be bad for you."

"Yes, it would."

"But if the two of us are recovering a consignment of pre-cut and individually packaged cocaine with a street value of tens of thousands of dollars …." He let the words hang there for a moment. "Well," he said, finally. "That would be a different story, right?"

"Absolutely," said Isaac. "Thank you for *not* telling me."

"You're welcome," said Sawyer. "We're a team."

"Where'd you get that product?" he asked.

"The original owner is currently incarcerated."

"How'd you end up with it?"

"Again," he said. "The less you know…"

"You're right," said Isaac, who stepped toward the door and readied his keys to lock Sawyer in.

"What are you doing?" said Sawyer.

"Closing time," said Isaac. "I like my job. Ain't no reason to get involved in the drug trade."

"What the hell?" said the kid.

"You never heard of Nancy Reagan?" he said. "Just say no, motherfucker."

33

Andrew tried not to look at the old lady. He just wanted the nurse to come in and take her away. The thing poking out of her stomach was the most disgusting thing he'd seen in his nineteen years on the planet—and that included his own ear after Sawyer had thrown the knife at him.

But this old gal kept talking.

She was on to Billy Graham and Bobby Weir now, making it sound like she'd been in close collaboration with them on some show they were supposed to do twenty years ago that never happened.

Andrew kept looking down at the tent of her dress under her sagging breasts. He couldn't help himself. And he couldn't help remembering what he'd seen underneath the soiled garment. And then he couldn't stop the feeling of bile from creeping up into the back of his throat before he had to swallow it down and listen to more of her nonsense. He couldn't take it anymore. He really had to leave—forget the cards, the revenge on Sawyer, the nostalgia for his uncle's gift. He couldn't be in the same room with this lady and her hernia for another minute.

He didn't know if there was a way to reclaim the bag anyway. With Helen out of commission, and this big Black dude in the picture, he was back to being on his own again. And it didn't seem worth the risk to mess with this dude who was bigger than an outhouse and seemed meaner.

But then Paul came walking across the waiting room, his eyes fixed on Andrew's, looking serious with the Billy Idol scowl, probably out of muscle memory.

"Hi Gorgeous," said the old lady when Paul was standing in front of them.

"Piss off," said Paul, then nodded at Andrew and said, "Let's move."

The old lady looked shocked for a split second before she said, "Eastwood talked to me like that once when he was shooting *Dirty Harry*, but then I—"

"Piss off," Paul said again, and Andrew got up and followed him out the door.

When they got in the hallway, Andrew said, "What about Helen?"

"I don't want to wake her up," he said. "She'll be in a lot of pain."

"But don't you think we should at least check in?"

"Are you a doctor, mate?" said Paul.

"Well, what are we doing?"

"She'll be here for a few days," he said. "She'll be doped up for hours. We can see her tomorrow."

Andrew felt like a bad person, but Paul was right. What was Andrew going to do to help Helen? It was his fault she was here in the first place. Kind of. It was also Paul's fault for giving her the gun. And, of course, it was *her* fault for taking it out. And the girl's fault for biting her. Lots of blame to go around.

Andrew nodded and wondered what was next.

"What else is in that bag?" asked Paul.

"The bag?"

"The bag with the cards," he said.

"Yeah," said Andrew, confused. "Baseball cards. What do ya'mean?"

"There's something else in there. Valuable. What is it?"

Andrew was still confused. "All I know is the baseball cards," he said. "They're worth a lot though."

"You don't know anything," he said and started rubbing his chin. "Your sociopath step-brother put something else in there that's probably worth more than the cards."

"What?" asked Andrew.

"That's what I'm asking you," said Paul, who looked around the empty hallway, craning his neck to make sure the elevators were closed. "Somehow, that big blood in there knows there's something else in the bag. I heard him talking to the girl about it." When he mentioned the girl, he reached up and touched his earring. For a moment, he looked like he was going to take it out but reached up and ran his fingers through his hair instead.

"Are we gonna try to get it before they do?" said Andrew.

"I like where your head is, kid."

"Where is it?"

"Your head?

"No," said Andrew, his head spinning now. "The bag."

"First we need to get my gun," he said. "It's in the bushes somewhere between your old house and the Jack-in-the-Box on Lombard."

"That's a few blocks," said Andrew, trying to picture the neighborhood in his mind.

"Lots of bushes?" he asked.

"Almost none."

***

It took only ten minutes to find the gun.

Paul spent a moment in the car checking the revolver, popping out the cylinder, spinning it, and looking in the chambers, before closing it up. "I'm glad to get this back," he said, smiling. "I was worried somebody'd get hurt."

Andrew didn't even like being near it. He'd seen what it had done to Helen's foot, which was nearly as disturbing as the old lady's hernia. There was so much blood immediately that he couldn't really see the full extent of the wound, but he knew there was a hole there. And frosh biology had taught him that there were lots of small bones all meeting up in the area from which the blood was flowing. He could only imagine the damage and wondered if bits of the bone had gone with the bullet through the hardwood floor and down into the basement.

"Where we going now?" Andrew said.

"I'm from LA," he said. "So, I don't know the city that well."

"Okay," said Andrew, finally understanding his role in the finale of this ridiculous caper—navigator.

"You need to bring us to the boathouse. We'll start there," he said.

Andrew sighed. "Which one?"

"Shit," said Paul and put the car into gear. "How many are there?"

"I know of two," he said. "One in Golden Gate Park at Stowe Lake and one way out at Lake Merced."

"Are they near each other?" asked Paul.

"Sort of," he said. "We can pass by one on the way to the other."

"Lead the way," said Paul.

Andrew gave him the first few directions and said, "What else do you think is in the bag?"

Paul looked over at him and shrugged. "You know your step-brother better than me."

"Probably something he stole," said Andrew.

"Could it be drugs?" said Paul.

Andrew thought back to some conversations he'd overheard in regard to Sawyer's real dad. Those exchanges were making some sense to him now. "I think his dad might have maybe done some dealing," he said. "I think that's why my step-mom left him."

"No shit?" said Paul.

"Take a right on Fell," said Andrew. "I'm pretty sure he's in jail now."

"No shit?" said Paul.

"No shit."

The Stowe Lake parking lot had eight cars in it. Paul had told Andrew they were looking for the kind of station wagon with wood paneling on the sides. There was only one station wagon among the cars in the lot, but it didn't have the paneling.

Paul parked his car in the shadows at the far end of the lot, away from the boat house and the picnic tables where a group of kids was huddled. Paul and Andrew rolled down the windows and listened. They could hear drunken chatter and an occasional burst of laughter.

"I know it doesn't have the wood paneling," said Paul. "But I think we should do a quick check in the back just to make sure."

"What do we do if we see the bag in the back?"

"We'll hope that one of the doors is unlocked," said Paul as he opened his door and stepped out quietly. It was dark, and they were under a tree, but Paul's bleached hair was like a beacon in the night. "Don't slam your door," he whispered. "Let's leave 'em open. We don't want these people to hear us."

They stayed low and scampered through the lot, ducking behind cars until they got to the station wagon. Andrew hid behind a rusted-out Camaro while Paul stepped up to the station wagon, made a visor out of his hands, and peered into the back. He turned his head toward Andrew but kept his hands on the back window.

"There's two bags back here," he said.

"Is the back unlocked?" Andrew whispered.

Paul pulled at the handle, and it slipped through his fingers. It hammered back into place and made a pop at the same moment there was a break in the clamor up at the picnic tables.

From where Andrew crouched next to the Camaro, he looked up at the tables. There was a lamppost next to the boathouse that provided a hazy glow through the fog above the picnic area. The people up there were only silhouettes, but Andrew saw them move suddenly, some standing up. He could see arms and legs now—more distinct—now that they were standing and pointing.

"Crap," he said. "Can they see us?"

Paul sat on the bumper and said, "How could they?"

But when Andrew looked back up into the blurry illumination, the shadowy globule was separating into individual forms, like something out of a horror film—a giant spider giving birth to a cluster of hatchlings, immediately prepared to wreak havoc on the world.

The spiderlings initially sounded like revelers at a backyard barbeque, but then Andrew started to hear individual voices: *They're trying to steal the car. Who the fuck are you? Get 'em!*

Andrew didn't say anything. He just started running toward Paul's car, but by the time he could see it, he could sense the horde closing in and heard Paul yelling, "Okay, okay, okay."

Andrew threw his hands in the air like he was about to be arrested and then felt fingers clamping down on his shoulder.

The group led Andrew and Paul back toward the picnic tables. Male and female voices were shouting in Andrew's ears as they were marched through the dark parking lot. Threats and promises. Taunts and jeers. Interrogation without expectation. Some of it felt like old school heckling, like they were players on opposing little league teams—*Batter's off his rocker, just like Betty Crocker...We want a pitcher, not a belly-itcher.* Andrew thought back to the parks and schoolyards and playgrounds of his youth. He knew in his soul that he was going to be humiliated tonight, like Sawyer had done to him so many times. But he was resigned to accept whatever these people were going to do to him. In the past, fighting back had always made it worse for him.

The hecklers shoved Andrew and Paul down onto the same bench so that the two of them were looking back across the picnic table at a semicircle of oddballs. It was different from the ER. Those people seemed to have plummeted, without control, into their desperate stations in life.

The people around the picnic table were different. It appeared to Andrew that they'd chosen to be who they were. In fact, many of them looked like they'd spent considerable time developing their individual styles, personas that would seem normal in any number of venues but were unsettling mixed together in this particular place.

One dude was dressed a lot like the Mexican guy in the ER waiting room, except this one had added a hair net and one of those chains that hung out of his pocket. Standing next to him was a surfer dude, wearing a thick puka shell necklace, a terry cloth polo, and a pair of Ocean Pacific shorts. A third guy was dressed like Alex P. Keaton on *Family Ties*: tweed blazer and tie. The biggest one, the one that had grabbed Andrew's shoulder, wore a long overcoat and a hat like Dick Tracy would wear.

The girls had their own unique multiplicity. There was a ghost-faced girl with dark black hair and heavy eye makeup; a dread-locked beauty with a Bob Marley tee-shirt, a big-haired girl with acid-washed jeans and a fluorescent pink jacket.

The most striking member of this eclectic group was a young woman dressed almost exactly like Paul. Apparently, she was also a Billy Idol fan. She had bleached blonde, cropped hair and a leather jacket. Her pants were tighter than Paul's, and she wore stiletto heels, but the overall look was comparable. From Andrew's perspective, she looked like she was snarling at Paul as the whole group sat in silence.

It was quiet only for a moment, and then Paul looked around at the posse and said, in his best English accent, "What've we got here? The island of misfit toys?"

The girl in the leather immediately walked around the table, wiggled onto the bench next to Paul, threw her arm around his neck, and said, "I think I'm in love."

31

"She *is* good-looking though, right?" said Dave and adjusted himself in the boat so that he could look back toward the parking lot.

"Who?" said Marcus. "Braids?"

"Yeah ... Amy," said Dave.

"I already said she's nice-looking," said Marcus, his breathing labored now as he continued to row.

Cheese was in the back of the boat and jumped when something splashed in the water behind him. "What the hell?" he said.

Dave laughed. "I think a fish just jumped," he said. "Sit down before we capsize."

Cheese shook his head and grabbed both sides of the boat when he eased back into his seat. "That scared the crap of me," he said. "For some reason, I don't think of this lake as having fish in it."

"What do you think the boats are for?" said Marcus.

"The boats?" said Cheese.

"They're for fishing, man."

"Yeah," said Cheese. "I know. I just thought—"

Another splash. This time closer to the middle of the boat. "Jaws," said Marcus and jabbed one of the oars into water as if he were fighting off a great white.

Then two more splashes, one right after the other, the second sending water into the boat.

"Those assholes are throwing shit at us," said Dave. "Row out farther before we get killed."

Dave could hear laughing from the shore, but he couldn't see very far through the thick fog. Visibility was only about ten yards, but there was clearly a Lowenbrau bottle bobbing on the surface near the bow. Marcus dug in to put them out of range.

"Are they throwing rocks?" said Cheese.

"Bottles," said Dave and then thought back to religion class earlier that day. "Let he who is without sin cast the first stone."

"Say what?" said Marcus.

"You guys know the one," said Dave.

"What one?" said Marcus.

"The one where they're gonna stone the lady," said Dave. "But Jesus shows up ..."

"Who's stoned?" said Cheese from the other side of the boat.

"No," said Dave. "It's from—"

"I know," said Cheese. "I'm just messing with you."

Dave laughed and looked at Marcus, who was still rowing away from the shore but also in the direction of Lake Merced Boulevard. He raised his eyebrows at Dave.

"What?" said Dave.

"Are you gonna finish the story?"

"You don't know this one?"

"I know that line," he said. "But I can't remember the story."

"Okay," said Dave. "But what's the plan here? How are we supposed to get to the car if those guys are waiting for us?"

"We'll row to the little beach by the main entrance," said Marcus. "Then we can just leave the boat there and try to sneak back to the car without them seeing us." He rested the oar handles in his lap again and let the boat drift through the black water. With no discernable moon on this foggy night, the water looked like oil. "Or we could just hide and wait for them to leave."

"I can't get in a fight while I have this cast," said Dave. "I got screws holding my wrist together."

"I know," said Marcus.

Cheese leaned around Marcus and looked at Dave. "If we have to fight," he said. "You need to just stay out of it, dude."

"We can wait 'em out," said Marcus.

***

Climbing out of the boat, Dave got his feet wet up past his ankles. His shoes made squishy sounds as he moved across the lawn, trying to avoid being detected by anyone from the party. He, Marcus, and Cheese found a hiding place behind a cluster of trees near the entrance. The wind was starting to push the fog out over the water so they had a decent view of the station wagon from where they crouched on the dewy grass.

The big kid, the one who seemed to be with Amy, was standing on the roof of Cheese's car now and looking out over the lake. Wham's *Wake Me Up Before You Go-Go* was rasping out of the old boombox, which seemed to be in between stations. Dave always yelled to turn it off when this song came on, but in private, he had to admit to himself that it was catchy.

"This is embarrassing," said Cheese. "He's just mocking us now." Cheese sat down on the grass behind the tree, pouting like a little boy. "I wish Jerry was here," he said.

"The hell with it," said Dave. "I guess we gotta go over and deal with this—defend Cheese's honor. We're seniors. We can't let underclassmen intimidate us." He hoped the big guy would see the cast and leave him out of it. Dave would simply tell the guy that Amy was a childhood friend, and that Marcus shouldn't have yelled that bullshit. Amy would prevent it from getting ugly.

"Can we wait five minutes?" said Marcus. "It's late. Maybe him standing on the car is the last thing he wanted to do to humiliate us before they leave."

"Five minutes," said Dave. "And we're not being humiliated. We're outnumbered."

"Tell that to your shoes," said Marcus and pointed to Dave's drenched sneakers. "And finish that story while we wait."

"What story?"

"The stoning," said Marcus.

"Oh, yeah," said Dave. "I think the woman was a hooker or an adulterer or something. And she got caught, so the law was that she had to stand there and let this group of men throw rocks at her."

"To kill her?" said Cheese, wiping the back of his pants and taking a knee behind the tree. He peered out toward the big dude still standing on the roof of his station wagon.

"That part I don't know," said Dave. "But either way, pretty awful, right?"

Marcus nodded and said, "So what's the Jesus part?"

Dave smiled because he thought in the story Jesus did some cool stuff before the men could start throwing rocks. Dave didn't need to whisper because the kids at the party had the radio going, but he kept his voice low when he said, "So, Jesus goes over and stands near the woman and says the famous line: 'Let he who is without sin cast the first stone'."

"That *is* good," said Marcus.

"Yeah," said Cheese. "It's a trap."

"How?" said Marcus.

"They're all sinners," said Cheese. "So, if they're being honest with themselves, they can't throw the stone." He took a moment to peek around the tree at the station wagon. "And if one of them does think he's a saint, what kind of saint would throw a rock at a woman?"

"True," said Marcus.

"It's a great line," said Dave.

"This asshole is dancing now," said Cheese, pointing back at his car. "This is a joke."

The big guy was doing a dance that everyone started doing last school year, bending his knees, and swinging his arms back and forth to the sides, snapping his fingers before swinging his hands back the other way. It looked like a girl-dance to Dave.

"You want to go over now?" said Dave.

"A few more minutes," said Cheese.

Dave looked back at Marcus. "So, Jesus delivers this great line," he said. "Then he picks up a stick and starts to draw something in the sand." Dave paused because he knew this was a weird detail to be in the Gospel, and Dave wanted Marcus to appreciate that it was in there.

"A stick?" said Marcus.

"Yeah," said Dave. "So, in class this morning Brother Willis tells us that Jesus picked up the stick because he was trying to give all the guys a chance to drop their rocks and leave. He wasn't trying to shame them. Like he was letting them preserve just a little bit of dignity after he totally burned them."

"Maybe," said Marcus.

"But then someone in the class asked what he wrote in the sand."

"I was thinking the same thing," said Marcus.

"So, Jerry raised his hand."

"Hawk?"

"Yeah," said Dave. "And he said, 'I think Jesus wrote a message to the woman."

"Interesting take," said Marcus. "That sounds like it could be true."

"Jerry said the message might've said something like, *I got this* to make it so the woman wouldn't be scared."

Marcus laughed. "The Bible should've said what Jesus wrote. I like Jerry's idea though. The son of God being confident as hell."

Dave peered through the trees, trying to get a better look at the party. Hoping to see Amy. Hoping that Amy didn't really like this guy.

"Why'd you tell me all that?" said Marcus.

"What?"

"The Bible story."

"You asked me to," he said.

Marcus shook his head. "No, man," he said. "How did we get on that topic?"

Dave thought for a moment. "They were trying to stone us," he said, finally. "With beer bottles."

"Like they never sinned," said Marcus.

"When we go over there," said Cheese. "I'm gonna say, *Let he who is without sin throw the first punch.*"

"I like it," said Marcus. "That might make them pause to think for a second before they beat the snot out of us."

Dave was still looking for Amy in the shadows when the party was suddenly illuminated. A car was pulling into the lot, and the headlights made the big kid turn to see who was coming. Dave caught a quick glimpse of Amy, leaning against the VW Bug, squinting into the oncoming lights, her braids resting on her shoulders.

Dave also saw that the back door of the station wagon was open.

32

After the initial pricks from the Novocaine needle numbing his scalp in preparation for the stitches, Jerry didn't feel any pain while the ER doctor secured the sutures. Jerry did feel some tugging on the skin at the back of his skull and also the coolness of the air on the spot the nurse had shaved. No pain, but the sensations were both odd—appropriate for this bizarre night.

When he stepped back into the waiting room, Billy Idol and Andrew were gone. Edgar was gone. The black guy was sitting next to Carolyn, and there was a new group of people with burns, coughs, broken bones, and allergic reactions.

Carolyn and the black guy stood up at the same time. Jerry thought Carolyn would show some compassion since she was the one who forced him to see a doctor, but she was smirking. So was the black guy.

After the doctor had closed up the wound, the nurse placed a gauze bandage over the stitches. She told him that she couldn't use an adhesive bandage because it wouldn't stick to his hair, so, instead, she was forced to secure the dressing by wrapping an ace bandage around the circumference of his head and clipping the bandage with two metal clasps. Though he hadn't passed by a mirror, he knew he looked ridiculous—like a Civil War victim. He felt like he should be playing a flute or carrying a tattered flag.

"Can't believe you're laughing," he said to Carolyn.

"I'm so sorry," she said and stepped up and hugged him. "I just wasn't expecting the bandage is all."

"I know," he said. "I feel like a fool."

The big black guy still had a grin and said, "The bandage does seem a little excessive."

Carolyn gestured toward him and said, "This is Ronnie. We need to go with him right now."

When they got to the car, Carolyn and Ronnie explained the situation.

Carolyn sat in the front seat with Ronnie, and Jerry sat in the back. He was pissed off that Edgar was in trouble, and he was worried about Dave and the boys.

"You don't want those guys driving around with illegal shit in the back of their car," said Ronnie. "Any number of things could happen, and most of them are bad." He was holding the wheel with one hand down at six o'clock but seemed to be in perfect control of the vehicle. "I'm making a phone call when we get close and find out what else is in that bag. If I don't like the situation, I'll drop y'all off, and *you* can take care of the merch for Edgar." A car started to swerve into his lane, and he used his other hand to tap the horn. The swerving car straightened up and faded back into traffic. "If it's something I can use," he said, "I'm taking everything back to Sawyer myself."

"I don't get why we can't take the cards for Edgar so he gets paid for all this. You can do what you want with whatever else is in there."

Ronnie took a deep breath and was about to talk, but Carolyn interrupted.

"Ronnie and Edgar were both hired by Sawyer," she said. "Apparently, he didn't think Edgar would go through with it. He got worried and asked Ronnie to get the bag for him. Did I say that right?" she said and looked over at Ronnie.

"That's the description of the predicament in which we currently subsist," he said.

Jerry wasn't sure all those words worked together, but he got the gist of what the man was saying. "So, is Edgar going to get paid?" he asked. "He did most of the work here, and now he's headed back to juvie because of this whole thing.

"Is that how you see it?" said Ronnie, keeping his cool, but weaving through traffic like he was being chased.

"How else should I see it?" said Jerry.

"I was there when the kid got arrested," said Ronnie.

"And ..."

"And Edgar didn't get arrested for breaking into the house to get the cards," he said. "Your man's going back to jail for bringing a keg into some people's backyard and also for having a doobie on his person when he was interrogated by the police."

Jerry caught Ronnie's eyes in the rearview mirror. Ronnie was correct in his assessment of the details regarding Edgar's incarceration, but his rendition certainly didn't tell the whole story. "If Sawyer Puck never asked Edgar to engage in this plot," said Jerry, "Edgar never would've encountered the police."

Ronnie had Gladys Knight playing softly on the radio, but he turned it down. "How's that?"

"What do you mean?" said Jerry, confident in his calculation.

"Again," said Ronnie. "I was there when they put the bracelets on him, and they didn't say anything about the cards. They talked about the breaking and entering of a different house. They also mentioned contributing to the delinquency of minors and possession of narcotics." The car was at a stoplight now, and Ronnie turned around in his seat to look at Jerry. "Did any of those crimes occur because your boy was retrieving Sawyer Puck's property?"

"Okay," said Jerry, looking at this thing differently now. He had no more interest in trying to get Edgar paid. If it happened, it happened. But Jerry wasn't going to debate Ronnie anymore, especially since Ronnie was right.

They'd gone to that party before they went to get the cards. Carolyn gave them the address that she got from Cheese. Jerry went along with the plan to bring the keg in the backyard. No one tried to stop Kent from climbing on the roof.

When Jerry tried to reverse engineer the evening to organize the dominoes in a row and ultimately be able to visualize which ones led to Edgar going back to jail, the exercise did actually lead back to Sawyer's job. Edgar never would have been at the ER and run into Kent's family and the cops if Jerry didn't need stitches. And Jerry wouldn't have needed stitches if he never went into the house. And he wouldn't have gone into the house if Sawyer had told Edgar that the door to the boiler room would lock behind him.

Jerry was doing it to himself again.

He knew it didn't matter at this point what had led to, as Ronnie would say, *the predicament in which we currently subsist.* But ever since the waterslides, he'd gotten in the habit of retracing incidents that led to other incidents that led to still more incidents, that caused outcomes for which Jerry either found punishment or reward.

He knew people did this when they reviewed what they'd done to obtain a winning lottery ticket. There was some fun in that. People shopped at particular stores because of a certain set of circumstances. They picked numbers for very specific reasons. They loved to wave the tickets in the air and talk about the string of events that led to their riches.

But Jerry was burning too much emotional fuel with this new habit. He felt like he was addicted to it and wondered if it would ever stop. *If he hadn't smoked Edgar's weed that day.*

Or if he'd stayed with Carolyn instead of following Chrissy Lang like a little puppy.

Or if he hadn't accepted his role as a distraction to Trixie.

Or if he'd been quicker to reach out to Chrissy when the slide started to separate.

He could go back four or five days before the waterslides to link all the episodes together. It was a toxic practice, and he knew it needed to stop.

"You okay back there?" said Ronnie.

"Yeah," said Jerry. "You're right. We'll help you get the bag, and then we're out of it."

"Good," said Ronnie and turned the radio back up. Gladys Knight was finished and now Marvin Gaye was doing *Sexual Healing.*

No one spoke for a moment, and Jerry listened to the words for the first time. He knew the refrain. Everyone did. But the other lyrics hit him hard tonight:

A sea was stormin' inside of me
Baby I think I'm capsizing
heal me my darling
heal me my darling
The waves are risin' and risin'

"Which place we headin' to first?" said Ronnie, looking over at Carolyn.

Carolyn looked back at Jerry.

"I think they're at the Boathouse," said Jerry.

"Lake Merced?" said Ronnie.

Jerry nodded at him in the rearview mirror.

"You sure?" said Ronnie.

"No," said Jerry. "Just a hunch."

Carolyn turned around in her seat. She put her arms around the headrest and said, "Is your hunch based on anything?"

"It's late," said Jerry. "Cheese won't want to walk all the way down the hill at The Grove. The Boathouse is just easier. He can pull the wagon right up to the party."

Carolyn looked at Ronnie and said, "I think he's right."

"How long you two been going out?" said Ronnie.

Jerry started to talk but stopped himself. He wanted to hear what Carolyn had to say about this. He didn't know *what* they were at this point, but he hoped it would go beyond tonight. He felt like it would. But he was mad at himself for letting her be involved in any of this. He just wanted to protect her though he had to admit to himself that she wasn't the type of girl who wanted or needed protection.

"I've been chasing him for years," she said. "He's only just realizing he's in love with me."

Ronnie was smiling. "What took you so long, homie?"

"I'm an idiot," he said and felt his face getting warm.

"Not anymore," said Carolyn. "He finally came to his senses."

***

Ronnie pulled into the 7-11 parking lot on Taraval.

Carolyn turned her head quickly to Jerry, pointed out the window with her thumb, and mouthed something that Jerry couldn't decipher. It looked like she said *Blow Eamon*.

"Y'all want anything?" said Ronnie. "I need to microwave a burrito and then make a quick call, find out if I want any part of that bag."

"Can I ask," said Jerry, "what contents would dissuade you from wanting the bag?"

"I'm not in love with baseball cards in the first place," he said. "And I don't want some other shit I can't move immediately. And I sure as hell don't want anything to do with heroin or crack." He was touching the door handle but turned to face Carolyn and Jerry. "Heroin's an opioid, y'know? Fucks people up. Ruined my cousin. So, I won't pick up that bag if there's heroin in it." Then he opened the door and said, "I'll be back."

As soon as the door closed, Carolyn said, "Blue Comet," and pointed at a car parked across from the laundromat.

Jerry looked over, saw the dent still on the front bumper, and knew it was the car his dad had sold months ago. He pulled his keys out of his pocket, showed them to Carolyn, and said, "Let's go."

33

Andrew just wanted to get out of there. It was clear they were at the wrong boathouse, and the more time they wasted at this one, the less chance they'd find the kids with the bag and get it back. Andrew appreciated Paul's proposal that, if they could obtain the bag, Andrew would get the cards and Paul would get everything else that Sawyer had stuck in the bag.

But they had to find it first.

On top of it, this tribe of wild weirdos might or might not be friendly. The girl in the leather was cozying up to Paul, but the rest were giving Andrew the collective evil eye, and he didn't like it at all. The big kid in the Dick Tracy getup was standing directly behind Andrew, so there was no way for Andrew to make a run for it if things got hairy. Andrew saw this as a clear case of unlawful imprisonment.

"You ever heard of Kid Wiggles?" the girl stage-whispered into Paul's ear.

Paul shrugged and looked over at Andrew for help. Andrew shrugged back.

"You might have to remind me, love," said Paul, smiling, but it was the worried kind.

"C'mon," said the kid dressed in a coat and tie. "Get your heads out of your asses." He paced in front of the group like an attorney delivering an impassioned closing argument. "How do you not know Kid Wiggles?"

"What about you?" said the Latino kid with the hairnet, pointing at Andrew. "You know Wiggles, right?"

Andrew was scared he might get slapped for providing an incorrect response, so he decided to pretend like he didn't know the question was directed to him. Then he felt the large hand clamp down on his shoulder again.

"Answer the man," he heard from a voice so low that it seemed contrived. It sounded like the butler from the *Addams Family.* Andrew was tempted to turn around to see if Lurch was hunched over him, ready to say *You Rang.*

"I feel like I *should* know," he tried, looking across the table at the assortment of faces staring back at him.

There was a quiet second. Then the group burst out laughing.

When they quieted down, a Filipino kid in baggy sweats and no shirt parted the congregation of eccentrics. The brim of his baseball cap was pushed way to the side, like Daffy Duck's beak after a well-aimed shot from Elmer Fudd. The kid's sneakers, which were peeking out from under the sweats, were bright white and seemed huge to Andrew. Like college mascot shoes.

"You fools don't know Kid Wiggles?" he said and jumped up on the table.

Andrew felt like there was a good chance this boy was, indeed, Kid Wiggles. But Andrew didn't want to offend anyone, so he held his tongue, hoping this would end in some way without his having to speak.

"Follow me," he said and added, "Wala kang silbi," then jumped off the table. He walked toward the lake in the direction of the docked pedal boats. Andrew assumed that he'd just been insulted in Tagalog and was fine with that. He just didn't want to get punched again tonight.

The kid in the coat and tie followed Kid Wiggles but turned to Andrew and said, "He had a part in *Breakin' II*, you idiots."

Andrew involuntarily whispered, "*Electric Boogaloo.*"

Andrew had not seen *Breakin' II: Electric Boogaloo.* Nor had he seen the original *Breakin'*. But he was familiar with both. They'd come out in recent years and seemed to him to be the most ridiculous films ever created. And adding *Electric Boogaloo* to the sequel seemed especially outrageous.

"So, you do know him now?" said coat and tie, smug sneer, like this little banker was ready to throw down.

"I appreciate his craft," said Andrew, really lost on what these people wanted from him.

"Then get up," said coat and tie. "He's about to put on a show."

Lurch pulled Andrew up by the back of his shirt while Andrew watched Paul's female look-alike slide off the bench, lean in behind Paul, and insert her fingers into his belt loops. She pulled up gently, and Paul complied.

The group, which now looked to be close to thirty people, walked en masse toward the flat area in front of the pedal boat slips. There was a large square of cardboard on the ground, probably from a new refrigerator or washing machine, and Kid Wiggles was standing on it.

"Get ready to have your minds blown," he yelled and pointed at a nearly identical Filipino boy, also bare chested. But this one looked to be only ten or eleven years old, out late with this bizarre congregation on a Friday night.

With both hands, the kid was holding the handle of a monster boombox. He let go with one hand and pressed play. The crowd went nuts when a carnival barker voice came out of the speakers and seemed to be introducing the act. There were strange noises in the background that didn't sound like instruments to Andrew. They sounded like they were coming from a human—not like whistling or humming. Something else. Almost like baby chatter and heavy breathing but producing a steady beat behind the barker's talking.

Andrew couldn't hear the words over the cheering.

Kid Wiggles was standing in the middle of the cardboard square with his feet together and his eyes closed.

Andrew heard Paul say to the girl, "What *is* this?"

"Just watch," she said.

Then the beat changed slightly, and the barker's words started to come out like he was chanting a little bit, reciting a bad poem with strange enthusiasm:

La-di-da-di, we like to party
We don't cause trouble, we don't bother nobody
We're just some men that's on the mic
And when we rock upon the mic we rock the mic right

The island of misfit toys closed in on the cardboard square when Kid Wiggles started to do a kind of move where he skipped in place. He had his hands out to his sides and was raising them, palms up, like he was trying to summon rain while the crowd got louder, and the miniature version of Wiggles turned up the music.

Paul asked the girl, "Who's that bloke on the radio?"

"You never heard of Doug E. Fresh?" she said.

"Can't say that I have," he shouted over the music, as more kids shoved past him to get a better look.

"You need to get out more," she said.

Andrew peered over the collection of bobbing heads to see Kid Wiggles down on the ground now, twirling around on his back, intermittently freezing in different poses to the delight of his friends.

Andrew recognized that he was on the outside perimeter of the throng now. He watched Paul whisper something into the girl's ear. She nodded and pulled a pink pen out of a tiny purse that she had strapped diagonally between her breasts. She handed the pen to Paul and stuck her hand out, palm up like Kid Wiggles.

Paul wrote a number on her palm and then handed her the pen. She smiled and suddenly looked very young.

Andrew watched Paul look out at the backs of the people watching Kid Wiggles. Then he looked at Andrew and gestured with his head toward the car. Andrew saw that Lurch was now part of the mob, pumping a fist in the air, high above the heads of the other revelers. It was the perfect time to make a quick exit.

Paul and Andrew both took a few steps backward, away from the show. Then they both turned and ran as quietly as they could toward the car. Andrew looked over his shoulder when they were halfway across the lot. He thought he saw some people looking at him, but he turned back around and focused on getting to the car. Paul was ahead of him, slipping around the back of the car and then opening the driver's side door.

Then Andrew heard the music stop and an eruption of shouts, similar to the ones they'd heard when they were first spotted—angry, almost barbaric, yelping.

By the time Andrew had closed his door, Paul was already reversing out of the parking spot at the corner of the lot. As he shifted into drive, Andrew saw the first individuals from the mob approaching Paul's side of the car. Paul didn't slow down, and three or four kids pounded on the hood and the roof as Paul skidded out of the lot.

Andrew turned around in his seat and looked out the rear window. The misfits were starting to fade into the fog, but Andrew got a good look at Lurch and Kid Wiggles, both waving their arms wildly, their mouths wide open as they shouted profanities.

When Paul finally drove off the bumpy dirt path and pulled onto a better-paved road with streetlights, he turned to Andrew and said, "Holy shit."

Andrew said, "What the hell?"

"What do you think that was?"

"Once I saw that it wasn't some kind of costume party, I couldn't figure out what would bring all those different kinds of people together. Some kind of weird club?"

Paul was quiet for a moment. Then he said, "Nah, man. It's easier than that."

"Oh, yeah," said Andrew. "What then?"

"Kid Wiggles," he said and then laughed loud and hard, like someone who'd seen something funny but also dangerous … which is exactly what they'd both experienced. Andrew hadn't heard Paul laugh the entire night and was taken aback by the sound. It was a nasally, staccato guffaw—not very English. It was an American belly-laugh that betrayed his Billy Idol persona. Probably the reason he didn't laugh much and, Andrew assumed, never on stage.

Andrew said, "Did you give that girl your phone number?" Then he squinted at Paul's profile, looking through the dark car to try to determine Paul's age, which had to be close to thirty.

"Hell no," said Paul. "That was definite jailbait back there."

He was casual now—no more English accent—but he didn't make eye-contact with Andrew when he asserted his denial.

34

Ronnie was a big man. On days when he missed a meal, he would sometimes get dizzy from carrying himself around all day. Tonight, he had a couple vodka gimlets in his belly and nothing else. He wasn't sure what he'd be dealing with at the boathouse, but he didn't want to be light-headed in the event that something went down. Also, he rarely passed up an opportunity to microwave a 7-11 frozen burrito.

All he wanted to do was run in, grab the burrito, and heat it up. Then run out and use the pay phone to call Isaac and find out if Isaac had gathered any intel on the contents of the bag. Ronnie felt like it would not be complicated. Once he knew what was in there, he would know immediately if this job was worth the effort.

After he had the intel, his two guides up in the car would lead him to the station wagon, tell the friends to hand over the product, and then Ronnie and the kids would part ways.

Something inside him wanted to let Jerry and Carolyn keep part of the take, but they probably knew better than to ask, and he needed the money more than they did. Once he unloaded the goods, he'd have enough cash to get out of San Francisco and away from Uncle Norris. If he couldn't get out now, he felt like he might get stuck in his routine and end up drinking gimlets at Shanley's and doing odd jobs for Norris until he met an early death or went to jail. He already knew plenty of guys who'd ended up in one of those two scenarios.

He knew there were other ways out, but a pocket full of cash made every plan easier.

A couple of middle-aged white guys were standing near the pay phone. They were smoking cigarettes and drinking tall beers wrapped with brown paper bags. One of them nodded at Ronnie as he pushed open the glass door and made his way to the frozen food section. This 7-11 could get crowded on a Friday night, but the line was short, so Ronnie was confident he could be back on the road in less than five minutes and in the boathouse parking lot in less than ten.

As he walked past the front counter, he eyed the hotdogs and then took a peek at the truck stopper sandwiches in the refrigerated section, but he knew what he wanted. Once he got to the frozen stuff, he was momentarily tempted by the pizza rolls, but he pushed them aside and grabbed a beef burrito.

While his burrito was in the microwave, he watched a couple of Asian kids playing Cobra Commander on the machine in the corner by the Duraflame logs and the racks of newspapers and magazines.

There was no line at all now at the register. Ronnie watched the microwave timer run down to zero. He heard the chime and then reached in to pull out the burrito, but it was too hot. He burned his hand and dropped the burrito on top of the microwave. He cursed and grabbed a handful of napkins out of the dispenser. He used the napkins as an oven mitten and carefully picked up his late dinner. For a moment, he considered pulling a runner, but he knew he had to use the phone right outside the store, so he walked toward the register.

By the time he got there, two teen boys wearing black t-shirts and ski caps had slipped into line. They were holding skateboards and using handfuls of coins to pay for their Slurpees.

Ronnie looked past them through the glass doors at a little white Toyota pulling up in front of the store. It was full of young girls, all of them laughing hysterically.

Ronnie looked at these two clowns in front of him, laying coins out on the counter as the old Chinese clerk did the math for them. Ronnie was about to reach into his pocket to pay for the two skateboarders and keep things moving, but he noticed some movement from the Toyota and turned his attention back to the front door.

The girl driving the car had her head turned over her shoulder like she was backing out, but the car pitched forward, jumped the curb stop, and smashed through the front doors of the 7-11 before it stopped abruptly about a quarter of the way into the store. The two skateboarders jumped back, one of them stepping on Ronnie's foot. Everyone in the store was screaming, including the kids who were playing Cobra Commander.

The clerk ran around the counter. He was waving his hands and yelling in Mandarin.

The four girls in the car, including the driver, were laughing so hard that, for a moment, Ronnie thought they were all crying. But they weren't. The driver was slapping the steering wheel with both hands and shaking her head, her long bangs covering her eyes. The girls in the back were leaning between the two front seats and hooting like they'd just gotten off the Tidal Wave roller coaster down at Great America.

Ronnie could feel the burrito sweating through the napkins as he watched one of the skateboarders take his cap off and say, "Whoa," then walk through the broken glass and lean down to look into the driver's side window.

The girl looked over at him with confused eyes. Then she rolled down the window and said, "We'll have four Cherry Coke Big Gulps and as many nachos as you can carry."

After a split second of silence, the other three girls lost it. They were laughing and screaming at the same time. The driver still looked confused before she eventually joined in with the others.

The skateboard dude was smiling when he looked at Ronnie and said, "Baked," and then walked to the counter and grabbed his Slurpee.

Ronnie took a bite of his burrito. Then he put a fiver on the counter and walked past the chips and pretzels display to get a better angle and see if there was room to exit the store. The clerk continued to yell and walk around the front of the car, which took up all the space where the double doors used to be.

Ronnie leaned down and looked into the Toyota. The uncontrollable hilarity had decelerated into uneven breathing with occasional bursts of feverish laughter. Two of the girls were holding onto the other two as if the laughter and the weed had suspended the laws of physics, and they thought they'd fall off the face of the Earth if they didn't hold onto something.

"How you doin'?" said Ronnie. And when the girl looked over at him but didn't say anything, he raised his eyebrows. "You doin' all right?"

She nodded her head. The girl in the back seat had her nose flattened against the window, trying to get a better look at Ronnie.

"Listen," he said. "I gotta make a very important phone call, and y'all are blocking the door."

The driver tried to look serious. She pursed her lips and said politely, "My apologies, officer."

Ronnie was going to correct her but didn't want to waste any more time. "Please back out if you can," he said. "You just need to reverse about five feet, and I'll be able to get out."

The driver said, "Absolutely, officer." Then she mechanically put her left hand at twelve o'clock on the steering wheel and turned to look over her shoulder through the back window. She put her right hand on the back of the passenger seat, and finally pressed on the gas.

The car shot forward again, this time ramming the front counter and knocking over the hot dog roller grill and a ChapStick display. The two skateboarders both had their hands on top of their heads as they watched the Chinese clerk jump up and down, making noises that, to Ronnie, sounded more like American Indian chanting than anything in Mandarin—noises that were angry and melancholy at the same time.

Ronnie had seen enough.

He walked past the car, pausing by the passenger window to say, "Thank you, miss."

Then he crunched through the broken glass and sidestepped the Toyota's rear quarter panel on his way out into the lot, where the payphone was posted up in front of the last parking spot before the sidewalk. The two dudes who were drinking beers out of brown paper bags crossed his path on the way out.

Ronnie knew where they were headed.

He'd seen this shit his whole life—lazy opportunists. They always found a way to get something for free when there was any kind of mayhem to create a diversion. They'd pretend they were confused, wander into the store, and just start grabbing stuff off the shelves. Total bullshit. Totally predictable.

Ronnie got Isaac on the first ring. "Any news?" he asked.

Isaac said, "Where you at?"

"7-11 on Taraval."

"You got those kids with you?"

"In the car."

"Puck spilled the beans," said Isaac.

"And ...?"

"Cocaine," said Isaac. "Lots of it. Ready for sale."

"Okay," said Ronnie. "I'm in. I got a guy for that."

"You might as well get the baseball cards too," he said.

"I'm gonna grab the bag and go," said Ronnie. "These kids'll bring me to the station wagon and then tell the owner that my bag is in the back. The owner's gonna pull it out and put it in my hand, homie. Then I'm gettin' outta Dodge."

"That's the plan," said Isaac. "Then you hold everything at your house, and I'll come by tomorrow."

Ronnie thought Isaac was losing it. "I'm not bringin' it inside the house" he said. "You want Norris to find it?"

It was quiet for a long moment. Apparently, Isaac hadn't thought this part through.

"I gotta get goin'," said Ronnie, "before these kids all go home and make me break into the station wagon outside some family's house. I'm not trying to do that."

"Okay," said Isaac. "Just leave it in your trunk for tonight, and we'll figure out something tomorrow."

"Yeah," said Ronnie.

"You're movin' out," said Isaac with a little laugh in his voice. "New life."

Ronnie smiled and hung up.

He ate the rest of his burrito in one bite and threw the napkins in the garbage can. Then he took long strides over to his car. The windows were steamed up, and he wondered whether or not Ken and Barbie were making out in there.

He opened the door and said, "Let's ride." But before he got into the car, he saw that they were gone. He took a quick look around the parking lot to see if they'd just stepped out to get some air, but all he saw was the two bums walking out of 7-11 with armfuls of merchandise.

35

Jerry saw Carolyn put both hands on the dashboard when he made a hard left into the Boathouse parking lot.

When he slowed for the speedbumps, the first thing he noticed was the fire.

"Pull over," said Carolyn, actually putting her hand on the steering wheel and pulling it.

"Okay," said Jerry and took the first open spot, about fifty yards from whatever was burning up ahead.

"What the hell is that?" she said and squinted.

Wisps of fog were drifting over the lake in waves, so the flames would go from vibrant to muted and back to vibrant again. "I think they must've lit a fire in a garbage can," he said. "Do you recognize any of the cars?"

"I see Cheese's station wagon," she said. "And I think I know that bug."

The fog cleared again. "Holy shit," said Jerry. "Someone's on his roof."

"I know that guy," said Carolyn in an anxious whisper.

"Who is he?"

"Justin Mifsud," she said. "He transferred into St. X at the beginning of the year."

"How do you know him?"

"He's from L.A.," she said. "He's friends with Annie's boyfriend. We kind of went on a double date about a month ago."

"Really?" he said and tried to do the math in his head. That was after the accident.

"I did it as a favor to Annie," she said.

"That guy dancing on the roof of Cheese's car?"

"Jerry," she said. "You fell off the face of the Earth. You never called me back. I thought you didn't like me."

She sounded like she was apologizing, but she didn't have to. Jerry knew it was his fault that he and Carolyn weren't together earlier. He even wondered if they were officially together now.

"Besides," she said. "He was a total jerk anyway."

Jerry was staring at the guy on the roof. Justin Mifsud. Jerry didn't like anything about this guy. He very much didn't like the fact that Justin thought it was okay to dance on Cheese's roof. Cheese was a moron, but Jerry was surprised that he would allow this nonsense.

"Why wouldn't Cheese tell him to get down?" said Jerry.

"Justin can be really persuasive," she said.

"How was he a jerk?" said Jerry, but the words came out slightly choked. He was having some kind of emotional collapse that was affecting his nervous system. The weight of the day was pressing on him, and he actually felt his knees shaking.

Her head was tilted slightly downward, but she rolled her eyes up to meet his. "He tried to get a little too close," she said. "Y'know?"

Jerry wanted to know where this happened and how she allowed herself to get into a situation like this. But he knew he had no right to ask those questions. When he should have been calling her and taking her to the movies and to Pier 39, he was sleepwalking through his life, not really talking to anyone. Just trying to figure out what was wrong with himself.

He had also been a little embarrassed.

He was a part of the group that had screwed things up for everyone.

He was part of the group that had caused so much heartache for so many people.

So, no, he didn't have the right to ask her about her date with Justin Mifsud.

But he did anyway. "How did you get yourself in a place with this guy where he could pull something like that?" As soon as he said it, he knew it was bad. He knew it would make her feel bad, even though she had no reason to. "I'm sorry," he said. "I'm losing it, I guess."

The two of them stood beside the car and looked at the fire for a moment.

"It's okay," she said and reached for his hand. Just like that. Like he deserved to be forgiven so quickly and so graciously by a person who'd done nothing wrong.

"I'm really just mad at myself," he said. "There's no reason for me to question you about any of that." He reached up to touch his forehead and felt a glaze of sweat even though there was a chill in the air. "I'm not sure why I did that."

"Why are you mad at yourself?" she said, and he could sense that she was looking at him now, but he kept his eyes on the flame.

"I feel like I wasted all this time," he said and paused because he wanted to explain it right without sounding corny.

"What do you mean?" she said.

"I should have been calling you every day," he said.

"That might have been a bit much for me," she said, laughing and pulling herself close to him, her face resting against his chest.

"For me, it would have been so much better," he said. "I don't know what I was waiting for."

"I do," she said.

Jerry watched Justin Mifsud do a terrible version of the robot and then sit down on the roof, his legs hanging off the side of the car. Someone handed him a beer.

"Are you gonna tell me?" he said.

"You were punishing yourself," she said. "There wasn't any *reason* for you to do that, but that's what you were doing. It was like you didn't think you deserved to be happy. And now that you feel that you've paid back at least some of your phantom debt to society by not letting yourself enjoy life, you're allowing yourself something and not sure how it's going."

He figured she was probably right. There were times when he'd actually committed to this self-punishment at the semi-conscious level. He thought back to moments during which he was laughing really hard or celebrating a tackle at practice or savoring a burger from Zim's. And how he would internally talk himself out of the momentary joy. He'd actually been doing this to himself. Stifling his laughter. Quitting football. Dropping the burger onto the plate.

It was all coming back to him now in a physical way. Even though he was standing next to this beautiful girl, who seemed to understand what he was going through, he was physically experiencing the happiness-deprivation to which he'd sentenced himself after seeing Chrissy's fall. After seeing Dave's wrist. And the feeling was weakness, or maybe fatigue. Like he had no strength in his arms and legs. They were just noodles hanging from his body.

Intellectually, he knew he wasn't responsible for what happened that day. At a certain level, he thought that nothing was ever just one person's fault. And intent actually meant something. Doing something by accident meant that you didn't do it on purpose. It was a circular argument that had been popping into his head for weeks during the times when he was trying to forgive himself. He might have even said it out loud a few times when he was alone. It was a preposterous statement: *Doing something by accident meant that you didn't do it on purpose*. It was like saying that he was happy because he wasn't sad. So stupid. But that's what was going through his head when Carolyn finally spoke.

"Jerry," she said.

"Yeah."

"If we're going to get the bag for Edgar and get the hell out of here before Ronnie shows up, I think we need to do it right now."

Jerry knew she was right, and he knew this was a bad time to try to figure out what was going on in his head. But he felt that he was a little closer. Carolyn was helping him get a little closer.

"Here's the plan," he said. "We pull up behind the station wagon. If it's unlocked, we just open it and grab the bag."

Carolyn had both arms around his waist and was looking up at him.

"If it's locked," he said, "we call Cheese over and quietly ask him to open the back so we can grab Edgar's bag." He put his arms around her and squeezed. "There's no need to engage with anyone else. We get right back in the car and get out."

"We can explain everything to Dave and Cheese tomorrow," she said.

"We gotta do this right now," he said and realized he was talking to himself. He had a feeling this guy on the roof of the station wagon was looking for trouble, probably trying to get Cheese or Marcus to engage. Dave couldn't fight with the cast on his arm, but the other guys wouldn't hesitate unless they were outnumbered. They were probably outnumbered.

"You're saying it has to be right now," she said. "But we're not moving."

He smiled down at her, and she reached up and put her hand on the back of his neck. She pulled him down to her, and they kissed. It wasn't a peck. And it wasn't a make-out kiss either. It was something different—long and sweet. Jerry got lost in it for a moment and then sensed that she had her eyes open, so he opened his.

Her eyes *were* open. "We gotta go," she said.

Jerry smiled and looked off toward the fire, but, out of the corner of his eye, he saw something white, moving down near the trees.

36

When Dave saw the headlights coming into the parking lot, he initially hoped it would be the cops and that they'd help get that asshole off the roof of Cheese's car. Dave just wanted to go home. It was fun to get out and see some people, but it was late, and he'd made it through the night so far without something really stupid happening, so he wanted to keep it that way. But his current predicament seemed to be shifting into the *stupid* category as he sat on the wet grass, hiding from the conflict that was surely waiting for him up at the car.

The location at which he was situated with Cheese and Marcus put him about midway between the party and the spot where the latest car had parked in the shadows near the entrance. Dave could tell it wasn't a cop car. In fact, in the fog, it looked a little like Jerry Hawkins' old blue Comet.

Dave felt like his group was safe from detection where they sat under the tree down close to the water. After a few minutes, the driver and the passenger got out of the car and looked out toward the party. It was too foggy to make out their faces, but Dave thought it looked like a girl and a guy, standing close together, maybe out here on a date.

Dave looked back and forth between the party and the couple, but the fog was too thick in both directions to see what was happening in either camp. Cheese and Marcus were a little stoned and were telling each other outlandish lies about the kinds of martial arts moves they intended to use on the kids who'd commandeered the station wagon. If the three of them made a group decision that they couldn't wait out the kids any longer, Dave was confident that the kung fu acrobatics Cheese and Marcus were slow-motion pantomiming would have little effect on the behemoth of a junior, who'd apparently staked his claim on the station wagon as well as on Amy.

Dave was trying to catch glimpses of her and thinking about the many moments they'd shared together when they were little, back when things didn't seem as important to him as they did now that she looked the way she did. Now that they were both at a high school party together and interacting in a way that seemed so distant from their childhood excursions.

Images of sandcastle building, egg tossing, birthday cake eating, and hide-and-go-seek playing were running on a loop through his mind, and Dave was trying to figure out how he'd missed her transformation. And since she looked so different now, he wondered how he was able to recognize her at all. It didn't make sense. Her face just seemed more adept at holding her features, which were always so animated—wide mouth and big eyes, always ready for an adventure.

The dancing bear on Cheese's car must have seen the same thing, and now he didn't want anyone moving in.

Dave was fairly certain that Amy wouldn't be hanging around this guy much longer. She was too smart for him. So, Dave was fine avoiding both of them tonight and hopefully getting a chance with Amy sometime in the near future.

The fog took a timeout for a moment, and Dave had a good look at the party, but Amy must have been on the other side of the cars, so he turned to take a look at the couple up near the entrance. He caught the end of a kiss and then saw them hold their embrace. When they eventually turned their faces toward the party, he could see that the guy was wearing a bandage around his head like some kind of lazy Halloween costume. And the girl looked a little like Carolyn, mainly because the girl *was* Carolyn. And the guy was Jerry.

Dave took another quick peek down at the party before he turned and gestured to Jerry and Carolyn. He was careful with his casted hand as he waved it back and forth above his head, beckoning his friends to come down the hill and tell him what to do.

With their heads ducked low, Jerry and Carolyn ran down the hill taking cover behind trees as they approached the spot where Dave, Cheese, and Marcus were stationed.

"What's going on?" said Jerry.

Before Dave could get the words out, Cheese said, "That big fucker's standing on the roof of my car."

Jerry looked over at Dave, then back at Cheese. "Why don't you tell him to get off?"

"It's a little complicated," said Dave.

Jerry nodded and looked like he was clenching his teeth. "Here's the thing," he said. "Edgar left a bag in the back of the station wagon, and by my calculations, I have about five minutes tops to get it and then get out of here before something bad happens."

Dave looked at his watch. "The big kid thinks I want to steal his girlfriend, and we're outnumbered, so it would've been a bad idea to try to fight these guys."

"*Do* you want to steal his girlfriend?" said Jerry.

"I do," said Dave and was surprised that he was willing to admit it without hesitation. He saw Carolyn smile and then heard Marcus behind him.

"Yessir," said Marcus. "I set this up for him."

"He didn't," said Dave. "What should we do?"

"We don't have time to create a complicated plan," said Jerry. "We need to go over there right now and get Edgar's bag. I'll get the guy off the roof. Then we're all getting in the car, and Cheese is going to drive us out of here fast, or we'll be dealing with a different problem." Jerry looked around at everyone and said, "No more provoking these guys. Got it?"

Dave nodded at him.

Cheese said, "Marcus took three beers off one of them."

"Forget all that," said Jerry. "Let's go."

They were no longer in hiding. Jerry led them up a path to the cracked asphalt, and they walked right down the middle of the lot. But no one from the party noticed them. The raspy old radio was playing Violent Femmes. Almost all the people in the mob were dancing around the fire like crazy people to the furious beat of *Add It Up.*

Why can't I get just one kiss? Why can't I get just one kiss?

To Dave, it wasn't even really singing, and the dancing wasn't dancing either. They looked more like broken machines, all malfunctioning at the same time. Dave wouldn't have been surprised to see extra parts littered across the lot.

He was happy to see that Amy wasn't a part of it, but when he got close enough, he didn't like the look in the dancers' eyes, glossy and bulging as they bounced around, dangerously close to the fire. He was pretty sure he heard Jerry in front of him say, "Where's Ralph and Piggy?"

Then, for just a moment, Dave focused on the words to the Violent Femmes song. He'd heard it before and knew it was one of those songs they didn't play on the radio because of the explicit lyrics.

Some of the guys were screaming the words, including the bastard on the roof of Cheese's car. The light from the flames was throwing out malicious shadows. The savage movements were larger than the kids and blended together into an amorphous dream phantom oscillating feverishly as the song's rhythm picked up speed.

Dave thought these guys were pissed enough to immediately come after him, but no one seemed to even notice they were there. When he looked over at Cheese and Marcus, they were transfixed on the fire-dancers. But Jerry and Carolyn were scrambling around near the back of the station wagon. Jerry was picking up tiny white pouches that were strewn on the ground and in the back of the car. He was throwing them in a duffle bag.

Carolyn was gathering up binders and sticking them in the same bag.

Just above them, the big guy had stopped dancing and was looking down at Jerry and Carolyn. He yelled, "Turn off the music," and the parking lot went quiet. Dave could hear the crackling of wood in the garbage can. Apparently, these folks were feeding the fire with the cardboard from their twelve packs and small branches from the closest trees. There must have been cans in there as well. It smelled like destruction.

"Look who joined the party," said the big guy, pointing down at Carolyn, who'd just put the last of the binders in the duffle bag.

Carolyn had her back turned to the car, but she looked up over her shoulder and nodded at the ringleader of this three-ring clown show. Dave could tell they knew each other, and that Carolyn had no use for the guy.

"Is this your blow?" he said.

"How much did you guys get into, Justin?"

"Is it yours?" he said.

"No," she said. "And you don't want to meet the owner." Then she looked at the rest of the group and said, "If any of you other idiots stole any of this cocaine, you need to put back in the bag whatever you don't already have up your noses." She stood in front of the car and held the bag open in front of her like a Salvation Army Santa Claus.

Dave was surprised that several kids came forward and dropped the little packets and half-filled bundles into the bag. Many of them apologized to Carolyn, who just looked at them, a little disgusted at their behavior.

Amy didn't move. She was taking furtive glances up at Justin.

"Why are you pussies listening to this bitch?" he said, clearly a challenge to either Jerry or Carolyn.

"Don't engage," she said to Jerry, who looked calm as he gestured to Cheese, Dave, and Marcus to get in the car.

"Let's go," he said. "It's time."

"Seriously," said Justin. "You guys are a joke, letting a girl tell you what to do."

Amy spoke up even though she didn't seem to be part of this. "They're just giving back what they stole, Justin."

He was quiet for a moment, clearly surprised that she was taking a stance on this. Dave had his hand on the door handle, but he didn't pull. He was worried about Amy. He didn't know this guy. Didn't know what he was capable of, especially since he was clearly high. Dave wasn't getting into the car until he knew she was safe.

"What about when these guys stole the little dude's Lowenbraus?" said Justin. "And Dave over here, trying to steal my girl." He was taking deep breaths, looking like he was ready to spring off the roof like a silverback gorilla and start tearing people apart.

Jerry had the car all packed up, and Cheese and Marcus were already in the car. "Everything's cool," said Jerry. "You guys can finish your *Lord of the Flies* party. We're gonna head out."

Justin looked down and said, "Who the fuck is this guy?"

"I'm nobody," said Jerry and looked over at Carolyn.

"That's what I thought," said Justin. "Are you with this bitch?"

Carolyn was holding the duffle bag up to her chest and already shaking her head before Jerry looked over at her.

"C'mon, man," he said. "Are you on crack? You know better than to talk to a girl like that." He was actually grinning up at Justin. He had one hand in his pocket and was using the other to signal for Justin to get down from the roof of the car—a backwards wave and a reassuring nod before saying, "You need to climb down from the roof so my friends and I can get going. We're in a bit of a rush."

Justin started laughing. "Fuck your rush," he said and spread his feet apart in a more athletic stance. "You and this bitch can—"

That was all he got out before Jerry grabbed the cuff of Justin's pants with one hand and pulled back hard. Justin fell onto his ass and said, "What the—"

And that was all he got out before Jerry took his other hand out of his pocket and then used both hands to pull Justin's foot. For a second, it looked like Justin was trying to use his free foot to hook onto something to keep him on the roof. The result was that he did the splits and then gave up.

Jerry jerked one more time, and Justin came down. He flapped his arms like an injured bird, but it didn't do any good. He hit his head on the side of the car and then again on the cement to complete the dismount.

Jerry put his arm around Carolyn and moved to guide her into the backseat so that they could go, but before they all could do anything, a car pulled in behind the station wagon and blocked them in.

37

On the way out of the 7-11 parking lot, Ronnie rolled down his window and yelled at the two opportunists, who'd opened a big bag of Doritos. They both had their hands in the bag at the same time when Ronnie said, "Get a job," and then rolled his window back up as he took a hard right out of the parking lot. He took the turn too sharply, caught a bit of the curb and skidded out onto Taraval in front of a guy on a motorcycle.

The motorcycle pulled up beside Ronnie, looked like he wanted to say something, thought better of it, and sped away across Sunset Boulevard.

Ronnie turned left on Sunset. Although he was counting on Jerry and Carolyn to direct him to the boathouse, he knew where Lake Merced was and drove in that direction. When he got to the lake, he had to make a choice—left or right. It was really a coin toss for him. He chose left and immediately felt that it was the wrong decision. He didn't have any reason to feel that way except that his instincts were messing with him.

He drove past Lowell High School, where he'd played a football game as a student at McAteer. Then he saw the road that led up to Stonestown Mall. He followed the golf course on his right. San Francisco State, where he'd been accepted as a high school senior, loomed on his left. His mind wandered back to his McAteer guidance counselor's office but quickly shifted back to the present, where he felt like he was moving away from the lake.

He considered making a U-turn and heading back to the original fork in the road. He also knew that if he kept going, the road would eventually curve around the south end of the lake and send him toward the entrance to the boathouse. So, he kept going, thinking you can never go back and do the fork in the road twice. It felt like a waste of time. Like stopping to ask for directions.

He went past Brotherhood Way and knew he was headed toward the A&W and Westlake Joe's. He could go for a couple of Papa Burgers right now. He rushed the burrito and was still hungry. He'd been to both these places a few times but couldn't remember if there was a way to get back to the lake off this road. He pictured the kids in the station wagon driving off to their next destination. He squeezed the steering wheel hard and then forced himself to keep his cool. Took one really deep breath, and there it was. He got his cool back again.

It was pretty foggy, but he was relieved when he saw the road in time, took the quick right, and got back to following the lake. He was a bit more familiar with this area. There was an apartment complex across the street from the police shooting range. It sounds crazy, but he used to deal weed out of the complex's intricate parking garage, which had a bunch of escape exits if one of those cops crossed the street from the range and tried to bust his ass.

Yeah, he knew where he was now. The boathouse entrance was just up the road.

He killed the headlights when he made the turn and saw the bobbing shadows of what looked like a bonfire party. As he got closer, he spotted a station wagon with a kid standing on the roof. With the only light coming from a garbage can fire glowing through the fog, he didn't have a clear view of what was going on, but as he pulled closer to the station wagon, he experienced what he could only describe as an optical illusion. A *now you see it, now you don't* moment.

Ronnie blinked, and a big kid on the roof of the station wagon vanished into thin air. Or maybe he was never there in the first place.

It didn't matter to Ronnie at this point. He just wanted to get the bag and move on with the rest of his life. He pulled in tight behind the station wagon, blocking it in—there was a curb stop and a grass island with a tree in front of the station wagon and Ronnie's car behind it. Someone was in the driver's seat, and someone else was getting in the back, but they had nowhere to go.

Ronnie had two options: go in hard and try to scare the shit out of these kids, or just calmly tell them that Edgar asked him to retrieve his bag from the back of the station wagon. All the kids were looking at him now, so he climbed out of the car and decided to try out the composed approach. It would be less work in the short term but could force him to expend a lot of energy if he had to change course.

He nodded at Jerry and glanced at Carolyn, who was holding the bag up to her chest. "You sly dogs," he said. "Y'all almost made it, huh?"

Jerry pointed at a big kid lying on the ground. "This asshole slowed us up."

The kid on the ground sat up on the cement and hunched forward. He rubbed his head in little circles.

"Try to pat your belly at the same time," Ronnie said and laughed to himself.

"Huh?" said the big kid.

Ronnie said, "Don't worry about it, homie."

The kid started to stand, but Ronnie stopped him.

"I need you to stay right there," he said. "I don't want there to be too many moving parts here."

"Huh?" said the kid, sounding like he was just waking up.

"Justin fell off the station wagon," said Jerry.

"You pulled my—"

"Shut the fuck up, Justin," said Ronnie, keeping his eyes on Jerry and Carolyn, who were standing close now. "I thought we were partners," he said to his former associates.

"Really?" said Carolyn, a half-smile on her cute, little face.

Ronnie smiled too. "At the very least," he said, "I didn't expect you two to cross me up. I thought y'all were my little homies."

Jerry looked disappointed. He was chewing on the inside of his lip, and his eyes were starting to droop. The kid knew it was over. He didn't get out fast enough, and he didn't have the stomach to go to battle with someone Ronnie's size. Jerry probably didn't want anything to do with the cocaine either. "We just wanted to make sure Edgar got credit for doing his job," he said. "He *did* find the bag, and we're worried the dude Sawyer Punk will go after him."

Carolyn jumped in. "And we're not a hundred percent sure you and us have the same objective," she said and adjusted her grip on the bag.

"It's Sawyer *Puck*," he said. "Like in hockey." He laughed a little when he realized Jerry said the name wrong on purpose. "I was going to give y'all credit," he said, feeling strange lying to these good people. "But I need to secure the bag. Your man, Edgar, got a little careless with the product, and I've been hired to be the anchorman in this twisted up relay."

The girl was a real looker, but she had a pouty face now, a funny little snarl to let old Ronnie know she disapproved of what was about to go down. Ronnie had to decide whether he would ask her to bring the bag to him, or if he'd walk over and take it from her. This felt like it should include a very official transfer of power, and he wanted it organized professionally.

The big kid was leaning back a bit now, his hands on the cement behind him, tilting him in a position where he was in the front row, looking up at the show playing out in front of him. The rest of the group was quiet, their heads shifting back and forth between Jerry and Ronnie, like they were watching a tennis match where only one player had the benefit of a racket.

A girl in braids and a kid with a cast on his arm stepped over and stood next to Jerry and Carolyn. The kid with the cast had his arm around the girl. He was avoiding eye-contact with Ronnie, so this was apparently more of a symbolic posturing.

Ronnie knew these kids could gang up on him. Some of them looked jacked up on coke, and he wondered if they'd gotten into Sawyer's supply. Ronnie did not want to get into a parking lot wrestling match with a bunch of coked-up white kids. But it seemed like this group was split anyway. Ronnie didn't believe they could come together in peace and unity to agree to kick Ronnie's ass. He was pretty confident it would all go smoothly.

He worried a little about Jerry. The kid was sure of himself. Not in a cocky way. Ronnie would say it was more in a mature way. Jerry seemed to be a kid who knew his strengths and weaknesses and seemed to be smart enough to utilize the strengths and avoid the weaknesses. Those were the hardest guys to beat at anything. Sports. Business. Love. The dudes who understood themselves seemed to win a lot more than the other guys. The delusional motherfuckers looked like this barrel-chested buffoon sitting on the ground.

"You gonna have to pass the baton, Carolyn." Ronnie said it like they'd been hanging out their whole lives and both understood things about each other without having to say them out loud.

"I hope things work out for you," said Carolyn and looked like she meant it.

"I appreciate it, girl."

Jerry's voice was restrained. He said, "I don't suppose you'd be interested in letting Edgar present Sawyer with the binders, and you take the other stuff?"

"No can do," said Ronnie. "I got my orders."

The fire was getting lower, and there was less light. The kids on the outskirts of the group were in the shadows, and Ronnie didn't like it. This had gone on long enough. He needed to get the bag and get out before these little Catholic school kids decided to unionize and take him down. He'd put up a battle and knock a few kids' teeth out in the process, but he was pretty sure he'd lose if the whole gang decided at the same time that they wanted more cocaine.

Time to leave.

"I'm gonna walk over to you," he said and looked Carolyn in her eyes. The last of the flames was making them change color as she held the bag out in front of her. "Jerry, you gonna be cool, right?"

"Like Larry Bird," he said.

"Shit," said Ronnie. "The hick from French Lick. He ain't cool."

"C'mon, Ronnie."

"I'll give him credit for being a top-notch *white* player," said Ronnie. "But he's definitely not *cool*." Ronnie looked around the semi-circle that had formed around the little one-act play that was about to conclude.

"Dude looks like a geek, right?" he said to the crowd, but all the white faces just stared back at him.

"The geek made nine 3-pointers in a row in the long-distance shootout," said Jerry.

"He can shoot," said Ronnie. "But we *all* takin' Magic if we got first pick."

"I'll take Bird," said Jerry.

Ronnie liked these kids, but it was time to go. "And I'll take the bag," he said and walked over to Carolyn.

She held the bag out in front of her and looked into Ronnie's eyes. "I hope you do something cool with it," she said.

He took the bag from her. "I will," he said. "I'm fixin' it so I don't have to do this shit no more."

"Good," she said. "Get out while you still can."

He nodded to Carolyn as she handed over the bag. Once he had it in his hands, he liked the feel of it. The weight of it. It felt like freedom.

He walked backward so that he could keep an eye on everyone. The big kid on the ground looked up at Ronnie as if to ask if he could get up now, so Ronnie shook his head and pointed at the ground as if to say *Stay put, big boy*.

It was almost completely quiet now except for the sound of the lake lapping up against the shore and the sound of a car pulling in behind him.

38

Now that things were coming to a close, Andrew took a moment to reflect on his personal motivations. Paul stopped talking when they turned onto Sunset Boulevard and headed south toward Lake Merced. So, Andrew had a moment to come to terms with why he was still involved in this convoluted quest to get his baseball cards back—a mission that ramped up significantly when he chose to walk into Helen's place for a psychic reading way back when he was just pouting on Haight Street.

Poor Helen. She didn't deserve this.

Andrew didn't like leaving her in the hospital. But Paul was right. Andrew wasn't a physician, so there really wasn't anything either of them could do for her at this point. Andrew made mental notes to visit her first thing in the morning and to give her a cut of the card sale if he decided to do that.

But even as he contemplated the idea, he knew that it was never going to happen. He had been working on being more honest with himself, and in this case, the honesty was exposing some hard truths. But better not to keep lying to himself. If anything, maybe this night had taught him that.

Helen had her own people. Andrew knew he wouldn't be giving up any of the money. She wasn't alone in the world. She was a grown woman, who'd decided on her own to take part in the shenanigans. For all Andrew knew, she'd planned to con him somehow after they found the cards. Andrew was more alone than she was. He kept telling himself this while they crossed over the streetcar tracks on Taraval and headed toward Ulloa.

But, deep down, he didn't fully believe Helen was that kind of person. He was just working really hard to justify abandoning an injured woman in her time of need. But he was failing, and it was bothering him at his core.

So much had happened over the past few hours, and he was so damn tired, that his mind was shooting off ideas in haphazard patterns—preliminary thought bursts, followed by crisscrossing notions that were only tangentially related. The bursts weren't like the big fireworks from a Fourth of July show. This neuroactivity was more nuanced, like the delicate flickers from a hand-held sparkler—the tiny, inconsequential specks of fire that can rain down almost undetected. The thoughts were coming in so quickly that he was only partially aware of them at all before another burst would send a cluster of new sparks that would converge with the others until it was uncertain which ones belonged together and which ones he'd pushed into mergers of convenience.

He was trying to force himself to believe that he was participating in this quest in order to retrieve a gift from his uncle. He was trying to jam that idea into his consciousness. Trying to make himself believe that he had a sense of nostalgia and respect and loyalty and love for his uncle, and that the cards were a manifestation of that love. In that case, he deserved those cards. It would be an injustice for him not to have them.

But tiny conflicting embers drifted in, and the cumulative effect kept driving him toward the truth, which was that this whole undertaking was about more than honoring his uncle.

It was also about his hatred for Sawyer.

And everything that had happened—including the hole in Helen's foot—was the result of that hatred. Nostalgia and loyalty for his uncle might have played a small role in his current saga, but he wasn't sure how much. He felt like he didn't really know himself anymore, that maybe he'd lost more than a fragment of his ear in that fight with Sawyer.

Another truth that he was finally admitting to himself was that he never expected to find the bag in the first place. He brought Helen into the mix just to make himself feel like he'd done everything in his power to get the cards and not regret anything later. But then the bag was there, and once he saw it, the other compilation of emotions hit him. All the possible factors converged, including the hate and revenge for his step-brother.

An additional factor he considered as they approached the junction at the end of Sunset Boulevard was that he wanted to finish this now. He wanted to complete the job. And he told himself this was as good a reason as any.

He didn't fully trust Paul, and there was a chance that the opportunity for redemption had already passed. But he was going to see this through. No reason for him to stop before the finish line.

As they slowed to search for the entrance, Andrew was convinced that the motivation for reclaiming his belongings was a combination of all the emotions. He wondered why he always assumed that people, including himself, made decisions grounded in a solitary intention. He'd seen it his whole life. Movies and books and history teachers promoted the idea that a single motivation triggered every individual action. *He did it for vengeance. He did it for pride. He did it for jealousy. He did it for greed.*

But Andrew felt that sometimes a person did it for a million reasons. For *every* reason. Multiple factors could converge at the right or wrong time, but after the person acted, it seemed that he was always judged only by the final factor. This happened invariably, even though nothing would have happened unless all the factors converged. Andrew could see that now.

When he spotted the tall, wooden sign welcoming visitors to Lake Merced and Harding Golf Course, he promised himself to stop overthinking his motivations and his decisions and to simply keep chasing the cards. Nothing else mattered now. It was happening whether he liked it or not.

"Do we have a strategy?" he asked Paul.

"For what?" said Paul, like he'd just woken up from a nap.

"For how we're getting the cards back."

Paul looked over at Andrew and said, "It depends, doesn't it?"

"On what?" said Andrew.

"Who has 'em."

Andrew let that wash over himself for a moment. There were only a few possibilities. The kids and the big black dude could still be together, and they could have beaten Andrew and Paul in the race to the boathouse. The three of them could have picked up the bag and left already.

Or the bag could still be in the back of a station wagon parked just up ahead.

Or the kids with the station wagon could have already gone home and were snuggled safely in their beds, and the station wagon they were looking at could belong to someone else.

Paul slow-rolled through the parking lot toward the blurry glow of the bonfire. He stopped about twenty yards away and looked over at Andrew.

"What?" said Andrew.

"You ready?"

"If the bag's just sitting in a car," said Andrew, "and all we have to do is say it's ours and grab it, then I'm definitely ready."

"Well, that looks like the car," said Paul.

"That's gotta be it," said Andrew. And as he squinted through the thinning fog, he got a better view of the situation. There were a lot of people. Someone was even on the ground, either passed out drunk or beaten into submission.

"Let's hope this goes smoothly," said Paul, both hands on the steering wheel, leaning in toward the windshield for a better look.

Andrew was having trouble swallowing. "What're you going to do if they put up a fight?" he said and kept his eyes on the scene up ahead.

Someone moved in front of the person on the ground, making it difficult to see what was happening near the fire.

Paul picked up the gun and did his best Billy Idol snarl, his eyes looking deranged in the flickering shadows.

"You're not shooting anyone over these baseball cards," said Andrew.

"Of course not," he said. "This is just for show."

Andrew thought back to the incident at the house. "I think Helen was holding that same gun *just for show*, and she's in the hospital right now."

"She didn't know how to handle it," he said.

"Which is why you shouldn't have given it to her in the first place," said Andrew, maybe stalling a bit now, rethinking whether or not they should be engaging with anyone if there was going to be a gun involved.

Paul leaned toward Andrew and said, "Don't bugger this up, mate."

"I'm ready to go," said Andrew. "I just think we should know what we're doing if there's any kind of resistance."

"Listen, mate," he said. "I'm a thespian."

"An impersonator," Andrew corrected.

Paul ignored the jab. "I'm going out there and putting on a show." He reached forward and tapped Andrew's head with the barrel of the gun. Apparently, the show had already started. Andrew didn't like the gun touching his head. It gave him a brief chill. He knew not to make any sudden moves, but he wanted to slap Paul in the face for messing with him.

"As long as it's not a wild west show," said Andrew, "I'm fine with you doing some acting."

Paul looked disappointed with Andrew, like he wished he had a better partner for this job. He pulled the car up right behind another car that was blocking the station wagon. Paul's car was sticking out into the road. The fire was in a garbage can, but it was dying—a dull beacon in the fog. It provided just enough light for Andrew to make out a figure backing away from the group toward the car that Paul had just jammed in. This person was large, and Andrew had a pretty good idea who it was.

When the large person turned around and squinted into the headlights, Paul said, "Showtime," and opened his door.

Andrew scrambled out his side of the car and heard Paul yelling in his British accent again.

"All right, you wankers," he said, waving the gun around like a guy who didn't know how to use one. "Let's make this painless, shall we?"

The big black guy was holding the duffle bag in one hand. He walked to the driver's side door of the car in front of them and said,

"Y'all are gonna have to back that up." He waved his hand at Paul's car and then focused on opening his door.

Paul shrugged and then said, "Hold it there, mate."

The big guy paused. "Oh, hey," he said. "You? Billy Idol. You gotta move this car, homie. I'm movin' out."

Andrew thought about the Billy Joel song of that title and wondered if the big guy had gotten the two Billys mixed up. Andrew wanted this to be over. He didn't like that this big dude didn't seem phased by Paul's gun and maybe didn't know the difference between Billy Idol and Billy Joel. Andrew also didn't like that Paul was waving the gun around. He looked like a fool.

"I need the bag, mate," said Paul and took a step forward.

"Not gonna happen, my brother."

"I don't want to use this," said Paul.

Andrew saw that some of the high school kids were running off into the trees and down toward the lake.

"Don't worry," said the big man. "You ain't killing a man over some baseball cards."

"What else is in there?" said Paul.

The big man shrugged.

"Cocaine," yelled a high school girl standing on the outskirts of the crowd. She had braids and looked like a little girl, putting her hands over her mouth after she said it, as if she'd blurted it out by accident.

The big man shook his head at the girl and then looked back at Paul. "Move it, homie," he said and opened his car door. "Or I'm coming back there and movin' it for you." Then he bent down to throw the bag into the car, but he was surprised, as was everyone in the boathouse parking lot, by the gunshot.

39

Jerry had already lost. As far as he was concerned, the game was over. He had no interest in fighting Ronnie, and he knew Carolyn would fully support that decision. Any physical conflict with Ronnie wouldn't just be a fist fight with some high school kid at The Grove. Ronnie was a grown-ass man. And a criminal. Even if Jerry were to land a lucky punch and was somehow able to run away with the bag of goodies, a criminal like Ronnie wouldn't just concede. He'd be back with more criminals, all looking for Jerry and the cocaine.

It just wasn't worth it to Jerry. Edgar was going to be all right, regardless of whether or not Ronnie was telling the truth and would be holding the goods for Sawyer. Maybe Ronnie had a deal with Sawyer that Ronnie would unload the drugs and get a percentage. Jerry had no idea how this was supposed to work. But when he was honest with himself, he didn't fully believe Ronnie was Sawyer Puck's partner.

He also didn't believe that Sawyer would try to hurt Edgar if Sawyer didn't get what he wanted. When Jerry was truly honest with himself, he had to admit that he was just enjoying the adventure. That's why he'd agreed to help Edgar in the first place. After feeling alone for so long after the accident, he was just happy to be hanging out with his friends again. And he was more than happy that Carolyn was there and appeared to like him. He could still taste her cherry lip gloss on his lips.

Jerry also couldn't conceive of a scenario in which Ronnie knew not only about the existence of the bag but also about the presumed location of the bag at the hospital. It didn't make sense that Ronnie found them at the ER. Even Sawyer wouldn't have known they were there. Jerry felt like there had to be a mole, but he couldn't come up with anyone who could be supplying Ronnie or Sawyer with information.

Jerry wished that Edgar hadn't forgotten the bag in Cheese's car. If Edgar had just grabbed it before he got out, Ronnie would have walked into that ER waiting room and simply taken it from him, and that would have been the end of it. The adventure would have come to its natural conclusion right there. Ronnie would either hold onto the bag for Sawyer or keep it for himself, but it would have been out of Jerry's control. He and Carolyn could have jumped on a bus and gone home with plans to meet up for ice cream the next day.

But because Edgar had forgotten the bag in the back of Cheese's car, Jerry was forced to commit grand theft auto, and he made Carolyn come along for the ride. And that was only after assaulting Andrew and leaving the scene of a shooting.

And now Ronnie was being jammed up by the Billy Idol guy.

Billy had stepped out of the car like a pop diva. But this diva was waving a gun around like a live microphone. Ronnie was mostly ignoring the gun, but Jerry didn't like the look of it. His next move was to open the door and hope that Billy was going to do as he was told.

But Billy didn't seem to like that. He pointed the gun at Ronnie, and just before Ronnie was going to toss the bag into the car, Billy pulled the trigger, and the sound echoed over the lake.

Jerry stepped in front of Carolyn for the second time tonight. He watched half the crowd run for cover. He could hear people yelling and sliding over the wet grass away from cars. Jerry should have done the same and pulled Carolyn with him, but he froze.

Instead of flipping the bag into the car, Ronnie fell forward onto the gravelly cement and let go of the bag. It slid over the hood of Ronnie's car and landed on the ground between the car and the station wagon.

Jerry's mind went back to a day game at Candlestick Park when he was little. John "The Count" Montefusco was pitching, and Davey Lopes from the Dodgers fouled one over the third base dugout. The ball bounced off the stairs and landed on an empty seat in the row in front of him. Jerry hesitated for just a moment, and a fat man in a Ron Cey jersey got the souvenir.

He stared at the bag for only a moment before he turned his attention back to Ronnie.

"You stupid limey bastard," he yelled, his hand on his right butt cheek.

Billy Idol held the gun down to his side and ran over to Ronnie. "I'm from El Segundo," he said. "And that was supposed to be a warning shot."

"Warning shot?" said Ronnie, his voice so high it sounded like a woman's. "You do a warning shot up in the air." His voice kept getting higher. "If you missed, you coulda killed one of these kids." His voice was so high pitched it was barely audible. He rolled onto his side, away from the car. "Motherfucker," he said in a whisper.

Billy knelt down beside him and said, "I was aiming at the car, dude."

Ronnie reached up with his bloody hand and grabbed Billy's earring. He yanked down hard, and Billy let out a rebel yell that skimmed over the lake and ricocheted off the steep hills on the opposite side. Then he grabbed his ear with both hands, stood up, and kicked Ronnie in the stomach.

"That was a rotten move, mate," he said and swore under his breath before he kicked Ronnie again and then put the gun up to Ronnie's head.

Ronnie laughed. Apparently, he still wasn't scared. He was breathing heavy and had his hand back on his ass. "Where's the bag, homie?" he said, and rolled his eyes over to where it had landed.

Jerry looked to the landing spot and then immediately noticed that Carolyn had slipped away like a thief in the night. When he looked over his shoulder into the fog, he thought he saw her disappearing behind a bluff, moving diagonally toward the lake. But there were kids scattering all over the place. It could have been anyone.

Jerry didn't know whether to go after her or to keep his eyes on Ronnie and Billy Idol.

"This is a bloody circus," said Billy, standing up and looking out toward the lake. Then he pointed the gun at Ronnie. "See what you did?" he said, his voice slipping back into his natural SoCal inflection.

For a moment, Jerry thought this guy might shoot Ronnie right in the middle of the parking lot. Instead, he ran back to his car, moved it about ten feet back, and ran back to Ronnie. In plain American, he said, "Get your fat ass in your car and get the fuck out of here. If I see you when I get back, I'll shoot you in the head."

Ronnie was leaning on one hip, looking up at Billy. He glanced in Jerry's direction but didn't say anything. "You're not a good enough aim to hit anyone in the head," he said to Billy and laughed. "But don't worry, I'm leaving." He got up on one knee. Then he grunted and hoisted himself all the way up. "I'm going to the hospital to get this son of a bitch removed from my ass," he said. "I'll check in on Madonna for you. Maybe she'll give me your address. Your place of employment. Something like that so I can find you if I need you."

He limped to his car, and Billy Idol ignored the threat. Billy ran past Jerry and then stopped short and came back to him. "You're coming with me," he said and pointed the gun at Jerry. Dave was standing to the side. The girl with the braids was gone. Dave nodded at Jerry to do what he was told.

"Where we headed?" said Jerry.

"We're going to find your girl," he said. "You're going to call out to her and tell her to come back with my merchandise."

"You think she's gonna listen to me?" said Jerry.

Billy smiled at him. "Let's get this over with," he said and pointed the gun in the direction he wanted Jerry to walk. Blood was dripping from his ear onto his shoulder, and his spiked hair had flattened out from the fog.

Jerry thought the guy didn't even really look like Billy Idol anymore. He was more like some down and out kid from LA, who came up north and bought some junky clothes at the Goodwill. His eye makeup was blotchy and made him look like he was sick. But his eyes were still intense. He was on a mission.

He pushed Jerry in front of him and then poked him in the back with the gun. "That way," he said and pointed toward the fishing pier.

Kids were still standing in small groups on the outskirts of the cluster of cars where they'd been dancing around the fire only a few minutes before. But most people were already in cars headed for the exit, trying to escape before the cops would inevitably appear and start taking down names to share with the deans of the local Catholic high schools.

"Okay," said Billy Idol. "Stop here."

They stood on a little bluff overlooking the lake. On the far side, Jerry could see the headlights of cars rushing around Lake Merced Boulevard, heading back from the peninsula to their houses in the Sunset. He looked over his shoulder and saw more cars leaving the parking lot.

Billy Idol tapped the back of Jerry's neck with the gun and said, "Say this … wait what's your girlfriend's name?"

Jerry didn't say anything, so Billy hammered the back of his head with the barrel of the gun. Jerry felt the stitches separate from his scalp. Then he felt the pain, which came on in a delayed wave and spread into his shoulders and down his spine. His reflex was to spin and hit this asshole in the mouth, but he fought it off and said, "Carolyn."

"Good job," said Billy. "Here's what you say. You shout out, *Carolyn, you need to bring the bag over here or I think this guy is going to blow my brains out with the gun he's holding up to the back of my head where the stitches are."*

Jerry turned his head and said, "That's a little long, isn't it?"

"I was making it up off the cuff."

"How 'bout I just yell out, *Carolyn, bring the bag over here or Billy Idol's going to kill me."*

"That'll work," said Billy, but before Jerry could say anything, Billy pivoted and ran toward the pier.

Jerry took a step in that direction and saw what Billy must have seen. Carolyn was holding the bag and running parallel to the lake. She was being chased by Andrew, who was taking long strides but didn't seem to be closing the gap.

Jerry ran in the same direction as Billy, who was trying to cut her off before the path opened up and gave her more options. "Just give it to him, Carolyn," Jerry yelled, surprised to already be taking shallow breaths after the first ten yards.

She must have heard him because she looked up in his direction. But she didn't drop the bag, and she kept moving until she saw Billy Idol coming down the hill in her direction. She should have just given up. There was nowhere to go with Billy cutting her off in one direction and Andrew chasing her from behind. But she took a hard right and ran down the pier. Jerry knew she didn't have a plan. She was just trying to delay the inevitable. One of Jerry's mom's favorite insults was to tell people to *take a long walk off a short pier*. That seemed to be Carolyn's last option, but she thought better of it and stopped at the end.

She leaned back against the wooden railing, the lake washing up against the pilings beneath her. She held the bag in front of her and tried to catch her breath. "You guys are total dicks," she said.

Jerry walked behind Billy Idol, who was taking his time now. Jerry heard Andrew on the pier behind him. "Give him the bag," said Jerry.

Carolyn smiled. "I will," she said. "I just wanted them to work for it."

"Well, nice job," said Billy. "You did that."

"Can you not point the gun at her?" said Jerry. "Just take your stuff and go."

"The man says, '*Your* stuff'," said Billy and looked back at Jerry. "Finally, someone's acknowledging that this is mine now."

"Take it," said Jerry.

Billy Idol took a step toward Carolyn and put his hand out

Carolyn leaned back and swung the bag to her side like she was going to throw it over Billy's head. But when she flexed her knees and twisted her torso, her rear end and the bag itself knocked the dry-rotted railing behind her. There was a loud cracking sound. It ripped through the air, and everything froze for a moment. The sound was familiar to Jerry, but he couldn't place it. It sounded maybe like a cracked baseball bat from an inside pitch. Or maybe a broken bone. He knew the sound. And he knew what was about to happen.

Carolyn dropped the bag in front of her and started to swing her arms, but there was no reason for her to fight it. She'd already lost her balance, and gravity was going to do its work. Whether she attempted to break the laws of physics or not, she was going in the water.

She made eye contact with Jerry, but she didn't scream. She just said in a normal voice, "I can't swim."

Before Jerry even heard the splash, he jumped over the duffle bag and used one hand on the still-intact portion of the wooden railing to vault himself into the murky lake.

Splashdown: The Pirate's Plank Disaster 25 Years Later

A Six-Part Documentary Series

Produced by NorCal Newsreel. Presented by Small Town Consortia in association with The Joint Center for Civic Review and The Sonoma County Film Institute

2010

Episode Six: Extraordinary
TRT 29 min

[Transcript]

Sister Margaret Miller (Former Principal, St. Mary's): We actually prayed a lot.

Narrator: Do you think that helped.

Sister Margaret: I know it did.

Narrator: Did the school do anything special to help with student anxiety?

Sister Margaret: No one really used that word back then. But you know what helped? They were good kids with good parents. And instead of letting the tragedy separate them, they got closer. There was some initial tension, but I'm not exaggerating when I say that it was the closest senior class in all my years at the school. Girls can be tough on one another, but that class loved each other.

Narrator: Did the school administrators set up grief counseling for the students?

Sister Margaret: Well, that's another thing we didn't really have back then.

Narrator: How do you account for the love you describe among the girls?

Sister Margaret: They had a couple of really strong leaders. Fearless kids. And I think God might have stepped in because these girls needed it. Have you ever heard of Catherine McAuley?

Narrator: Tell me about her…

Sister Margaret: She was our founder. And she said, "We must strive to do ordinary things extraordinarily well." I've always liked that. And I think we did it after we lost Chrissy. We weren't lazy about the simple stuff. Of course, we took it easy on these girls who'd been through so much, but we didn't talk about it. We didn't spend any time patting ourselves on the back for our compassion. We just did it quietly. We kept acting like we were still strict and had to challenge the girls to make them into strong women. But we nurtured them in such a way that maybe they didn't even notice what was going on. At the risk of sounding like a braggart, I would like to say that the St. Mary's faculty and staff were extraordinary in the ordinary act of caring for those girls. I'm proud of that.

40

For a moment, Carolyn felt like a little kid. Like she was playing *steal the bacon*. She almost giggled when she swiped the bag and slunk away while everyone was either scattering or watching Ronnie yell at the guy dressed up like Billy Idol.

But she checked herself. This nut-case had a gun and actually fired it. She almost felt guilty because *she'd* told him where it was. She'd been trying to protect someone from grabbing it out of the bushes and hurting someone, but that notion seemed silly now after she'd watched Ronnie get shot in the ass by the very same gun.

Once she had the bag, she took a quick look at Jerry, but he had his eyes on Ronnie. She knew Jerry was going to be pissed that she got herself involved again, especially since there was a gun as part of the equation now, so the threat of violence against her had escalated considerably. But something, a misguided but extremely strong instinct, pushed her to pick up the bag and see how far she could get before someone would notice her.

But nobody did. She kept looking back at the dying fire and the shadows moving around the garbage can and the cars, but no one seemed to notice that the bag was missing, so she kept moving. She wished she'd had time to develop a plan, but it all happened so fast that she was winging it, hoping some scheme would magically work itself into her consciousness.".

She knew that if she could get up to the golf course, she could run up the 18th fairway, past the clubhouse, and use the bridge on the other side to get over the lake and away from Billy Idol and Ronnie. But when she started to climb the grade up toward the golf course gates, she saw a figure looking down at her.

Andrew.

She had to pivot. The short-lived plan was not going to work. Andrew ran at her, and she took off back toward the pier. She was trying to buy time so that she could devise plan B, but all she could come up with was to outrun Andrew and hope that no one else got involved.

If she could get past the pier, there would be more trees, which could help her elude Andrew, but then she saw the Billy Idol guy's stupid hair bouncing down the bluff. It was more or less over for her now. She knew that. The bag felt like it contained bricks. But she took the only available route that didn't involve her running into Billy Idol or running back at Andrew—she turned hard right and jumped onto the pier. She listened to the thumping of her own feet as she slowed to a jog and made her way to the end of the pier.

A part of her wanted to get to the end and throw the bag into the water, but she didn't want to piss off the guy with a gun, so she just waited for them to get to her. She leaned back, felt the railing bend a bit with her weight, and took deep breaths, the foggy air cooling the back of her dry throat.

Billy Idol was first to hit the pier, and Jerry was next, shaking his head at her from fifty feet away. And then came Andrew, who must have been really slow. He was walking, probably aware that it was only Billy Idol with whom he'd be negotiating for his cut of the cards and the cocaine.

When the Billy Idol guy got close, Jerry said to Carolyn, "Give him the bag." Carolyn was surprised at the sound of his voice. He was stern. She hadn't heard that before, but she understood how he was feeling. It had been a long day, and he was worried about her. She knew she was acting like a fool. She couldn't even figure out why she was being so impulsive. It wasn't really her thing. She wondered what was motivating her considering she hadn't had a drink in hours, and the idea of somehow trying to save Edgar didn't make as much sense anymore.

She knew Jerry probably didn't like this side of her, if it was, indeed, a side at all. There was no reason for her to be messing with these guys, but something in the way, way back was nudging her in that direction. She wondered if she was just trying to extend the night to spend more time with Jerry. And she also didn't like the jerk in the Billy Idol getup, whose ear was dripping blood all over the pier. She wondered if he'd run into a tree branch trying to chase her down, and the thought actually made her smile.

He gloated a bit and then reached out for the bag. She was going to hand it to him, but she started to pretend that she was going to throw it instead. She wasn't going to do it. It was just one more move before the bag would be gone forever, and Billy Idol would walk off with it into the fog.

But something happened. When she bent her knees, her backside bumped the guard rail, and the railing snapped. The crack was louder than she would have imagined from the splintery wood, hollowed out by lakeside rot. There was a moment when she thought she'd be able to catch her balance. She let go of the bag, thinking the release of the extra weight would help her cause. It did not. She windmilled both arms for only a second before she was resigned to what was going to happen.

She caught Jerry's eye. She knew he'd be in the water with her in a moment.

She had no knowledge of how to land in the water. She never took lessons. She made the mistake of flattening out her back and doing what was, for all intents and purposes, a reverse belly-flop. A back-flop. The noise she made hitting the water sounded like a slap in the face. She heard herself grunt.

And then things slowed down.

The shock of the cold water stiffened her from her shoulders to her toes. And then she sank. She felt the water coming into her ears and covering her face. She closed her eyes. She knew the worst thing you could do was panic. If you panicked, you could drown anyone who tried to save you. So, she just sank. Her back only hurt for a second, but now her ears were starting to ache.

If she weren't in the cold water, she knew she'd be blushing from embarrassment. She was both mortified and horrified at the same time and imagined her cheeks heating up and betraying her cool, but that was all happening in her mind. She wasn't blushing. She was sinking. She knew enough to start kicking if she went any deeper, but there was a sudden explosion in the lake just to her left.

She felt the underwater vibrations moving into her. The undulations. The wake of Jerry's fierce intrusion into the lake. She imagined the ripples buoying her to the surface, but they weren't. She was still sinking.

Then she felt his hands on her body. As soon as he touched her, she felt herself curl into the fetal position so that she'd be easy to cradle and bring to the surface.

The experience didn't follow the rules of time. It was slow. She never panicked. None of the sensations made sense. She was actually smelling mildew as she was being lifted to the surface, but she questioned how she could smell anything underwater.

Nothing made sense except for Jerry's arms around her and the clean air that she took in when they reached the surface.

She was doing mythology in English class, and Ms. Dalton was telling the class about the goddess Aphrodite, who was born from the sea foam after a guy named Cronus castrated his own dad and threw his genitals into the sea. Poseidon felt sorry for Aphrodite and brought her to shore. Saved her from drowning.

Carolyn felt sorry for the guy who'd lost his genitals.

But she was indebted to her own hero, who was carrying her now. She wasn't coughing or gasping for air. She was smiling and looking up at him.

"What were you thinking?" he said and put her down on the grass.

And then she started to shiver. Uncontrollably. The grace she was feeling just a moment before was replaced by involuntary twitching and muscle spasms. She wiped her eyes and then started to lose her breath.

"Are you okay?" he said and moved a strand of her hair away from her mouth. "Did you hit anything when you landed?"

"The water," she said and worried that her hair looked like seaweed. She didn't like that he was seeing her like this.

Dave and Cheese came running down the hill.

Dave said, "Did that asshole throw you in the water?"

"No," she said, and the word came out in several syllables because her teeth were chattering.

"We need to get her in the car," said Jerry and picked her up like she was a small child.

"I can walk," she said, but her hands were wrapped tightly around his neck, and he ignored her.

"Run up and blast the heat," he said to Cheese. "Do you have any blankets?"

Cheese was already running, but he looked over his shoulder and shouted, "No." He slipped on the wet grass, caught his balance, and sprinted to the car. He was the only one who seemed rattled.

When they got to the top of the hill, Jerry carried her across the parking lot and put her in the back seat like her dad might have done when she was little and sleepy. Then Jerry ran around and got in next to her. "Your dad's gonna kill me," he said.

"He's at the firehouse tonight," she said. "He'll never know that I almost drowned while I was in your care." She tried to smile, but she knew it must have been contorted as she was still shaking.

Jerry looked at her like he wanted to ground her for two weeks. Then he leaned forward and said to Dave, "How did it end with Ronnie and the Billy Idol impersonator?"

"The black guy's probably on his way to the ER," said Dave. "He could barely walk."

Cheese backed out of the space and said, "Billy Idol got in his own car and screeched out of here."

Then Dave pointed over past the garbage can at Andrew, who was standing alone with his hands in his pockets. "He left that guy pounding on the window," he said. "He chased the car for a few steps and then threw his hands up in the air. He looked like he might cry."

Carolyn was dripping all over the back seat and the water was activating some of the odors that had gone dormant in Cheese's car. "I knew it," she said through chattering teeth. "Billy Idol is a snake."

"Edgar was the only pure one in this shit show," said Jerry, who was shivering as bad as Carolyn. She put her hand on his leg to stop it from shaking. “He was just trying to do a friend a favor,” he said. “And now he’s back in jail.”

Carolyn said quietly into Jerry’s ear, “He was supposed to get paid though, right?”

Jerry took a deep breath and looked like he was trying to will away his shivers. “I didn’t say he was a saint,” he said and wrapped his wet arms around her.

41

Edgar's mom was so mad at him that she hadn't come to visit yet, but he didn't blame her. She couldn't read his mind. She had no way of knowing that he was done with all the craziness. He was going to take the GED and go to San Francisco State in the fall. It wasn't a difficult plan, but he needed a few things to go right for him in order to make it happen. State was cheap, but he'd need to get some kind of a job to pay for tuition, and then he could win back the respect of his family and friends.

His advisor from the SF Department of Children and Families told him that Kent's parents weren't going to press charges. Kent must have gone out on a limb for him, and Edgar appreciated that. Made a mental note to buy the man a beer if he ever saw him again. And also tell him to stay off the roof.

Edgar was still in violation of his probation for possession of narcotics, but the advisor told him one doobie might not be enough for them to hold him after his hearing next week. He was probably going to walk. Edgar was more worried about his mom than any prosecutor they could throw at him.

He was happy that Jerry and Carolyn were coming to see him in a few minutes, but he didn't know what to expect.

Isaac had told him that two friends of his were out there for a visit and that one looked like a model. So, Edgar knew who it was. He'd last seen the two of them when he walked out of the ER with Ronnie, who'd claimed to be working with Sawyer. But now that didn't seem to be the case.

Edgar had spoken to Sawyer the day after he was booked. Sawyer was a sneaky conman, but Edgar could tell the kid had no idea what Edgar was talking about when he mentioned Ronnie.

"A black guy?" he'd said.

"Big black guy."

"And he told you he was working for me?"

"He knew everything about you and the baseball cards," he said.

Sawyer had blinked and rubbed his temples with his fingers. "Well, shit," he said. "He got me."

Edgar didn't know who he was talking about. He said, "So you believe me?"

"He fucking bent me over."

"I did what you asked," said Edgar. "But he kept telling me we were on the same team."

"I'll bet," he said.

Edgar couldn't tell if he was mad. If anything, Sawyer Puck seemed mad at himself. Like someone had outsmarted him, but he didn't want to give the other guy any credit.

"Are we cool?" Edgar said as the two of them sat next to each other on a bench in the rec room.

Sawyer almost looked surprised to see Edgar sitting there. "Yeah," he said. "We're cool." Then after a minute, he patted Edgar on the shoulder and said, "Thanks for trying. I might need you to help me with something else though. I just don't know how to do it yet, but having some help would be good."

Then Sawyer got up and walked over to talk to Isaac, and that was the end of it. Edgar just hoped he'd be released before Sawyer asked for any more favors.

When Jerry and Carolyn arrived, Edgar didn't know how to feel. Isaac put them in a glass visiting room and said, "Fifteen minutes."

Jerry was excited to see them when he first heard they were here, but now that they were in front of him with nervous smiles, he felt his stomach drop. They shouldn't be in this place with these people. Edgar felt that everyone here was a loser, even though he liked a lot of them.

Jerry and Carolyn weren't losers and shouldn't have wasted time coming down here to see him.

"What's the haps?" said Jerry when he and Carolyn sat down on the other side of the metal table.

Edgar suddenly felt very sad. He had to swallow down what felt like a sob. He took a deep breath and said, "Kent's parents aren't going to press charges."

Carolyn's face lit up like a little kid about to blow out candles. "Does that mean you're getting out?"

"I hope so," he said.

"When will you find out?" asked Jerry.

Edgar shrugged and stared right at Jerry. Edgar was trying to get a read on his old friend. Jerry didn't look away but didn't show anything either. "Maybe this week," said Edgar, but he didn't like the way it sounded, like he was feeling sorry for himself. He didn't want these two to feel sorry for him. They had their own stuff to worry about. They had homework and tests and college applications. They didn't need to worry about him. "I feel pretty confident they won't keep me here for having a joint in my pocket."

"It seems ridiculous," Carolyn said and made a comically angry face. She still looked cute, but it was more like Shirly Temple when she scrunched her mouth up like that. "There's people out there committing real crimes," she said. "Like that Billy Idol jerk, running around discharging a pistol with a bunch of kids around."

Edgar raised his eyebrows. "Really?" he said.

"Things got pretty ugly down at the boathouse," said Jerry. "Billy Idol ended up with the bag."

"I thought Ronnie would've gotten it," said Edgar. "He seemed determined. And big."

"Yeah," said Jerry. "It didn't work out great for Ronnie."

"Jerry saved my life," said Carolyn.

"Really?" said Edgar.

Carolyn said, "Yes" at the exact time that Jerry said, "No."

"I almost drowned," she said and put her arms around Jerry's neck.

Edgar looked at Jerry, but Jerry looked away this time, embarrassed for some reason that he'd done something important.

Jerry patted Carolyn's knee and said, "How's the Sawyer Puck situation?"

"We're cool," said Edgar.

"Did he say whether or not Ronnie was working for him?" said Jerry.

"He'd never heard of the guy," said Edgar. "Said he'd been screwed, but I didn't ask by who."

"Andrew got screwed too," said Jerry.

"Billy Idol took everything?"

"That's what it looks like," said Jerry.

"Unless he gives Madonna something?" said Carolyn. She didn't sound confident. When Jerry and Edgar shook their heads, Carolyn said, "Maybe they were in love."

"So in love that he left her in the hospital?" said Jerry.

They were all quiet for a moment .

Edgar thought about all the people who'd been involved. Andrew had his team of Madonna and Billy Idol. Sawyer had his team of Edgar, Jerry, and Carolyn. Ronnie was some kind of free agent. And that's what Billy Idol became in the end. Just a selfish piece of crap.

Edgar felt sick to his stomach. He'd pulled Jerry and Carolyn into this mess. He didn't know what he would have done if either of them had gotten hurt. He felt pins and needles down his back. He knew that nothing happened to them. He could look at the two of them and see that they were fine. But the thought of them being in danger was doing something to his biology. He clenched his hands into fists and got some control of himself.

"I feel like Billy Idol was the last person who deserved anything," he said.

Jerry nodded. "He came into it late," he said. "The gun helped. He was calling all the shots at the end."

"At least he didn't get *everything,*" said Carolyn.

"Ronnie didn't get anything," Jerry corrected. "Dave said Billy left with the bag."

"I understand that," she said. "But Edgar's still a winner here."

Jerry half-smiled and said, "I don't think he wants to hear anything about the gift of good friends."

"That *is* a gift," she said and winked at Edgar. "But so is this." She had a little purse that was hanging from her shoulder. Without moving the long strap, she put her hand in and pulled out a sandwich bag with something rectangular inside. For a moment, Edgar thought she was giving him a picture of herself to have while he was locked up. But she held it up to Jerry's face and said, "Roberto Clemente, right?"

Then she turned it around for Edgar to see.

"Holy shit," he said, and then quickly, "Put it away." He looked over his shoulder to see if Sawyer Puck was lurking anywhere.

Jerry looked surprised too. He was staring at her like she was some kind of puzzle that he had no chance of ever solving. "How'd you keep it dry?" he said.

"I didn't have it with me at that point," she said.

"Where was it?"

"When we first got to the boathouse, you were cleaning up the cocaine, and I was putting the binders back in the bag."

"Cocaine?" said Edgar.

"Long story," she said.

Jerry first nodded at her and then shook his head like he couldn't believe what she was telling him.

"I grabbed the card and slid it under the seat."

"Why?" said Jerry.

"I knew there was a chance we might not get out of there with the bag."

"Well done," he said, still with the same confused look on his face.

"I'll have it for you when you get out," she whispered to Edgar. When she smiled, she looked like she did that day at the waterslides. She was dazzling. "You deserve it," she said finally and reached across the table and held Edgar's hands.

Edgar couldn't help smiling back big, like he was a free man or something. He was initially just excited to see a famous baseball card worth so much money. Then he was ecstatic that the money was going to be his. But when he looked across the table at Jerry and Carolyn, he almost cried thinking about how great and improbable it was to be in the company of these two amazing people. How incredibly significant and extraordinary and blessed he was to have friends like these.

About the Author

Tim Reardon was born and raised in the Sunset District of San Francisco. He received his Catholic school education in that westside neighborhood. He is the author of *The Improbability of Sainthood*, *Infinite Worth*, *Part of the Game*, *The Wrong Idiot*, and *Shadow Lessons*, all set in SF, where Tim is the President of Archbishop Riordan High School.

ALL THINGS THAT MATTER PRESS

FOR MORE INFORMATION ON TITLES AVAILABLE FROM
ALL THINGS THAT MATTER PRESS, GO TO
http://allthingsthatmatterpress.com
or contact us at
allthingsthatmatterpress@gmail.com

If you enjoyed this book, please post a review on Amazon.com and
your favorite social media sites.
Thank you!

www.ingramcontent.com/pod-product-compliance
Lightning Source LLC
LaVergne TN
LVHW050535160826
845677LV00011B/2051

* 9 7 9 8 9 8 9 4 5 1 3 4 0 *